Three to Tango and Other Tales

Books by Branka Čubrilo

Dethroned
Fiume – The Lost River
The Lonely Poet and Other Stories
The Mosaic of the Broken Soul
Three to Tango and Other Tales

Three to Tango and Other Tales

Branka Čubrilo

SPEAKING VOLUMES, LLC
NAPLES, FLORIDA
2020

Three to Tango and Other Tales

ISBN 978-1-64540-357-9

Many thanks to
Irina Dimitric-Stojic and Althea Kuzman

Part One

Three to Tango

The Twain Shall Never Meet

Tatyana Yuryevna Torasovaya and Jorge Rubio Rivera had been living under the same roof for a very long time without seeing each other. The hostility between the two flourished like some rare flower watered by a strong dose of contempt and bitterness caused by lies and deception.

The First Story: He, Who Cured a Dog

Jorge Rubio Rivera came to Madrid from his native Argentina with one suitcase. What was inside could barely be called 'possessions' or 'belongings'. One doesn't call two old pairs of underwear, two pairs of worn-out socks and an old towel—possessions. Fine, that wasn't all he brought with him in that old, smelly suitcase, which belonged to his distant relative who gave it to him in the firm belief he was going to give it back within a reasonable lapse of time. There were some old pictures, too, probably of family members; a portrait of an unnamed woman and a drawing of an unknown saint; then, several books and a ring that belonged to his late mother. It was never confirmed that the ring was made of eighteen carat gold, as he claimed. Of course, he claimed so, but I would not take his word as a guarantee because when it came to social status and etiquette, he liked to exaggerate, especially upon meeting someone for the first time or someone he thought he should impress. He wanted to leave the impression that he would never wear clothes bought in a second-hand shop or, God forbid, picked somewhere from the garbage (which he did!).

There was a big colourless comb, made of real, *real* ivory which was, indeed, the most treasured possession one could find in his suitcase. It was shiny, heavy and it smelled of almond oil. A wealthy man, the one who had a fine clothing store, gave him a bottle of almond oil as a token of gratitude because on one strange occasion Jorge Rubio Rivera rescued his beloved dog. Yes, Jorge almost threw himself under the wheels of a speeding car when the dog's owner finally understood that his dog didn't belong to the most intelligent breed. It was almost as if a miracle had happened: the traffic stopped and the people cheered! On that occasion the wealthy man said, giving him a bottle of fragrant almond oil, *"In case you meet someone famous in the near future."*

If he wanted to meet someone famous, then he had to move elsewhere, for in this small town of his no one was famous except the district judge's wife… and even if providence were kind enough to bring them together, even for a moment, he knew that such an encounter with the judge's wife wouldn't bear any significance or commence a miraculous journey for him.

As he yearned for a miraculous journey and yearned to meet someone famous, he took a pencil, opened the folded map of the world and closed his eyes. When he placed the tip of the pencil on the map he carefully opened one eye. The pencil showed a place, somewhere in Africa, a place where dark mountains breed only thick trees and dangerous animals, so he decided to cheat and to try his luck again, therefore he closed the opened eye and tried his luck once again. This time the tip of the pencil showed barren land on a continent that was too far to hold any dreams for him; he decided to cheat once again and closed his eyes.

This time he said a quick little prayer:

"Father, thy will shall be done this time."

The sharp tip of his pencil this time landed close enough to Madrid, therefore he thanked the Father to whom he prayed and started, first in his mind, to collect his belongings. When he was certain of what he was to take with him, he visited a distant relative, the only one he assumed might have possessed a decent suitcase. He heard his relative travelled on a few occasions somewhere to the USA … if that wasn't a myth. His family tended to weave myths as if myth weaving was their paid profession.

Before he packed his suitcase, he went to knock at the wealthy man's door, the one who gave him the bottle of almond oil as a token of gratitude for rescuing his dog. They let him in only because the wealthy man was in a lot of distress and no one knew what to do to soothe his pain.

Jorge Rubio Rivera came into his room, found him lying in his bed, crying.

"Señor ... do you remember me ... you do, don't you?" he commenced his stuttering presentation.

"Yes. Miguel. My dear fateful Miguel, where have you been all this time?"

Jorge Rubio Rivera swallowed an excessive amount of saliva and stuttered again:

"What is wrong with my master?"

"Oh, pain! My little darling is going to die."

"Your little darling?"

"Miga. Miga ... buenita Miga."

"Buenita Miga?"

"Si, Miguel ... mi buenita Miga." He showed a framed picture on his bedside, and Jorge Rubio Rivera recognised the little dog he rescued for an unusual reward.

"What would you give me, master, if I could cure your little darling?"

"Ask, Miguel, just ask!"

"If I cure your little Miga, would you be willing to buy me a one-way-ticket to Madrid? I have to go to Madrid, for my dear mother, just like your Miga, has been bedridden for a long time, waiting for me to come before she closes her eyes forever?"

"Everything, everything, anything ... just save my Miga, she is all I have."

Then Jorge Rubio Rivera asked for seven white candles, he demanded six cinnamon sticks, five quail eggs, four sparrow feathers, three cat hairs hairs, two drops of almond oil, and one page of his favourite book.

What he asked for was delivered within a few hours. They let him into the kitchen; he locked himself in, demanding to be left alone for another two hours.

Exactly at seven that evening, he announced, *"The remedy is ready"*. Miga was brought to him on a silk cushion.

The wealthy merchant insisted to be present during the ceremony, therefore Jorge Rubio Rivera told the servants to take the dying dog to the wealthy merchant's room. Then he whispered to him:

"One spoon for the dog, one spoon for you, master."

Forcefully the dog swallowed the portion; reluctantly, the wealthy merchant took his serving.

Nothing changed!

They all remained silent.

The dog didn't move, he kept his eyes closed.

By nine o'clock that evening, the fire had consumed the remainder of any rational thought left in the wealthy man's mind, so he started believing the dog was getting better. It was hellishly hot in the room, but that was the temperature Jorge Rubio Rivera insisted on; that was the temperature where miracles start to boil and to manifest.

They were served every half an hour with a spoonful of Jorge-made-medicine.

When the dog swallowed his fifth spoon, still forcefully, he almost barked. Yes, almost, for a tiny sound came out of this little lifeless bag of skin and bones.

The wealthy man and the two servants almost went into panic-mode out of sheer happiness or excitement, but Jorge Rubio Rivera lifted his index finger and looked sternly, first at the servants, then, a little less sternly, at the wealthy man. He said:

"Open all the windows!"

They quickly obeyed.

The dog hiccupped, once.

Jorge Rubio Rivera gave him, this time not so forcefully, the seventh and last spoonful of his medicine.

The dog hiccupped again!

No one was allowed to say a word.

Jorge Rubio Rivera brought the seventh spoonful of medicine to the wealthy man's lips and after swallowing it, the man took Jorge Rubio Rivera's hand and passionately and thankfully kissed it.

Jorge Rubio Rivera said loudly:

"Now, open all the doors wide."

The doors were opened, and in a short while the dog barked as a real dog would.

The wealthy man lifted his body, leaning against his elbows, he started to cry silently.

Jorge Rubio Rivera said:

"Let the dog run, let the sick man walk, close the windows and reassume your daily life. The dog has been cured, the heart of his master has been restored to happiness."

The wealthy man offered Jorge Rubio Rivera to work for him as his dog's and his own personal physician for a generous reward, but all Jorge Rubio Rivera wanted was a one-way-ticket to Madrid as they had agreed before the cure took place. He knew that his happiness was somewhere else, waiting for him; he knew the wealthy man didn't know how he had ignited a passion for a different kind of life. He was certain he was going to meet his destiny prophesied by the wealthy merchant's words, *"In case you meet someone famous in the near future."*

It is only logical, by the flow of this story and the strangeness of his character, that Jorge Rubio Rivera never again uttered a word about their earlier encounter.

That same year, in the month of July, when the days were almost as long as the nights, Jorge Rubio Rivera received a one-way-ticket to Madrid. He already had his suitcase ready to go.

When he landed, the scenery took his breath away for two very different reasons: the first was—the absolute beauty that his eyes met and the second was an uncertain fear which nestled in the pit of his stomach.

He resolved, long ago, that this strange, but vincible enemy wouldn't nest under his hat.

He resolved, and it was foreseen, too, by the wealthy merchant, on the day he gave him a small bottle of almond oil with a simple sentence which was his guiding star, that he was going to meet someone famous in his near future.

Upon his arrival, Jorge simply said, *"Welcome me Madrid, Jorge Rubio Rivera has arrived."*

The Second Story: She, Who Just Arrived

When Tatyana Yuryevna Torasovaya arrived in Madrid, she was grossly annoyed—it was too hot, the air was sticky, yet there was an unexpected wind blowing into her face, fuelling her dissatisfaction mingled with undisclosed anger. She was never allowed to show such marginal feelings like anger; hence she opted to stay silent. If one doesn't use words, one is not suspected of harbouring fringe emotions. Yes, she learned that a long time ago; her grandmother was the queen of suppressed emotions, therefore she learned this art from the most skilled artist. Her grandma was called *'Duchess'* and when Tatyana was a little girl, she believed that was her grandmother's name. Except Tatyana, no one called her anything other than *'Duchess'*.

So much had changed since the time of her childhood. Everything had changed since then. She sighed. Now, she thought, she had to do what she had to do.

It was her father's idea and wish; she simply had to do as he wished.

She found herself in Madrid, with only one suitcase, as seven big containers of her belongings were sent two weeks prior to her arrival. The house was aired, impeccably cleaned after brand new furniture was brought in, furnishings she had picked months earlier; the walls were freshly painted and the parquet floor in all the rooms was polished to the extent that one could see their own image when paying close attention to it.

For someone who had never seen a house of such beauty and opulence, this house could have looked like a palace, but for Tatyana Yuryevna Torasovaya who grew up in her grandma's house, this one looked like a modest house fit for a young student with wealthier parents.

But Tatyana wasn't a young student.

She was a well-known *prima donna.*

She wanted to be called Tatyana, for she couldn't stand when people, apart from those in her own country, butchered her names mispronouncing or wrongly annunciating them. Therefore, she would say, *"Just Tatyana will do."*

Sometimes she would say, *"Tatyana, the prima donna."*

There were only two people that *Prima donna* Tatyana really respected—her father and his mother, the *'Duchess'*. When it came to the rest of the world, she never showed her real feelings or her deeper thoughts.

No one really knew how old Tatyana was—give or take ten years. She looked perfectly preserved; she never aged since she turned twenty-two. If I really let myself into speculations about Tatyana's age, I could say that without make-up she looked perhaps twenty-five years old, but then, on closer inspection, one could find those fine lines and an expression that pointed towards thirty-five, and on a third look, or third thought, she was a *prima donna,* which calls for the question: *"Can a prima donna be such a young woman?"* There was an army of admirers, and countless times men had proposed, but Tatyana stayed faithful to only one love—her love of music. Men, to Tatyana, were people that wanted something from her, *something* she was never fully aware of. When it came to love, she loved men but not with her heart, she opted for a game in which she could gain something. Not of a material nature as she had no need for material things, but rather something of an unusual nature, like an uncertain feeling, like a completely different and non-existent compliment or an adventure that was destined to end in unexpected boredom, a notion unnecessary to explain to anyone.

That was Tatyana in a few superficial words.

Should I say—there was much more to Tatyana than what has just been described? … but the pleasure of knowing who Tatyana really was, and what her gifts were, was reserved only to two people and to a mesmerised audience when she was performing—that grateful but faceless cheering and clapping mass. Sometimes, she gave the impression that this faceless cheering and clapping mass was the fountain of her everlasting youth.

Every day she commenced with a yoga session: centring her body, calming her mind. That routine was followed by a short meditation and warming up her vocal chords. She would sit, after the just described short ritual, at her piano and kept on sitting there for hours, lost in the invisible world of tones, floating numbers and feelings that needn't be limited by any kind of description, or better to say—any kind of restriction.

Someone else prepared her breakfast, answered her calls, her mail or the door.

If I didn't know the story, I could easily have said that Tatyana's best-hidden secret was—she never had the need for love. She was loved! The *'Duchess'* adored her from the day she was born: she showered her with love and affection, with gifts, holidays and with only the best education. Her father nodded his head in approval and agreement; he wasn't a distant figure at all, but wasn't the one who would interfere, he just observed and nodded, for the *'Duchess'* knew all sorts of arts hidden from commoners' knowledge and awareness.

If I let myself into a little deeper analysis of Tatyana's character, I could say, that Tatyana, like some women throughout history, of her rank and status, was preoccupied with the same theme which, like a coin, had two sides: her happiness and her unhappiness. Shelter and a temporary cure was music; the audience was the distraction from one end of the extreme to the other.

The chauffeur held the door open for her, placed the suitcase in the boot, and said nothing, he waited for her to commence a conversation if and when she chose.

Tatyana closed her eyes, then all of a sudden, as if someone whispered something important and urgent, she asked:

"Megé? No one has said anything about Megé?"

"Lady Tatyana, Megé arrived an hour before you. Olga said she needed a rest; she should be rested and happy when you arrive."

"Thank you. I know seeing me will make her happy."

She put her sunglasses on and soon after it seemed as if she had fallen asleep; the chauffeur kept on driving slowly as if he were driving a basket of freshly cut roses whose petals had to retain the dew before delivery.

His hands were firmly holding the steering wheel; his voice manly but kind, his eyes never looked at her longer than needed; somehow whenever he saw her, his heart skipped a beat under his immaculately pressed uniform. His most hidden thought was: a lock of her hair on his pillow. Yes, it was one brave thought but the most intimate, and no one would ever suspect that he, Tatyana's chauffeur, could ever have had such a thought.

I almost forgot to say: Tatyana loved Megé more than any other living being, considering that her love was most generously given to her grandmother, then to her kind, but seemingly distant, father.

That was the Holy Trinity which carried her through the excruciating loss—the premature death of her beloved mother Ekaterina. It was Megé who licked away her pain that was dispersed all over her body. It ached so much, only Megé's soft, small, tongue could touch this pain without interfering with Tatyana's exaggerated wish to follow her mother to where she silently went. It was Megé who cried with Tatyana for days curled up in her lap, licking her hands, howling and calling Ekaterina's soul.

When she walked in, Megé couldn't contain her excitement; a nurse was called in, but the only one who could calm Megé down was Tatyana, only Tatyana, and the attachment she felt for Megé exuded from Tatyana's pure soul.

There were two women who took care of Tatyana and Megé: Olga Engenyevna and a young girl, only known to Tatyana as Anya. Tatyana remembered Olga as far as her memory stretched, for she was in the family even before Tatyana was born, she was to Tatyana a competent adviser, someone who had Tatyana's best interests at heart. With Anya, Tatyana couldn't be bothered—she was just a girl who did invisible but necessary chores, including preparing meals or cutting Tatyana's eclair exactly in the way she was told.

Olga read loudly what the local paper said about Tatyana's stay in Madrid. Tatyana just waved her hand commenting, *"That excitement won't last long."*

She demanded her room to be darkened; only in a darkened room could she gather her thoughts together. She needed time to reflect on her new home, on the question: *Would this new adventure bring more happiness or unhappiness to her?*

She disliked uncertainty, utterly, completely disliked it, yet paradoxically, every move, every concert, every journey was just a journey into uncertainty. Oh! How she longed, after her mother passed away, that she could be in charge of things, people and events that appeared or unfolded in her life.

Only in a darkened room could she regain this calm state of mind, which always came over her after clarifying a situation.

First, she took a cold bath, brushed her hair and bid *"Good night!"* to Olga, even though it was only half past seven and the sun was still up colouring the sky red.

She hugged the curled up Megé pulling her closer, and said:

"The terrifying thought, Megé, is that I am absolutely uncertain of what I feel: Am I happy or unhappy right now, and will this move bring happiness or her ugly sister along?"

The Third Story: Jorge, the Healer

It took him a while to figure out what that remedy was (the one he prepared and prescribed to the dog and his master back in Argentina):

Seven white candles, six cinnamon sticks, five quail eggs, four sparrow feathers, three cat hairs, two drops of almond oil, and one page of the man's favourite book.

The first one to thank was God himself, for what had happened on that odd day in the house of the wealthy merchant could only be described as a miracle. He knew nothing about psychology, medicine, healing or the placebo effect. He was a simple, poor peasant with a big dream of meeting *'someone important or famous'*, and the first important and famous accidental patient of his was the wealthy man and his dog. *'Must have been providence'*, *'It must have been God's will'*, *'Maybe I was chosen'*, those three were his most serious speculations when he pondered about the miracle which took place in the house of the wealthy man.

That unearthly moment gave him the feeling of superiority even though the cracks were thickly filled with fear. He thought, if that miracle was by God himself, then he must be very grateful, but frugal and careful, too, in his dealings with future customers.

He was a smart man, no one could claim the contrary, but he was not aware of the magnitude of the adventure he was planning to undertake. He had never even heard of the word *conman.* He never wanted to be one, even if he had known the full meaning and weight of the word, all he wanted was to perform the work God had assigned to him, and to be paid handsomely for it. No, God does not carefully select a man every day giving him a special assignment! He was ready to serve God's will to the best of his abilities.

On his very first day upon his arrival in Madrid, it looked to him as if God started showing him signs of His appreciation. He found an envelope. It was next to a car, nothing was written on it, he looked to the left, he looked to the right—there was no one around, he squatted and opened the unaddressed envelope. There was a card in it. The knotted letters, obviously written by a trembling old hand, read:

"Dear Pablito,
My beautiful rainbow Pony, I love you so much
and from the depth of my trembling heart I am
sending you a thousand kisses for your magnificent Birthday.
Your rainbow Abuela Carolina."

Abuela Carolina placed a handsome sum of money, licked the envelope and instead of putting it into her handbag, with her trembling fingers she dropped it on the street. That was his first thought.

There was no one in the street.

Wasn't that, a sign of God?

There was no one in the street, no name on the envelope, and the handsome sum of money? *If they were poor, she couldn't have afforded such a sum for a boy's birthday*—he soothed the tiny voice of guilt.

Recognising God's will as a sign of welcoming him into this bright city, he quickly folded the money and shoved it into his pocket.

This money would keep him afloat for a fortnight, at least.

He found a cheap place, paid for ten days and had dinner; afterwards he slept a deep, innocent sleep; he knew deep down that a fantastic life was about to unfold.

The next day, he went out to look for a job. He headed towards a big park where beautiful, big dogs run free, and well-groomed owners sit reading newspapers or chatting to each other.

The dogs were good-looking, pedigree dogs, well-groomed just like their owners; he feared that he wouldn't have much luck in this park that God created generously for everyone to enjoy and use. He said to himself, *'God has a plan for each of us, he didn't create this beautiful park just for dogs and wealthy men, just be patient, Jorge, and God will give you an opportunity, right here.'*

The day was long. No one really talked to him even when he tried to be helpful, kind and friendly.

He visited several parks, but on that day, it seemed to him his skill was not needed. God didn't show much interest in him today, but he knew his new life had just started and patience was a lesson the kind God wanted him to learn.

He visited all the parks in the vicinity but came back to the Inn tired and slightly disappointed. A young woman greeted him upon entering; he stopped for a chat. She gave him a lot of information about local parks and places where people take their pets on weekends.

Whilst he was walking through the streets of Madrid the following days, he carefully looked not only for wounded dogs, but he looked at the pavement as if God might offer him a second sign, a token of appreciation for his courage. In the end, didn't he show extraordinary bravery coming to Madrid and starting a new life? God had to recognise acts of bravery and heroism!

On the seventh day, he started to worry a little; he started to doubt his gifts and the possibility that they would be recognised and acknowledged. Fear crept in at night: when the lights were out he could see the light-bathed streets, he could hear people talking, sometimes laughing, he could hear the sound of heels on the pavement … this wasn't home … but he promised himself that he would make it home, he would realise his dream! With such thoughts under his brow, he would fall asleep with a faint smile in the corner of his lips.

That *big break* he was waiting for in the first ten days after his arrival didn't happen. But luck appeared in a much smaller size when he encountered an older lady walking her dog. Both were already tired, not to say old; Jorge followed them making a speech in his mind. When the lady stopped to catch her breath, he came closer and asked:

"Is your dog all right?"

She told him that they were two old girls living together. She complained about the stairs, about the steep street and about the recent, sharp pain in her left hip. He listened, nodded his head sporadically and told her in the end that he was a *dog healer*, but when the old lady didn't show a real interest in his skill or art, he asked if she needed any kind of help—like walking her dog on the days when she was unable to go out or to move with ease. He said he would do it for very little money, to which, in the end, she agreed.

That was how he started his modest career as a dog walker. But again, he knew that was the perfect opportunity God gave him: he was amongst dogs and their owners every day, accompanied by a dog. Now he was an equal player on the field.

He met a woman with two hounds. One was a little bigger than the other, his fur a little shinier, his body swifter, faster when running. He asked her if she knew why they were slightly different to the trained eye. She was surprised that he detected it so quickly; his observations were accurate and *professional*, as she put it, and Jorge nodded his head in agreement. He simply said:

"I am a dog healer", and started to explain his profession in detail to the very interested woman. He said that *'without any obligation, promise or reward'* he was willing to examine her dog and give his honest opinion.

"I'd be delighted, but you have to charge something ..."

"Let's first see how it'll go ... how he will respond ..."

Upon examining the dog, two days later, he said:

"I have good and bad news ...", to which she screamed; he put his arm around her shoulders continuing reassuringly:

"Everything will be all right with your dog, he needs better nourishment, there are some things missing in his diet, plus I would say he is a little bit sad, as well. What happened to him ... let's say ... four to six months ago?"

"What happened? Nothing really happened."

"Think back one year, let's say."

"Oh, we moved. My mother passed away and we moved houses."

"Exactly! You moved houses. Let me sort it out for you."

"Are you sure you can fix the problem?"

"I won't promise anything right now, but bring your dog on two different days next week and leave him with me for a couple of hours ... then we'll see. Is this something you can commit to?"

"Absolutely, I would do anything to help him, he has changed ..."

"Of course, he has ... he has been through a lot, plus his diet should be modified."

That evening when he came to the Inn, he went on his knees and prayed to God. He thanked Him for offering yet another opportunity of showing his skill and improving his financial situation. He prayed hard and he thanked Him numerous times and sometime after midnight he fell asleep on his knees.

He didn't know what to do to change anything regarding the dog's vitality, his speed was a way in which he showed his nature, but Jorge believed that a miracle would happen, that the dog would become swifter, faster and livelier, or, that the owner would believe it to be so.

Maria Victoria was her name and Mosca was the weaker dog's name.

They met in the park and she, almost reluctantly, handed the leash whilst Mosca was howling and pulling at the leash.

He whispered:

"Stash, analline volle, malline Mosca."

"What?"

"Those are just soothing words."

"In which language if I may ask?"

"Well. I know it would be too silly if I tell you, given that you are yourself in the medical field. But, let's just be open-minded; let's just show a little bit of trust. I know your mind is a scientific mind, but show just a little bit of trust."

Now, obviously, she was hesitant.

He bowed his gaze down and silently prayed, pretending he was tying his shoelaces with his mind.

The silence lasted for a short while, then the dog came and brushed his backside against Jorge's leg slowly, almost flirtatiously. Jorge nearly jumped up out of excitement or surprise, but he managed to stay calm and collected. He went down on his knees and commenced a long whisper into the dog's ear. He spoke in an Argentinian dialect, he talked about God; he begged the dog to be kind and calm. He called him a *'pal'*, a *'comrade'*, and a *'smart boy'*. He gave him handsome compliments and unbelievable promises telling him that only if he wanted to obey he could win any beauty contest and much more. The dog appeared to be an attentive listener, and after short but attentive listening the dog lifted his left leg and relieved himself on the kneeling expert.

That scene didn't provoke any reaction: Maria Victoria said nothing, nor did the healer, the dog whisperer.

The dog walked off.

To cut that long story short, Jorge won this first battle and walked away with Mosca on the other side of the leash. He promised to bring him back in a few hours. The dog whined, Jorge whistled loudly and in the end their song blended and rhymed perfectly.

He was so desperate to penetrate into that locked-dog-language that he even considered learning Hebrew, or some other exotic language, anything just to help him get closer into the dog's inner life.

Why did he suffer? What was his malady?

He fed him an ice-cream, he fed him with a small sausage he bought at the butcher's, he sang to him an old folk song, but still, the dog wouldn't give in and wouldn't show more sympathy.

When he came back to meet Maria Victoria, the dog ran fast towards his owner. Jorge smiled and said:

"This is just a tiny sign, soon you'll see a brand-new dog. Almost as if I have taken ten years off his back."

She just smiled and stroked the dog's back.

When she was leaving, Jorge put his hand into his mouth and bit hard, then called her back:

"When I see you tomorrow, please bring with you seven white candles, six cinnamon sticks, five quail eggs, four sparrow feathers, three cat hairs, two drops of almond oil, and one page of your favourite book."

He saw a plain, unhidden disbelief in her eyes, so he hurried:

"I know it sounds funny, almost like I am some sort of a wheeler-dealer, a quack, but please, give us a chance, to all three of us. For the sake of your beloved Mosca let it be the last thing you do for him. Have a bit of faith in me."

"It is not about faith! It is just something ... Oh, never mind! Tomorrow I'll bring what you asked for, and if the dog doesn't show any sign of even the smallest improvement, I shall cease our cooperation. Is that all right? Have you understood me clearly?"

"Absolutely, thoroughly and totally. But, let me tell you one thing—you won't have any regrets, my friend, you won't regret it!" and off they walked, each in a different direction. Maria Victoria with a light step and Jorge Rubio Rivera walked as if the heaviest rock was chained to his feet.

His money was running out. His rent had to be paid. His stomach was rumbling, and he was disgusted by Madrid's tap water. He longed to buy a bottle of reasonably good wine, he longed to eat a good chunk of meat; he couldn't believe people could survive on a vegetarian diet until he proved it to himself. Never before his arrival had he heard the term! Who would ever give up meat willingly!

He spent the whole night on his knees. He even cried a bit, but then he thought, if God could really see him, he would be rather disappointed by his crying. *God likes dignified and graceful people.*

That thought, in the middle of the night, came almost like a revelation, so he decided he was going to be *a dignified and graceful man* (on his own terms, though! as he never had a measuring stick). Maybe that was the way which lead to God's heart, as if God were some sort of heavenly negotiator.

Be it God, or Luck, or some sort of real, undiscovered talent, by the end of the second 'session' the dog looked more cheerful.

Maria Victoria handed him her beloved dog together with the items he listed the day before. She shrugged her shoulders, saying:

"Look, here are the things you've asked me to bring ... I thought about what you've said, it doesn't really make sense ... but look, somehow, I thought, I might just let you prove otherwise ... It is my dog, and I believe you wouldn't harm him."

"Please, please, my friend. Please trust me only today. One more day, please."

But when they returned two hours later, Maria Victoria noticed a slight difference in the dog's demeanour, therefore she said, *"Yes, at the same time."* when he said, *"See you tomorrow."*

With the last of his money he bought a better brand of multivitamins and fed the dog with a sausage filled with a powder of a finely crushed multivitamin pill. He talked to the dog, he sang to him, prayed for him and cuddled him as if the dog was his best pal or a former lover found again.

And the dog, previously lethargic Mosca, responded in a way any living creature would respond to love, kindness and care—he flourished in a very short time. Only after seven days of the *'treatment'* the dog was fonder of Jorge than of his original owner.

It was proven and confirmed: Jorge Rubio Rivera *was* a Dog Whisperer.

But, alas! He was broken like an old silver coin which exchanged a million hands. He was poor as a church mouse, desperate as a wide desert. So, he said:

"I am happy I restored his health and vitality. Happy for you two. Now I have to go back to Argentina, for I can't stay in Madrid any longer."

"Why is that so?"

"Well. I came here only to bury my late mother. She left my father many years ago, for she was from a wealthy family and married a handsome but poor Argentinian doctor. She couldn't live an average life in Argentina as a wife of a poor doctor, so she went back, remarried a successful lawyer ... when she passed away, I was advised to be her only heir. Only upon meeting her lawyer, I heard a heartbreaking story. She lost all her fortune due to a horrible illness called—gambling. She gambled away all her money, her houses and her horses. Everything! Everything! There was nothing left to me, not even her noble name as she brought shame to the family."

"Is that true?"

"Do you think I made up such a sad story?"

"Well. I suppose, I have to believe you. Why would you make up such a story?"

"Exactly! Why would I?"

"When are you going back?"

"When I save some money for the ticket."

"Hang on! You don't have money even to buy your ticket?"

"No. I lived in a hotel when I heard that there was nothing left ... Now I have to go, but even in Argentina I don't know what I shall do, for there are not many people who care for their dogs. Who would pay me for my services? Over there I did that out of my kindness and love for animals."

"There is a shed in my garden. You can stay for a few weeks. Mosca loves you ... Aron would grow fond of you in no time, I bet he would ... Stay with us for a few weeks and look after their diet ... you'll see what will come up for you."

In a very short time word spread: *There is a renowned dog healer in Calle de la Pasa;* soon after, whoever needed his help and knowledge simply asked for the Dog Whisperer which became the name he was known by.

Jorge's luck was twofold: whenever he had a 'lucky break' it was short lived, only to be followed by new uncertainty. When any uncertainty unfolded, he would lose all resemblance to the young man who came to Madrid just a year earlier with a firm resolution formed in his mind on the day when he received his first present for rescuing a dog, a bottle of fragrant almond oil given with the words, *"In case you may meet someone famous in the near future."* Understandably, the resolution was: *I am going to meet someone famous and such a meeting will change my life forever!*

In his mind, he never specified of what nature that encounter should be: he never thought of love, but rather of some sort of great, yet unidentified, success. He never cared much about love, for he was a handsome man, he knew he could find a woman only if he wanted to, but he also knew that one can't find remarkable success anytime, anywhere. He needed immense success first and then he would be able to choose a woman he could only dream of: a creature of indefinite beauty and style, a movie star, any sort of celebrity or perhaps, a duchess of some sort.

After several generous months of successful business as a dog whisperer, operating from Maria Victoria's shed, the circumstances changed. They changed the day she came home with a man she claimed she was going to marry. The man was a veterinarian. Alas, a veterinarian!

The very same moment the two men shook hands uttering their names, Jorge Rubio Rivera with this handshake lost all his self-confidence as if Maria Victoria's fiancé's hand was made of the strongest steel with which the sword of justice was minted. He felt an instant weakness in his knees, his voice became puny and croaky, his brow beaded with sweat, even his thick, heavy hair started to ruffle and dance, even though the day was still and the tops of trees in the garden were wholly motionless.

Alas, a veterinarian!

A vet!

He had piercing cynical eyes which looked straight into Jorge's quivering mouth; then he observed in his fine literate Spanish, in an accent Jorge would never be able to mimic:

"So, the Dog Whisperer, huh?"

"Yes, señor."

"Oh, please, don't call him señor, call him ..." Maria Victoria couldn't finish her sentence as she was interrupted by Artemio's voice:

"No, no, call me señor for now, we are not colleagues. Only with some of my colleagues am I on a first name basis."

There were no clearer words to indicate to Jorge that his stay at Maria Victoria wouldn't be extended any longer, woefully he walked into the shed and packed his several belongings into his old suitcase, the one he had borrowed from that relative who apparently visited the USA twice.

He left without a word; he just sneaked out, not even the dogs noticed his ghostly departure.

The advantage he had, in comparison to the days when he just arrived in Madrid with a half-empty suitcase, was the fact that he had some money, earned honestly during that year when he was known as the Dog Whisperer, or shall I say— a healer.

The Fourth Story:
An Unexpected and Fatal Hysteria

A tall and dark-haired man was seen around the house and he was, in Olga's opinion, the prime suspect. He was seen on two occasions: Olga saw him both times, and the chauffer saw him once. The description they gave was exactly the same and no one knew the man. No one could even fathom why he was seen around Tatyana's house, therefore, they suspected he was, most probably, an obsessed fan. Regardless of all speculation a horrible truth remained: the beloved, one and only baby, one and only love, one and only solace, Tatyana's most cherished friend Megé, had been poisoned!

That would be the second most perplexing task in Olga's life: the deliverance of such news to Tatyana, if providence didn't give her a helping hand, since she dreaded delivering unpleasant news to Tatyana. When Tatyana's mother passed away, it was Olga who held her hand and walked her to the Duchess's room. It was asked of Olga to stay in the vicinity twenty-four hours a day, for months, and to respond accordingly. The most devastating thing for Olga, apart from her own feelings of sadness and loss, was the knowledge that she wasn't able to do anything to relieve the pain Tatyana was going through. Tatyana refused to eat for days and her intestines swelled in her tiny stomach that resembled the stomach of a gravely pregnant woman. Her unevenly swollen intestines played a loud symphony of embarrassment, but at that time Tatyana's grief took over any other feelings that she had, so embarrassment wasn't really what she cared about.

Apart from the devastation caused by such news, Olga harboured a feeling of guilt as well, for when Tatyana said she was going to lunch with Giancarlo, it was Olga's suggestion to leave Megé with her. *"Why had Olga suggested this?" Tatyana* asked herself over and over. But there was nothing to do! She had to face the reality of the situation with all its consequences.

It happened as follows: at around four o'clock Olga remembered that Tatyana went out without Megé, and remembering this, she went to see why Megé was so quiet, for her initial thought about the quietness in the house was wrongly associated with Megé's absence. The thought was corrected, the awareness of the dog's presence in the house acknowledged, the only question Olga had at that moment was—*Why was the house so quiet and what was Megé up to?*

She looked around and she finally found the little dog in Tatyana's room. Lying flat on the small Persian carpet which ran beneath the longish, opened window.

Olga ran to the dog, but it was evident that she was unconscious. Alas! Olga screamed and at the same moment the entrance door opened, Tatyana walked in with a big bunch of roses in her hands.

When she heard Olga's scream, she dropped the flowers on the marble floor.

When Olga understood that Tatyana had just walked into the foyer she screamed again, this time louder. Tatyana wanted to run towards the distressed Olga, but her knees betrayed her and she fell on the marble floor squashing several white roses, the red roses appeared to have run away of their own will anticipating Tatyana's heavy fall. She looked at her distressed image in the mirror, but the third of Olga's screams broke the mirror into a thousand pieces which fell amongst the white and red roses and some gathered around Tatyana's scratched, bleeding knees. Now that the mirror was in a thousand pieces, she couldn't crawl through the corridor and reach the room from which Olga's distressed screams were coming from, therefore she chose to scream and to cry at the same time as she understood that Megé didn't bark. In such a situation Megé would be loud and present.

The door was wide open and through the door a tall, dark-haired man walked in and kneeled next to Tatyana.

All she could gather at that crucial moment was that the man wanted to help her and that he was very handsome and tall. He saw her broken skin, her blood on the white roses, he picked her up tenderly as if she were a cut, innocent rose and brought her into the room from where cries and screams were coming in circular waves. Tatyana, usually stern and distant with strangers, did not object but surrendered her body and will into his arms. When she saw Olga holding the lifeless Megé's body, Tatyana scratched her rescuer like a wild cat would in the face of alarming danger and he almost dropped her on the floor. But he did not! He held her tight as if she were a disturbed child who had just heard the most distressing news: the unjust and horrifying news, impossible to untangle or undo. When he cautiously laid the wounded Tatyana on the nearest sofa with a swift move, he approached Olga and without a word took Megé from her hands and walked out with the dog onto the patio. He was well aware that the dog was going to survive, for when he measured the amount of tranquiliser he knew it was not going to harm the dog.

Everybody's attention was on Tatyana, even Olga momentarily lost awareness of what was happening with the little dog, but after a short while a bark changed the whole scene: Olga stood frozen and Tatyana jumped to her feet.

In a slow confident walk, still holding the dog to his chest, Jorge walked back into the room and smiled at both women a wide, seemingly warm smile. His smile was rather a sly, winning smile.

"What happened? A miracle?"

"No, señora, no miracle. I, Jorge, am a dog healer." he said and extended his hand.

Tatyana extended her arms to take her dog, whispering *'My precious'*, giving Jorge one of her sincerest smiles.

In the salon drinks and finger food were brought out and Jorge was treated like a hero; she said she couldn't find the words to thank him.

But let me tell you what lead to this *heroic* rescue of Tatyana's dog.

After Jorge Rubio Rivera was faced with the brutal fact that Maria Victoria's fiancé was a veterinarian, he had to pack his few belongings and find another destination.

He walked around the big city, still strange to him, not knowing what would happen next. There were posters all over Madrid saying: *'Where the Extraordinary Happens'*.

A picture of a beautiful woman dressed in red—at once he was mesmerised, he kept on reading the first two sentences, unable to finish the whole advertisement, for her beauty confused the clarity of his mind. Below her beautiful face and piercing blue eyes two sentences were dancing: *'There is a place where time stands still. A place where exceptional talent meets world-class talent."*

He kept on reading the dancing letters which were reluctant to form, for him, a coherent, meaningful sentence; he kept on staring into her eyes and after some unspecified passage of time he noticed only one name—Tatyana Yuryevna Torasovaya.

'Should be Russian or German' he thought unaware that the two languages did not belong to the same linguistic group.

With the little money that was left from his heyday as a Dog Whisperer he risked purchasing a ticket, but alas, he was told that the tickets were sold months before the concert.

He followed the car from which beautiful Tatyana was escorted. He followed it for a few days and when he learned where the diva lived he examined the property and its surroundings.

Luck smiled at him once again!

Oh, merciful One! Tatyana had a dog! And, he, Jorge Rubio Rivera, was a well-known Dog Whisperer, a dog healer should she prefer a simpler version.

Now he was sitting next to the beautiful Tatyana looking at her smile, at her small hands that were stroking the dog tenderly, and thinking, *"Here I am, moving just one step at the time."*

He refused the second glass of sweet wine, said he had to go, to which Tatyana worriedly asked:

"How am I going to repay you?"

"It was my pleasure. It was just pure coincidence and luck that I should be passing by. Don't you worry about paying or repaying, as long as your little darling is fine, I am fine, too. But, what worries me is whether she is going to be completely alright."

"Do you want to come again and check on her? Would you?"

"Well, I would. I can't just leave it as it is, even though I am very sure that Megé is going to be fine. I think I can come by tomorrow, let's say, late afternoon?"

"I won't be home, but Olga will take care of everything."

Before he left, he turned and said:

"Señora ... I just realised. I can't come over tomorrow late afternoon, for I have a client who called me late last evening. It slipped my mind."

"Would you want to give me your number, I can call you ..."

"How about you give me your number and I'll call you as soon as I check my diary."

Jorge Rubio Rivera left the house of the *Prima donna* with her number in his pocket.

Olga said:

"This man looks familiar."

Tatyana said with a faint, grateful smile, *"He is a miracle worker"*, and Olga knew that the best thing to do was to put an end to the conversation.

After only a few weeks Jorge almost became Tatyana's best friend. He proved to be a real expert in dogs' health and happiness.

One thing was blatantly obvious but not to his admirer Tatyana: the dog wasn't unhappy when Jorge left, he was simply medicated. It was clear to Olga, it was clear to the maid, to the chauffeur ... but not to Tatyana.

They gossiped behind her back, they laid out a plan how to tell her and who would tell her, but in the end, they wanted to keep their well-paid positions and didn't dare to interfere with Tatyana's private life and her decisions. After all, it was her dog and she knew what was best for her little darling.

Each afternoon, when the table was laid out, the two new friends sat together and discussed Megé's health and wellbeing. As if she were mesmerised by his lazy drawl, Tatyana looked straight into his plump lips which, in a slow movement were delivering the most amazing stories.

He told her how he ended up living in Madrid.

He said his mother was born and schooled in Madrid, but when her father was appointed as a diplomat in Buenos Aires she fell in love with the city. And when she was only sixteen she fell in love with his late father who used to be a gifted dog healer. He told her a story about how his father rescued her dog and was given a bottle of expensive almond oil, a gesture accompanied with words, *"In case you meet someone famous one day."*

He said that his mother wasn't actually *'someone famous'*, but after all, he raised his eyebrows and said, *'she was a diplomat's daughter, close enough to be someone famous.'*

Further into his story, he claimed that his father died and unfortunately didn't leave much money, for he was very sad and disappointed when mother simply left the country after ten years. Her love affair with Buenos Aires wore thin, even her love for his father wore out and she left, believe it or not—without a word. Not even to her beloved son. Father suspected that she might have met some other man, and alas, he was right. He hired a private detective from Madrid who charged an unreasonable sum of money, but he said his father was willing to pay, no matter how high the sum, just wanting the truth regardless of the cost.

"Sad." He said, *"Sad!"* looking at the bread crumbs scattered on his plate.

He told Tatyana how he received a letter one ordinary afternoon whilst sitting on his veranda looking at the sunset. The postman came late that afternoon; he was tipsy. Customary to Buenos Aires, postmen are often offered a drink at every home, which they never have the strength of character to refuse. When he handed a letter to Jorge and when he gulped down the offered drink, he left a puzzled Jorge with an envelope written in neat steady letters. He skimmed the letter three times and smiled.

He smiled, for he had the precognition that it could be his very last smile.

He learned that his mother passed away and that her lawyer wanted him to come to Madrid where the will was going to be read.

With tears in his eyes he confidently told Tatyana that his late mother had remarried, she had three other sons and she left them all her fortune, leaving him only her wedding ring which his father gave her many years ago.

Tatyana grabbed his hand and gently squeezed it.

"When did that happen?"

"Two weeks ago."

"You have been here for only two weeks?"

"Yes. I had hoped she had left me something, I was her son just like the others, but she had forgotten me, she betrayed me for the second time, left me with nothing, I have to go back to Buenos Aires ... well, I wish I could stay here a little longer, a year or two, to find a job, to pay off some of my debts ... In Buenos Aires, no one waits for me, just a big city without opportunities for Jorge ... But my intent wasn't to upset you señora ..."

"Oh, stop calling me señora. Tatyana, call me Tatyana." She said whilst still holding his hand.

And this was the story about how Jorge Rubio Rivera secured his second rent-free abode.

Jorge Rubio Rivera prayed all night: down on his knees for several hours thanking his well-disposed God and unnamed saints who always cared about someone who was kind to people and animals.

The Fifth Story: Oleg and Olga

Tatyana might have called him *Chauffeur* and never even known his real name, but Olga knew Oleg since he was a young child. He was the illegitimate son of her distant relative, who initially intended to commit suicide when she learnt she was pregnant. Thank heavens she never proceeded with such an idea, for Oleg turned out to be a kind, honest and loyal young lad. When the old chauffeur retired, Olga first begged, then sincerely recommended the services of Oleg Rudinoff to Tatyana's father, *'an honest, loyal and discreet young man who will stay in the job for the rest of his life.'*

Oleg, on the other hand, felt deeply indebted to Olga and was therefore almost like Olga's right-hand man.

"Prior to Megé's so-called illness, I saw this man snooping around the house twice. He obfuscated her brain. It is not the same Tatyana any longer. She doesn't practise as much as she needs; she spends too much time with him. He is not who he claims to be. We need to find out who this creature is. Phoney, pathetic man."

"He never healed the dog." Said Oleg.

"Of course he didn't! Hell, he poisoned the dog, I am telling you he did."

"What's your plan?"

"I have no plan yet, but let me think. We need to prove that he doesn't heal animals, and he isn't even the fine gentleman he claims to be, he uses the wrong cutlery, he drinks from the wrong glass and he doesn't use a napkin. What kind of a gentleman does that? But he doesn't know one thing: you can't mess around with Olga; no one mucks around with a

Russian maid! Since I was a young girl I've served in the house of an aristocrat, I know who's who at first glance. You know what he is, Oleg? He is a scumbag! A conman and I am going to show all his true colours to our Tatyana. This is going to be their first and last Christmas together."

Well, there are all sorts of gods out there. The sky is populated by them, so it was not only Jorge Rubio Rivera who had his own God who looked after his good fortune. Olga Engenyevna had her own God to whom she prayed and conversed with on a daily basis. She would tell him all her concerns, fears, sinful thoughts or small mistakes she committed on a particular day. She even begged of him, every night, that he look after Tatyana as well, for Olga knew Tatyana never had the time to talk to God, and had too much pride to go down on her knees. Those chores were Olga's delightful duties that no one had really assigned to her.

Oleg, the chauffeur, took Tatyana and her friend to the jeweller. He was waiting in the car and opened the door when Tatyana walked out. The man, the conman, the one Oleg never wanted to call by his name, was walking behind Tatyana when a woman stopped him, greeting Jorge with the words:

"Jorge, is that you, my friend?"

They stopped and talked for a short while and Jorge introduced the two women; Oleg witnessed it. They almost said *'Good-bye'* when a man approached the woman and she delightfully asked:

"Do you remember my fiancé Artemio? We got married two weeks ago."

Artemio looked down at Jorge and said:

"Is that the man who claimed to be an animal healer? What nonsense! I'll wait for you in the car."

And he left without a word. Maria Victoria cheeks were painted red and said:

"Merry Christmas, Tatyana and Jorge!" and hurriedly entered the car.

Tatyana looked at Jorge, who said:

"Some men never let go even when they win."

In the car, in a few brief sentences he said that Maria Victoria was a woman he dated briefly, and this man couldn't get over it even though between the two of them Maria Victoria had chosen Artemio.

"Bah, some man!" he said and grabbed Tatyana's hand.

But, Oleg heard something else. He clearly heard the man call him *'a phoney'*, *'a so-called dog healer'*. He memorised the licence plate and sank deeper in his seat with a smirk on his face—This story would be music to Olga's ears.

When Tatyana and Jorge left the house just after seven that evening, Oleg walked into the kitchen and said:

"Make a feast, and take out your best wine, your faithful Oleg has a story worthy of a banquet."

"Tell me, tell me now."

"No, not right now. Set the table worthy of an emperor."

"You, devil! You better tell me what you have, you better spit it out right now or you'll go to sleep hungry."

"Set the table for the two of us, we have reason to celebrate."

In the two next days they gathered some vital details.

The car belonged to a doctor, a veterinarian, Artemio Moreno Martinez. Olga commented:

"Sure, a veterinarian. Should be easy for him to detect a phoney 'dog healer'."

The right opportunity came just a week before Christmas, which Olga promised to be their last.

Oleg took them to the airport but no one knew where exactly they were going, all Olga knew was they were not going to be back the same day. *Perhaps tomorrow*. She overheard *'Paris'* but Tatyana was secretive, lately. Lately she didn't feel the need to talk to Olga more than to confirm the usual protocol.

They found the address; they took the dog and appeared at the door of a veterinarian clinic exactly at ten.

Upon examining the dog, the doctor, the veterinarian, said:

"I see nothing wrong with your dog, are you giving him too many vitamins?"

"No." they simultaneously answered. Olga continued:

"The reason why we came is not just for the health of our dog. But the other day you met with Tatyana Yuryevna Torasovaya ..."

"Tatyana, who? Are you talking about Tatyana, the opera diva?"

"Yes."

"You must have made a mistake."

"Your wife, a lovely lady called Maria Victoria met with her friend Jorge the dog healer, and the healer was in the company of Tatyana Yuryevna Torasovaya."

"No! No way!"

"Well, all the same! Shame, isn't it? But we need a little bit of your help."

"With the utmost pleasure."

"You think what we think—he is simply a conman."

"He certainly is."

"How can we prove it?"

When *señor doctor Moreno Martinez* learned Tatyana and the con-man, as he called him, were coming back from their trip sometime tomorrow, he suggested they leave the dog with him, then they shook hands and the odd couple left the clinic with matching smiles of deep satisfaction.

***

"On the contrary, Jorge, I love her more than I love any other person, even more than Megé."

"Isn't she just a servant?"

"A servant! We don't call our faithful employees servants, I remember Olga as far as my memory goes. She loves me with all her heart, I know it."

"Well, I have my own reasons to dislike her. She has an agenda. She never looks me in the eye, she mumbles something in her language."

"You mean, in Russian?"

"Yes."

"Jorge, don't even try! Relax and co-exist."

"Don't get me wrong ..."

"I did not, and please, just be aware to what extent you entitle yourself ..."

"I apologise, my dear Tatyana, I sincerely apologise if I have offended your servant, but that wasn't my intent. I just wanted to tell you that she is not always what she appears to be."

"Jorge, just be a fine gentleman."

"You are right. I am."

When they arrived, Olga was in a state of panic once again.

It was early morning, they arrived in a taxi, she didn't want to call for Oleg, but when they walked in, Olga and Oleg were in the house with matching worried expression on their faces; Oleg went out quickly, whilst Olga said to Tatyana:

"I would like to talk to you in private."

"What is the matter?" asked Jorge.

Olga held Tatyana by her elbow and walked her into Tatyana's piano room.

There, once again Olga was to deliver the unpleasant news. She cautioned her but at the same time she assured her that they found the best veterinarian, and Tatyana, once again, nearly fainted. Jorge was called in, and in the voice of an expert, as if he were a graduated dog healer, he said:

"Who said you could leave Megé with a complete stranger? She is an intuitive dog, she is extremely intelligent and a private little darling. Did I ever say she could be left alone with a stranger?"

"Jorge, calm down."

"How can I calm down when your servant made the wrong decision? A decision that might be fatal for poor Megé?"

Olga's blood was boiling but she didn't dare utter a single word.

"Let's go! Hurry, hurry up, we have to go and get the poor little girl, take her back home. I have to examine her, calm her, she can be calmed only with my soothing voice."

Tatyana repeated:

"Jorge, calm down and be kind."

"Kind, I am but extremely worried, for this woman made the wrong decision."

"She never makes wrong decisions, for many, many years she has never made a single one."

"Well, she has made one now. Hurry up, I hope the driver is waiting ready to go."

He turned to Olga, saying:

"Address, address", to what Olga calmly replied:

"Oh, address, I have forgotten the address ... but I know the way."

So, there we go: in Oleg's car, there were four people ready to witness the epilogue to their story.

When they entered the clinic, there were approximately ten people sitting in the waiting room. Jorge said:

"Quick, quick, we have no time to waste! We have to see her immediately. Call that person who claimed she was ill."

Two more people joined this nameless and faceless crowd in the waiting room. Tatyana recognised the woman she met in front of the jewellery store and the man who made a rather unpleasant remark. They sat on the chairs, in front of the waiting crowd.

Then, another two people walked quietly in—Oleg and Olga, Tatyana's maid and her chauffeur. They sat simultaneously on the chairs without being told.

Tatyana raised her eyebrows and looked at Jorge, who said:

"What are the servant and the driver doing here?"

"Calm down, Jorge." said Tatyana quietly.

"I need to see Megé, immediately", he demanded.

Doctor Artemio Moreno Martinez said:

"Hello, dog healer."

Jorge started to talk louder but doctor Moreno Martinez cut him short in his sentence:

"Now we are going to talk, and you, dog healer, are going to listen. You'll listen to me first and then to my wife. Then, you will listen to

another ten or twelve people whose dogs you've healed for a hefty sum of money. Then those two kind people, who saw right through you, will speak, señor Oleg and señora Olga. Let me start: Megé is doing well, dear Tatyana. She was given tranquilisers for a prolonged period of time and high doses of vitamins that are prescribed for human consumption. On the day I met you, I understood that you were a simple crook without any education in the field where you were claiming to be an expert. You conned my, then fiancée, claiming that you improved her dog's health, whilst that dog was by its nature calmer and slower than the other one. You ran away the same day you met me, for you knew that your stay at my fiancé's was going to end, you knew I read through you and that my knowledge and education was something you couldn't fight. You can lie only to two groups of people: those who are too naïve, trusting and desperate if their pet is ill, or you can con those who are uneducated. Your bad luck is that you met educated people, who were just good citizens, good dog owners who cared. Genuinely kind and open-hearted people who fell for your stories that aren't true, for I have investigated you in the last few days and discovered who you really are. Just like me, you've never been to Buenos Aires, let alone lived there in a nice house with an honest family. You took advantage of a heart full of kindness that often makes my wife act silly and she opened the door to her home and let you live in her shed, for she believed your story. She believed because she had never met a scumbag before and was raised to believe that people were good and that a good Christian had to help a brother in a dire situation. You met me, you saw in my eyes that I could read you like a picture book; you cheap bastard, you unscrupulous liar. Do you recognise those people? You do! I found all of them easily, I even found a witness who saw you pick up an envelope that fell out of señora Mandez's bag, you counted the money and you threw away the birthday card. How much money was in that envelope? Look at all these people, regardless of whether you recognise them or not, now you are going to listen to their stories, for they are very interesting to all of us, including the police and the immigration department as some of their officers in plain clothes are sitting here. Let's start with señora Garcia Rodriguez."

In a very faint, trembling voice she started to narrate her story and the other stories followed in the thickest silence that ever fell upon any area of Madrid.

There was no police officer there or any immigration staff; there was just an endless river of humiliation that poured in his direction.

Olga was constantly wiping the corner of her lips hiding her little smile that barely noticeably played as if pulled by invisible strings, and Oleg just sat there without any facial expression.

Tatyana looked tired and somehow bored.

When each and every person finished their story, Tatyana asked for her dog. Megé happily ran towards Jorge first, licked his shoe, jumped up hoping he might pick her up, but Tatyana collected her into her arms and walked out. After Tatyana, Olga, then Oleg and finally Jorge left the office.

They sat in the car and Tatyana said:

"Come in, Jorge." and he did.

They drove home in silence.

Tatyana went into her room and started to play her piano; Jorge went into his room.

A few hours later Olga entered Tatyana's room:

"Dear Tatyana, what are you going to do? Am I going to tell him to leave the house now? Tell me."

"No, Olga. He has nowhere to go. I knew from the beginning who he was ... but Megé liked him ... she still likes him. He is a poor man; he did

what he did because he did not know any better. Let him stay until he decides when and where to go."

"But, Tatyana ..."

"Olga, please, do as I say. Thank you.

Margarita's Garden

Since no one was there to stop him, William Wildwood followed the girl to the garden, planted with various beautiful flowers, though the margaritas dominated and unintentionally, his mind labelled it as Margarita's Garden.

She sat on one of the two benches, the one furthest from the house, the one that looked directly into the colourful margaritas, and closed her eyes. She left the impression as if she was singing a soothing song, chanting a prayer or as if she remembered something of a very pleasant nature, or for that matter—anticipating something of a very pleasant nature.

He looked at her features, unintentionally, he thought again—*She appeared like a rose among the weeds; she looked otherworldly.*

He had met various kinds of women since his wife left him. Yes, she left him in haste when she learned that *'With such a man she would never acquire anything'*, that *'anything'* referred to extreme material wealth, including the finest art and jewellery. He never knew how he felt regarding her sudden and unexpected departure, for he was a wildly popular lawyer, yet she never worked a day, for she assumed that her apparent beauty had to be paid for and rewarded excessively. When she learned that William Wildwood was a very pragmatic and almost stingy man, sharp and analytical about every thought and decision, she decided to leave and find a better opportunity where she could again offer or sell her assets that were mainly sculpted by a fine surgeon's knife.

William Wildwood liked attractive women, he couldn't help himself, but there was another thing that always spoiled his choice—lots of them were not natural beauties, but as I stated above, the scalpel helped to get them those looks, which were considered by modern men to be attractive. He needed several fake looking beauties before he grew tired of such ridiculous masks which only masked their inner ugliness. That ugliness showed in a lack of empathy and kindness in general, and in an excessive, extreme thirst for someone else's wealth and status. Those beauties never read nourishing literature, never enjoyed a visit to the opera or any kind of fine art, only the price of things was what mattered and it sealed the ugliness of their empty souls.

There, in Margarita's Garden, whilst looking at the girl with closed eyes, he remembered Christa, a woman with the largest breasts one could buy, with lips like two vertically sewed up, oddly red, bananas. She bought and sewed up all the assets she showed off, hoping those assets would make wealthy men believe she was a desirable woman, yet she behaved like a domineering, heartless, calculating man. What a paradox! She would grab him by his manhood under the table and he would say, *'No, Christa, not here!'*, *'What a pussy!'* she would bark back and laugh loudly. A confident woman! There was no grace, no poise, no kindness or leniency, the attributes his mother possessed, her friends too and both of her sisters.

He shook his head in the hope of shaking off this memory that awoke shame every time he thought of that woman or of any other who chased after him, after his money and status, to be precise.

After a while he grew tired.

On rare occasions, when he had time to think about other things that were not related to the law and legislative decrees, he thought with a strong dose of nostalgia about the times when his mother moved around the house with such ease: effortlessly, elegantly, looking healthy and natural. His wife demanded, commanded, and showed off her breasts to everyone who wanted to have a look as they were on constant display, like some rare trophy in a glass vitrine. Even her nipples could be seen through her thin or transparent dresses; dresses he bought for a really ridiculous amount of money.

He met several Christa-like women on a dating website, the one Martin, his colleague, recommended, the one Martin used to resort to, where he lied he wasn't married, and a father of two children.

William said:

"Fine, fine, I'll give it a go."

And as if he was cursed (or the website bred only such creatures!) all women he met looked alike, behaved in the same manner and had similar needs.

When he really grew tired, he gave up his search for a companion.

So, now, on this fine afternoon, at a christening party, where he had found himself by sheer mistake as he believed, he laid his eyes on a young woman, almost a girl, who looked as if she had come from somewhere where women were taught some other art of being.

He barely noticed the beads of sweat slipping down his brow, and he struggled to form a sentence in his head, *"Hello, I am William Wildwood, a lawyer ... "*

'What the hell! Why would I introduce myself as a lawyer! What an idiot ... OK, another try—Hello, Wildwood. William Wildwood ...'

No, that wasn't the best introduction either; he thought it was dry, formal. What if he pays her a compliment?

No, not a compliment—that would be such a cliché, a cheap nasty cliché …

Why was he so confident when around unnatural, large-breasted women with masculine characteristics, yet he despised them and compared them constantly and unmercifully to his elegant, feminine mother?

A light wind changed the scenery: the butterflies flew up and danced on the wind's wings, the petals of the margaritas started dancing, the leaves started rustling and the wind chime gently sang; the girl opened her eyes and combed her hair with her fingers as if they were a thick but useful comb. A leaf of a paper, which was lying in her lap, the one William never noticed, rose up in the air and started to dance with the butterflies. The girl jumped to her feet trying to catch the leaf of the paper that William suspected might have been be a letter. He rose up, and being a tall and swift man, he caught the letter and handed it to the girl.

When she smiled, she showed the dimples in her cheeks and a row of uneven teeth. His first thought was, *'She's never heard about cosmetic dentistry'*, but that was a positive statement rather than putting her down for not taking enough dental care. Those uneven teeth added charm to her natural beauty.

Now he said:

"William Wildwood."

"Margarita Manning."

Short silence. Margarita had a little mysterious smile resting on her lips. She looked down and after another few seconds, she said:

"William Wildwood, a lawyer?"

"Indeed."

She smiled and was about to leave the garden, but he grabbed her by the wrist and observed:

"Looks like we know each other already."

"We don't. I've just heard about you."

"I hope you heard positive things, for I am a lawyer, often bad things are said about my kind."

"No, no. When I asked if you were a lawyer, I just needed confirmation that you were the William Wildwood I heard about before."

"May I ask, Margarita, who would be the person talking about me with a young ... woman." (he left out the word *'beautiful'* after a quick thought).

"I am not sure that'd be appropriate conversation."

Now William took her by the hand and led her back to the bench. They sat down looking at the margaritas.

"Is this your house?"

"This is my garden."

"Margarita's Garden?"

"Yes."

"The house is someone else's and the garden is yours?"

"Yes, sir."

"Don't call me sir. I am not an old man. Older than you, certainly, but still, I don't deserve a young woman calling me sir."

"I'll call you William, if you wish so."

"I'll call you Margarita."

"D'accord."

"I came here, to this christening by sheer mistake."

"How come?"

"A client of mine called me to write his will, obviously, I was given the wrong time. I was let in, still I don't know where he is at the moment."

"Is he changing his will?"

"Apparently."

She smiled. To William she smelled of wild roses rather than margaritas, even though they were sitting in the garden of margaritas and she bore the name of the beautiful flower. She smelled of wild roses. He said:

"You smell of wild roses."

"I beg your pardon!"

"I said, you smell of wild roses."

"And you talk nonsense."

"Often, I do."

"Lawyers, you talk nonsense."

"We do! More often than not, we do. But still, you smell of wild roses."

"If you are trying to flatter ... please don't."

"May I ask for clarification?" and without waiting for her permission he continued:

"The house is someone else's and the margarita Garden is Margarita's? How is that possible?"

"I am a gardener, and I look after this garden. It was I who planted it with margaritas."

"Let me look at your hands. No, you are not a gardener, Margarita."

"No, I am not."

"Okay, try again. Is there any good explanation to this situation: the house belongs to someone else, and the garden is yours?"

"Yes, sir."

"Yes, William."

"Yes, William, the garden is mine."

"And may I ask to whom the house belongs?"

"To the owner."

"To the owner?"

"Yes, to your client. The one who invited you to the christening."

"No, no, that is not correct. I am here, at this event, by mistake. I was called in at the wrong time. Just like you, I was bored and wanted to see this beautiful garden."

"You wanted to see me."

Now, William Wildwood was taken by surprise. His mind was quick but hers was quicker:

"You said nothing."

"Oh, no, no ... not nothing. I said, you are quite right. I wanted to see you."

"Why?"

"I thought you were bored, just like I was."

"I am never bored. I always write stories in my head."

"You write stories in your head? Do you write them down on paper? On your computer?"

"Mainly in my head."

"Is it then that you made up the story that you know me? That you already heard about me?"

"If you had followed what I said before you would have understood that I haven't made up this story, for I asked you if you were a lawyer. How could I possibly have known that you were a lawyer or that you have a hound called Arrow?"

"You know I have a hound?"

"Yes, sir."

"Yes, William."

"Yes, William, I know about your dog."

"Hmm, Margarita, now it is not a question of who I am, but I am puzzled with the question of who you are, young lady."

She smiled and showed her dimples again, and a row of slightly crooked teeth.

"Your teeth are uneven."

"Yes, they are."

"It is quite charming, isn't it?"

"If you say so si...."

"William."

"If you say so, William."

"And it doesn't bother you?"

"Should it?"

"No. You don't need to strive for perfection, you are almost there, and you are well aware of it."

"The strangest thing is: you are a lawyer yet your language is almost poetic, almost like the language of one of my characters that appears on the fringes of my imagination, in my head, where I write my stories daily."

"Do you write them in your garden?"

"Yes. Predominantly."

"Where else?"

"Everywhere. Wherever I am, wherever I go, I take my stories with me, and on the go I add to the story or I take away words, I edit and rewrite."

"So, that would be your daily duty?"

"Yes, William."

"Are you paid for your skill?"

"No, William."

"May I ask you a very personal question?"

"Hmm, I am not sure about that ... Let me think."

After a short while, she opened her eyes and said:

"Yes, you may ask a very personal question but I reserve the right not to answer if I find it inappropriate."

"I understand that you are an exquisite writer who writes all day long. If you are not paid for that fine work, how do you pay your bills ... or, to be more precise, hopefully not too rude—who pays for your living?"

With a gentle smile, Margarita stayed silent. It sounded as if she hummed a gentle melody, she looked as if she conversed with invisible friends. He waited for a long time, yet she stayed silent.

A woman came out. In a brisk walk, she approached.

"Mister Wildwood?"

"Yes."

He stood up and extended his hand.

"M. Moreau will be available soon. If you would like something to drink, a maid will bring it out."

"I am very happy right now. Whenever he is ready, let me know."

"Margarita, would you want to come in the house?"

"I would not."

"But I am asking you nicely to come in."

"Equally as nicely, I am declining your invitation."

"It is cold."

"Not for me. You can go in and get warm, I am fine."

William Wildwood said to the woman:

"I am enjoying young Margarita's company."

"She can be such a bore." she answered scornfully.

"You can be, too.", said Margarita with her trademark smile.

The woman walked into the house.

"Let's continue with our conversation. Do you remember my question?"

"Yes, I do remember, but as I said before you phrased it—I am retaining the right to remain silent. Not to answer it."

"Who was this woman?"

"Just a woman."

"Is she related to you?"

"No. I would hate that."

"Is she related to Mister Moreau?"

"How do I know?"

"So far, all you know about this household is: the house belongs to someone else and that Margarita's Garden belongs to you."

"Correct, William Wildwood."

William Wildwood wanted to ask another question, but the young woman stood up and walked towards the other end of the garden, she took off her dress and regardless of the coolish autumn day, she jumped into the pool which was hidden to William's eyes until she jumped in, and the drops of water flew easily up together with luminous butterflies and dreamy dragonflies.

"A mischievous, capricious and mysterious woman", he said almost loudly, and the voice above his head approved and confirmed his statement:

"You are right Mister Wildwood, capricious above all. Would you be so kind as to follow me, M. Moreau is waiting for you."

William Wildwood was pleasantly surprised by Mr Moreau's appearance: he was in his mid-seventies, yet he retained a fresh look of a man at least twenty years younger: he was tall, solidly built, yet his stomach was lean and his shirt was tucked into his neatly pressed trousers; his eyes were brazen but warm enough and a comfortable smile rested on his lips. He extended his long arm and William enjoyed his strong, manly handshake.

"Let's sit! What would you like to drink Mr Wildwood?"

"I don't want to waste your time, let's get down to work, I bet you are tired by now, all those people."

"Quite the contrary, I enjoy having people around me, it energises me. Nevertheless, I called you to rewrite my testament; just a few slight changes."

"I am well aware of your status, of who you are ... I was sincerely flattered, yet very surprised you summoned me for such a task."

"I don't want my lawyer to get involved in such a matter. I need someone else and I heard from certain people that you would be the most suitable person for this task."

William Wildwood opened his mouth to thank him, but he was interrupted with another question:

"Did you meet her?"

"Margarita?"

"Yes."

"In the garden. She said it was her garden."

The Frenchman, *'M. Moreau'* as the other woman addressed him, smiled and said with a hoarse voice in his thick accent:

"She said 'it is her garden'! She says many things Mr Wildwood; don't get charmed by this little adorable puppy. We'll see what we'll decide about the garden. I think ... I think, I suppose, I have to leave something to her as well ... she made up, all in her head, all of her stories whilst sitting in this garden, or that is what she claims ... you never know what's what when she talks ... but who really cares, Mr Wildwood, who really cares?"

"Is she related to you ... or is she Mrs Moreau ...?"

"I see, Mr Wildwood, you are keen to hear the story about this young beautiful flower that sits in my garden and thinks up her stories. She did tell you that she only writes in her head? No evidence of her stories on any piece of paper or any computer. But I was happy she came in and stayed in my garden. Yes, I did promise her the garden on one very

special night, very, very special night, you understand what I mean ... No, no, it is not what you think, Mr Wildwood, it is not! I am not saying that, that would be dishonest, it would be a lie, a flat out lie and a man of my status and reputation or age shouldn't lie. I swear, it is not what you think ... but, never mind, you can think, in the end, whatever you want, I'll tell you measured portions, which means what I choose to share ... I met a woman, the kind I would never get involved with, but somehow she knew things that were not intended for the general public to hear or to spread around. No, no, she never blackmailed anyone, not me, but she came to talk, and talk we did. You know those women that have large breasts, but they are not natural breasts, they enlarge them et cetera. Yes, she was one of them, I really didn't know what to say to her, I just wanted to give her some money and we could have finished that story there and then. But ... yes, she came up with some names ... people that I knew and respect and those whom I wanted to protect, so I offered more money, but she asked me to buy a nice little house for her, in exchange, she said, she would forget that story and all the names she had in her book ... there was more to that story, but let's keep it short, without too many unnecessary details. You know such kind of women, I bet you do. Soon after her visit to my house, a young woman came knocking at my door, Aveline let her in, she was stubborn, refusing to see anyone else but me, in the end they showed her in ... that's how I met Margarita, a lovely girl, with a great story ... a story that I started to believe to be true, and in the end I decided to believe and trust her... for, my dear Mr Wildwood, even without a degree in psychology I read people, I read them like an open book, any person to be precise I read like an open book. Her mother, Christa, the woman with the large breasts, the one who came to my house and told me a very peculiar story, the woman you were married to quite a number of years ago, was a cunning one—once she knew a secret, she would keep it to herself only if one was ready to pay a very high price in order to keep the story under a veil of secrecy. You know that, I bet you know it all. I wouldn't be surprised if you were the one who told her the story, the details, gave her the names, addresses and telephone numbers. I wouldn't be surprised, but look, maybe I am not right ... it is just a speculation, I am not accusing anyone of anything ... oh, Mr Wildwood, have I asked you if you wanted a stiff drink? Yes, I have! Fine then, I can continue with some parts of this story, just to inform you before we get down to our work, to the reason why I called you, as I said before—to rewrite my will, the testament as you would call it. The girl asked for the garden, and in haste I promised her the garden, and I am a man who never breaks his promises, so most likely the garden will end up in her name. What I want to say precisely—it will become her rightful, legal possession. And, that would be the right decision, my dear Mr Wildwood, I assume you don't mind if I call you 'my dear Mr Wildwood'."

William Wildwood tried several times to squeeze in some words, between the minuscule gaps Mr Moreau marked by his inhalations, without any success. Therefore, William Wildwood took out his cigarette box and lighter, believing Mr Moreau would stop him in his attempt to light a cigarette in his living room, giving him a chance to say something, but Mr Moreau, absolutely indifferent, continued stringing his sentences together. Without feeling guilty, William Wildwood blew a smoke ring towards his interlocutor's stony face which stayed unchanged.

"Whatever the girl told me, we checked those stories out, they turned out to be true, I gave her shelter, yes, I did, she was a good child, a good young woman, no, she wasn't a cheat. I thought initially she was your daughter, but it wasn't the case, I witnessed, as well, today's encounter, you couldn't have acted so perfectly, nor could she; it was obvious you two never met; you were not her stepfather either! I estimate that the

woman never even told you she had a daughter, for she was a liar, I bet you know it better than I do ... but on the other hand, I don't know how much you told her, way back when she was your wife, when you two shared a marital bed. I know, my dear Mr Wildwood, that people say all sorts of things in their marital bed, it is such a strange place ... anything can be shared there, anything. Let's get back to the girl now, we call her Margarita, but we checked that out too, it wasn't her birth name, her name was quite a strange name, Tallulah; she changed it when she came to New York to Olivia ... and eventually she became Margarita. We'll still call her Margarita, for it really suits her, her character, her whole personality ... she loves margaritas, she asked the gardener to plant margaritas and I can tell you, even though I am not an expert, nor an admirer of gardens—the garden looks nicer, more colourful and fresh due to the margaritas in general and to Margarita in particular. She sits there all day long writing her stories in her head. She is as innocent as one can be; she is a real angel, thank God, she never really knew her mother the way you knew her mother, isn't it so, Mr Wildwood? No, no, don't say a word now, you'll talk later when we get down to bona fide business, the real reason why I called you in today, on the exact day of my grandchild's christening; it was a mistake, almost a mistake, but you are here now, and we don't have to worry about another day or appointment. The will has to be rewritten, anyway. Let me gather my thoughts, Mr Wildwood ... according to Margarita's story she met her mother, the former Mrs Wildwood, three months ago. Finally, she found her with the help of a man who was an honest man, a good lawyer and a good father, but, Mr Wildwood, we all have weaknesses, don't we? That honest man who helped the young Margarita to track down her birth mother was Mr Berreau, yes, Mr Wildwood, exactly that Mr Berreau. I never asked about the details how my, of-many-years-in-service lawyer, Mr Berreau, met the girl, I mean, young Margarita. I never even felt entitled to ask, I would never even ask such a private question ... but, nevertheless, they searched for her birth mother and Mr Berreau spent long nights with the girl and possibly, probably ... I can't say what had happened, but ... let's say he succeeded in finding her mother about the same time when a woman who claimed to be Mrs Christa Pitt-Barlow came to my house with quite an indecent proposal because she knew ... let's say some fragments of my dealings, some of my associates ... let's leave it there. We do a background check on each and every person we come in contact with, you have to know that, Mr Wildwood. Yes, every person, even you. Because we checked you out, I know what a good lawyer you are, I know about your success rate and I know the gossip that housewives read in the yellow press about your, let's call them, adventures. On one particular evening Margarita persuaded Mrs Pitt-Barlow, I mean, her birth mother, to have dinner together. I know it was true, for we were following Mr Berreau for some time, we were aware he was spending long evenings with a young woman; we knew who the young woman was and we knew everything about the so-called Pitt Barlow woman. They came to my door with different stories, but they didn't know the stories were checked out thoroughly long before they appeared on my threshold with absolutely different agendas and aims. Let's cut the long story short: the so-called Pitt-Barlow was turned down with all her offers, I dislike saying anything more about it, but I kept the young girl, for she, at the time, couldn't find any better place to write her stories but in my garden. The one I promised to be hers one day; yes, I promised it in haste, almost with a dose of excitement, for this game was so delicious and the girl so gifted and plain. Hence, I called you, we need your help—my testament has to be re-written. Do you agree? You do agree, why wouldn't you, for you are going to be handsomely rewarded, just don't fall into the trap, into the illusion that the girl might have any interest in you. For she doesn't have any. No, no, don't even try, just listen, I dislike it when people interrupt my sentences; I dislike it when the current of my thoughts is abruptly changed. So, do not try! Thank you!"

William Wildwood felt as if thousands of yellow bitter ants were crawling up his back—from the base of his spine up into his head, angrily marching on the highway of his spine. Paradoxically, he felt spineless. He needed a stiff drink but his lips were stiff and sealed. With his sharp eyes, Mr Moreau sized him up once again and said:

"I'll call a maid, I see you need that stiff drink I offered earlier. I'll leave you here for a moment, as I have to go to the safe to fetch my old testament. Then you'll read it out loud, we will agree, together, what has to be changed and how you will rewrite it. Be patient, enjoy this lovely music, I bet you love jazz, if not, tell me what would you prefer, we have all sorts of music, we love the late Pavarotti, for goodness sake, who doesn't? Am I not right? Who doesn't adore the late Pavarotti? We went to all the major opera houses to attend his performances and recitals, once we even travelled to Sydney, to their extravagant opera house to hear him sing. Have you been to the Sydney Opera House? No? Oh, marvellous building, you know the one that looks like giant shells clumsily glued together, emerging from the sea ... well, something really nice to see, something different and almost special. We never slept there, in Sydney, when it all finished we went back to the States ... we flew on a private jet, actually, it was such a long flight. Never mind, I will be back in a few minutes and you'll get your drink and you'll gather your thoughts together, so when I come back with the paperwork you'll be prepared in your mind. By now, you have enough information, you can refresh your memory and we can go on with our business. Yes, in the end I called you for business, so far we have just indulged ourselves in a friendly chat."

The music didn't help his concentration; he couldn't believe that he ever, ever uttered a word about Mr Moreau to his former wife Christa. Whilst waiting, his body was heavily pressed against the innocent sofa, his forehead frowned, adorned by numerous drops of sweat; he almost jumped up when someone tapped his shoulder:

"May I sit next to you, William?" but without waiting for an answer, Margarita comfortably sank into the soft leather, curling her legs up and offering a handkerchief, *"Wipe off your brow, William."*

"You are Christa's daughter, why didn't you tell me?"

"Why didn't I tell you? How on earth would I have ever known you still remembered Christa? I am not too sure if she was my real mother, my birth mother. That's what Jean-Luc, I mean, Mr Berreau, said a few months ago. He helped me track her down, in the end she was reluctant to admit anything ... look, I dislike talking about my mother, I have peace of mind in my Margarita Garden, and I don't want to remember disturbing things and people. She talked about you; you have to know that! She tried to convince me that my father was a famous lawyer ... but it wasn't true ... stay relaxed William, you are not my father ... The whole episode will end up in one of my stories, but they have to stay locked in my head, for they are not intended for a wider audience. Especially Mr Moreau would be upset if I ever wanted to write those stories down. Unacceptable! I will inherit the Garden, and I am very pleased with such a prospect, that was all I ever wanted. I never asked for money or for your head, like my mother did. Anyway, I like you; you look like a decent man, just caught up in the web of legal dishonesty, lies, controversy, corruption and all those heavy deeds, or misdeeds, that go hand-in-hand with success in your field."

"Your story, Margarita, or whatever your real name might be, is quite confusing, it doesn't add up."

"I know! It's so strange. Yours likewise! Who would ever marry someone like Christa? Sorry, none of my business, but you were her fourth husband, and now she said she has remarried and bears the Pitt-Barlow surname. Who on earth is Pitt-Barlow? Do you know anyone by that name? A lawyer? A judge? A sophisticated crook? Some bankster? Never mind, William, those are such boring topics, in the end all I want is to sit in my garden, my Margarita Garden, and write my stories in my head. Now that I know the testament is going to be rewritten, I can sigh a sigh of relief. Would you like another drink? It looks as if he was caught with guests again; he was so busy all day long. You see that tall man over there? The one leaning against the windowsill? Do you recognise him? Yes! That's him! He is the godfather of the child. To shorten your boredom of waiting, do you want me to entertain you with one of my stories, knowing Mr Moreau is never in a hurry? I can give you insight into my latest piece of writing which happened in my head, yeah? I can tell you a story that was already written or, if you prefer, I can make one up in your honour? What would you prefer, William?"

"Feel free to choose from your repertoire." Said a sullen William.

"Let me see ... I think I will make up a story, just for you. You can give it a name when I finish it. When I was born, my mamma left me in front of my father's mother's door like a loaf of bread wrapped in cellophane paper that smelt of the margaritas she was given that same day. No, not as an acknowledgment of giving birth to a child, but someone had stolen her moped on that day and left a bouquet of margaritas together with an apologetic message: 'I am sorry, I need it more than you do at this weird moment, this early hour of the day. Accept my apology and the beautiful margaritas, for that is all I have right now. If I ever amount to anything in life, believe me, I swear, I plan to, I shall bring the moped back with an even bigger bunch of margaritas, xx Al.' No one knew who the mysterious Al was, was it a woman or a man, it doesn't really matter

for the plot of the story. Mamma left me at the threshold wrapped in cellophane, and she used the same piece of paper on which Al had written a message for her (that's how I came to know what Al had written in haste to Mamma). On the other side of the original message my mamma had written in her tired handwriting (she was tired for she gave a birth to me on that very same day). She said: 'Hey Betty, I won't start with Dear Betty, we both know that you hate me and that I hate you in return. Betty, I have given birth to this baby girl, she is your son's daughter. I wrapped her nicely in nice paper, like a flower, if you wish you could name her after a flower, something like Rose, or Rosemary, or Violet would make quite a name. I got to go elsewhere, Betty; I can't stay stuck here, with your son. He is as mad as a mad dog. He is mad like you, Betty. I always believed that he drank your madness through your milk when you were breastfeeding. That is partly a reason why I won't breast-feed this child, who knows what seeds of madness she could take in whilst suckling? Look after her, Betty, for I might be back one day. If I don't come back, let the child know my name, only my first name.'

At least, Al had signed their message, my mother never even signed hers; I bet my papa's mother never knew who had written that message to her. They said my father chased after every woman in the County and wider. That's that! No, you don't need to know how Betty had got rid of me. Irrelevant! I wasn't an orphan either; I grew up in a nice family with three other siblings, but one day, it was late summer, I decided to run away. I couldn't stand the idea that I was, like a bad seed, planted in someone else's beautiful garden, a garden of roses and gardenias where I was a weed. There you have it! You don't need to know more of this part of my life. I changed my name and had a little bit of luck doing it, for I met a very nice man who wanted to marry me. I really never wanted to be called someone's wife, I just wanted to stay true to my real self, without any wish or aim to tailor myself around someone's life, career or good name. He had it all: a good life, a promising career and a solid name, a whole lot of people knew who his papa was, believe me, he wasn't a Mickey Mouse guy. For several years I lived under his roof, I told white lies avoiding mentioning my family, I just simply told him they passed away. With him I met sophisticated, educated people, he taught me how to mingle with those kind of people, I wore beautiful clothes and was happy, temporarily. Then the defect of my character started to creep in on a daily basis and I couldn't control anything any longer. I wasn't dishonest! No, I wasn't. I told him, but he refused to believe it, I told him my bad self was coming out more and more and I couldn't control it, and that destructive-self was calling me to wander around New York and look for that woman who left me wrapped in perfumed paper in front of someone's door. I can't tell you why I desperately needed to find this woman. Why? Why was she ruining my daily attempts at happiness even though she was just a big fat lie nestled between my imagination and fragments of my remembrance? You, William, won't figure it out, just like I couldn't, so do not frown, recline comfortably in this soft sofa and listen without interrupting. The man I left, who believed back then, that he would go mad if I ever left him, survived, and as I heard he said he was going to find me. That was the reason why I changed my name again. You do not need to know what my previous names were, for it doesn't help to improve this story in any particular way. It could only bring more confusion, for by now you are well aware that my stories are not an easy read; yes, you are right, quite complicated. But to cut a long story short let's get to the moment when I changed my name to Margarita. It was just before I found my mother with the help of my lawyer. I mean, Mr Moreau's lawyer, which is Mr Berreau. French names, they make me struggle pronouncing them sometimes, even though my former partner took care of everything, so I even had private French lessons to give my English a mellower rhythm and posher pronunciation. He liked sophisti-

cated women and did everything to squeeze me into this perfect model he tailored for me. As I hadn't had much money at that time, for no one lives from writing and selling stories, I promised Mr Berreau that every day I would tell him a new, exciting story in exchange for his services. He thought I had an aristocratic background and I never really attempted to make him think any different, so I started to narrate stories about the Prussian royal family, and I was astounded how much I really knew about them as I liked reading about European history and old royal families. A very, very strange habit and need for a modest American woman, you may say, William Wildwood, but you never heard any of my made-on-the-spot stories, therefore you can't judge my talent. When you put talent and rare knowledge together, you can easily fascinate any man.

She moved closer, and whispered in his ear:

"All right, dare I say, she blackmailed him, but this is strictly between you and me. No one ever mentioned the word 'blackmail', but your name came up several times in different contexts and narrations. That's what I heard. Even though it appeared that he was quite angry with you, he picked you to rewrite his testament. Let's forget for a while about Mr Moreau, and let me tell you how I met my mother. Mr Berreau, the lawyer, the man I was narrating my stories to in exchange for his services, finally tracked her down, he said it wasn't of my concern how he had found her. I never asked. I just kept telling him stories, he would pick a topic and I would come up with a story on demand. Some of his ideas were quite weird, but I learned not to label people, things or stories. Just to take everything as it comes. You know, life gets utterly uncomplicated and easy when you stop judging and calculating. We met on a very ordinary day, as I remember it was a plain, uneventful Wednesday. All I did that day was manicuring my hands and nails, for I always believed

that hands show who you are: it is entirely different, the hand of a writer in comparison to, let's say, the hand of a waitress, social worker, housewife or even a lawyer. I combed my hair and applied a little bit of make-up, in case she was a natural beauty, in the end I had to inherit those genes from someone. I wore a nice dress. Not too expensive, in case she came casually dressed. We all see people differently, don't we? Especially men see us differently to what other women see. I really don't know what impressed you, for I believe it wasn't her physical appearance. I laid my eyes on her and shivers went down my spine. Or up. I just felt so uncomfortable. Not the creature of infinite beauty, the way I imagined someone who gave birth to me. I know, William, it sounds silly when I say that, almost as if I am an utterly vain person, but if I am honest in my narrations, I must say it the way it was. Let me now use plain language: she was a plastic woman ... her breasts were so large, popping out of her dress ... making me feel almost hysterical. She looked at me with a pair of cold, cold eyes, opened wide, her fake eyelashes were for some reason uneven, her face was without any wrinkles, and her lips were the biggest embarrassment on that stretched out face. She couldn't control her lips; I barely understood what she wanted to say. It took me a good half hour to get used to her way of speaking as her sentences were not coherent, I suspected that silicones, Botox or other poisons leaked and were carried through her blood into her brain, which was thick like the foam one stuffs garden bench pillows with. Among other things she said was that she didn't get anything from you when she divorced you. She said 'Nothing' and it sounded through her lips as if she said 'Nofin'. Whenever she mentioned you she would say 'Nofin', even though I couldn't read anger on her ironed-out face, I could detect it in her voice, for anger coloured it dark and heavy. Why did she mention you? Well, she was retelling her wedding tales. She claimed she had had four husbands, but only you were a lawyer. So, no one else knew as much as you knew. Her face was grotesque, her body, I would say, ridiculous with those oversized breasts, her hair extensions too long ... but, you know, William, she wasn't actually poisoned by Botox or silicones or any of those poisons, for she knew what she wanted. She really knew! The only reason why she really wanted to meet me was to see Mr Berreau, for she knew whose lawyer he was! Cunning one, hey? She was not naïve in the slightest, but William, nor was I. As soon as I joined the dots it all clicked! She wanted to frame you because you never left her anything, and she wanted to cash in on the stories you told her way back when you two were married. We met once again, without the presence of my lawyer, I mean Mr Moreau's lawyer, just the two of us. She asked if I wanted to get rich overnight. Not just rich, but she said, 'obscenely rich'? To which I said, 'I do' and she told me what I had to do in order to get rich overnight. It involved Mr Moreau, Mr Berreau and, strangely—you, William. I told her I had to think about it a little, which I did. I couldn't tell you how much and what Mr Moreau believed, but after a while he warmed up to me and started inviting me to his house almost every day. One day he said, 'You know, young Margarita, I believe all of your stories. Way back from the time you were called Tallulah, Olivia and Margarita. We checked your stories and we couldn't find the smallest discrepancy or lie. You must be a master storyteller, the type born once a century. Or, you are telling the complete truth.' It turned out to be the latter; he gained my trust and offered a garden, to stay in it as long as I wished, for he knew that my stories were worthy of his garden ... and the garden worthy of my presence. What do you think, William, is it worthy my presence? Of course, it is! I am glad we are on the same page, or figuratively speaking—in the same garden. Here, take this handkerchief and wipe off your brow; it is quite a humid day today, isn't it?

The strange thing is—I never perspire. Even when I was a young child, we would play all sorts of sports, everyone would get damp with sweat but me. As dry as dry martini. You are not a chubby man, you shouldn't perspire that much, but hey, we are all different."

She leaned towards William Wildwood and pressed her body against his. This move had only intensified his, already excessive, sweating and increased his heart rate. She whispered, *"Everything's going to be all right, William, just do what you are told."* She rewarded his eyes with the most beautiful smile and the most innocent direct look. At that moment, to William, the look in her beautiful green eyes was the look of a fallen angel.

William was about to open his mouth and ask the first question from the list he had formed under his sweaty brow, but he noticed Mr Moreau approaching with an unforced smile and some papers in his left hand. He waved those papers towards them and said:

"Here, all is prepared."

He pushed himself between the two of them and asked, still with an unforced, almost friendly smile:

"Did she entertain you fabulously, Mr Wildwood? She is such a storyteller, pity she is reluctant to write her stories down. She wants them to stay locked in her pretty head, which to me is quite a selfish act, but if I were her, honoured with such a gift, I think often I would be as selfish as she is, for—why share those gems with ordinary folk? I would probably be just like her, saving my stories for a selected few. Let's move a step closer to the closure of today's meeting. I bet you have places to go and people to see, and when it comes to time management I am not the best at it. Here are three copies. One is for you, Mr Wildwood, the other is for the young Margarita and the third one, naturally, for me. Have a good read and if you have any objections or suggestions, we can go through it together. All three."

William Wildwood was not convinced from the beginning that all his host wanted was to rewrite his testament, but reading the papers, his sweat drops multiplied and turned into a flowing river and the spot under his rear end was drenched as if he had wet himself. Maybe he did, we will never know such a private detail. This was not a testament, the usual testament he would write or rewrite. It was a kind of testament … yes, there was a mention of Margarita's Garden transferred in Margarita's name, some paragraph on margaritas and gardenias, total nonsense, Margarita's Garden in the context of his house. This was not his house; William's house. He read it again, Mr Moreau cleared his throat, asked for a bottle of Moët & Chandon and three glasses and looked at the melting William Wildwood.

"Any questions, Mr Wildwood?"

William remained silent. Margarita said:

"It looks like Mr Wildwood agrees with the testament ... don't you, William?"

Still, William Wildwood remained speechless and that wet patch below his bottom grew bigger and wider. It grew quickly; it looked like he would drown in it by the end of the afternoon.

"But this isn't my house, Mr Moreau."

"What do you mean, it is not your house? Don't skim the document, please, read it again, for goodness' sake you are a lawyer, you should understand a plain document, go, go back to it and read it one more time. Read it slowly, thoroughly; take as much time as you need to figure it all out."

The Moët & Chandon and five glasses arrived on a silver tray. Mr Berreau, Mr Moreau's lawyer, joined them and a tall nameless man too.

Very tall, not only nameless, but speechless as well. He never uttered a word. He was just standing there with his big arms crossed on his chest, his legs apart and his big, solid-built body upright, he looked as if he was showing his physical beauty and superiority. The Champagne cork catapulted and hit the opposing wall, it almost hit one of the Picasso paintings, the glasses were filled up and everyone rose their glass up but William.

"We will salute when he signs it. C'mon Mr Wildwood, you've had enough time to read it, sign the testament, I am not an impatient man, but look, there are other people here waiting for me, I have dedicated enough time to you. All I have time for now is to salute you on your fantastic decision."

"What have I decided?"

"Gentlemen! Did you hear the question? He is asking what he has decided! Dear Mr Wildwood you are a serious man, a lawyer, yet you are asking me, us, what you have decided. You know what you have decided. You have decided to sign the garden into Margarita's name. You are giving her the Garden as a present. She does deserve it, doesn't she?"

"I don't know if she deserves it or not, Mr Moreau, but the Garden isn't mine, you know that."

"I told you to read the document carefully, you are a lawyer, I emphasised that a number of times; Mr Wildwood, don't waste our time, my patience is growing thinner ... if you think you need another look into the document, fine, read again but read it this time with full awareness."

"This is your house, Mr Moreau ..."

"It is not mine anymore. You have bought it. Actually, we have exchanged houses. Here, you said we will swap houses as they have similar market value, I am not a petty person, give or take a hundred thousand, who cares, I am quite happy to relocate as I miss living close to water."

"According to your plan, where am I going to live, Mr Moreau?"

"Where are you going to live? How can I answer that question, Mr Wildwood? That's entirely up to you. Now, sign it so that we can move on, here, our glasses are ready."

The excessively tall man came closer and stood behind Mr Moreau's back. With his legs spread wide, he was now looking directly in William Wildwood's eyes.

"You want me to sign this house in her name?"

"You are the one who wants it, Mr Wildwood. It says in the document that you are signing over your house in Ms Margarita's name. It was your decision. I am the one who will sign this beautiful garden over to her name. We negotiated houses, not a garden, so, according to our agreement, the house is yours and the garden is still mine. I am giving the garden to Margarita, as I promised earlier, and you are signing your house into her name. What is so difficult here to understand, Mr Wildwood?"

The champagne was still in the glasses; the bubbles disappeared. The butler brought, on a silver tray, another bottle of champagne, and two more men in double-breasted suits joined around the low glass table. William recognised the taller man. His name was Laurence Malmassari, a dirty cop, confident and outspoken as if there was no law above him.

"Witnesses. We need two witnesses, don't we?"

Margarita took off her dress and went out. William noticed a flock of birds flew up as water splashed high.

It was one of the happier days in Margarita's life: she got, not only the garden of her dreams but a house as well, for kind Mr William Wildwood under the pressure of his conscience corrected a cruel decision he made in his past when he coldly told his wife Christa, *'You are free to go but the same way you came—empty-handed.'*

Margarita was convinced Christa was her mother, she said to herself whilst swimming with the goldfish and dragonflies buzzing above her head, *'Blood is thicker than water."*

Back in the house she heard the *'chin-chin'* rattling of five glasses, kind Mr William Wildwood had signed *his will*, which was to be implemented as soon as it was signed.

Portia's Bad Habit

When Portia de Huante was a little girl, she developed the bad habit of biting her nails. She was particularly keen on her thumbs.

Usually lunch was served at noon, and she developed such an attuned feeling of sensing those ten minutes before the clock started clanging its first strikes. She ran fast, as if she was chased by her, often angry, grandmother and hid behind the shrub dividing two houses: their house and her grandma’s house.

She would squat or kneel as if in a prayer and commence dedicatedly biting her left-hand thumb, first. It lasted precisely four minutes, as her inner, unmistakable, clock would count; then still hungry, she would swap thumbs and repeat the exact routine dedicatedly. It was all done in eight minutes precisely; she would lick the wounds and the droplets of blood, straighten her dress, brush the dirt off her knees and run into the dining room.

Her grandmother would fire at her:

“Show me your hands!”

Portia De Huante always ran to her father, as he was the only one who could calm his mother down with words:

“Let me handle it, Mamma.”

Portia would spend some time in her daddy’s lap; he, stroking her long hair always started with the same phrase:

“This is a bad habit, you’ve got to stop it.”

A year earlier, her grandmother took a clove of garlic and smeared her thumbs. That practice was applied every evening before going to bed.

But it didn't stop her from biting her thumbnails and the pinkish skin around them. Grandma strengthened her medicine when she realised that garlic wasn't a strong enough remedy to turn Portia off her favourite pleasure. Chilli pepper was the next remedy, and that made Portia vomit, and if she touched her eyes with her fingers they would unstoppably shed tears. They were red and itchy the next day and Father strictly forbade such a practice.

Her thumbs were always swollen, red, inflamed and bursting with puss around her tiny fingernails, or shall I say, the remains of her nails.

Her nails were a topic at the dinner table; they were a topic at family gatherings and in her school, too.

When she was seven, they took her to a psychologist to fix the problem.

It was a successful attempt, for Portia de Huante had stopped her bad habit.

For an entire week!

The following week, she not only bit the nails but she bit off the skin and the flesh around the nails as well; one could see pink and red flesh turning into a pussy puddle, which clearly indicated that the painful grimace on her face was the result of the puss.

A few weeks after that, they took her to a priest.

They all thought he might put some sense into her; he talked about things that would scare some other kids, they could scare Portia too, only if she weren't that fond of her fine entertainment.

Wherever they took her it had to be after noon, for she needed those ten minutes of loneliness, hidden behind the shrub which divided the two houses: their house and her grandma's.

They told her that she would lose all her friends and would grow old all alone, they told her no one would be willing to marry her, or no one would ever consider her pretty … but it didn't help. She kept on biting her nails, skin and flesh around them. Her thumbs looked like warriors who came from a bloody battle. She pitied them, she promised them to treat them better, she talked to them the way one talks to their best friends: sometimes with the sweetest words, and sometimes scolding them or promising better treatment.

Then, guests arrived one day.

Portia de Huante was seventeen years old and her thumbs looked like the thumbs of a seventy-year-old woman. She learned how to hide them, and she invented all sorts of lies to tell when asked *'What happened to your thumbs?'*

"Nothing!", or

"The neighbour's dog bit me!", or

"I touched a hot tray from the oven..." she never looked in the eyes of anyone who asked. Then she would run away, or behind the shrub or down to the riverbank.

When the guests arrived, Portia de Huante was hiding in her room.

She was beautifully dressed. In her red polka-dot dress with ribbons and bows, it barely reached her knees showing her bare, beautifully crafted legs.

No one ever told her she was beautiful. They always told her she had a *'bad habit'*, all her thoughts were concentrated on such a simple sentence, all her energy went into hiding her thumbs.

Grandma would yell:

"One day a doctor will chop them off!"

Or she would say:

"They'll get infected so badly the infection will spread through your blood into your body and you will die, you silly, silly girl."

She was petrified at the thought of dying, but it didn't prevent her from continuing her favourite ritual which always brought the best and the strangest enjoyment, and clashing emotions like fear, pain, pleasure, guilt and extreme puzzlement over her future. What will happen in the future? Was she going to live or to die because of such a dangerous practice or, as they called it—a bad habit?

But the future she feared and secretly waited for revealed itself on that day when their guests arrived, containing in itself a coded message.

They came in a big dark-coloured car, and two cats lazily dropped out of the back seat. A fat woman came out; she needed a helping hand to pull her out. It was her dad who pulled the big woman out. They hugged and kissed. Another fat woman came out from the other side of the car, Portia couldn't see her fully—she saw only the upper part of her body as the big car hid her. Father rescued her as well, he hugged her too, and, as Portia caught with a corner of her eye, he kissed her too, twice. The driver of the car came out. He wore a wide-brimmed brown hat and sunglasses. He took the sunglasses off and hugged the man who looked like a tiny rabbit compared to him, his older brother, Horatio.

They came back from America a few weeks ago. From the Big Apple. Grandma said, *"Such a stupid, stupid name, why would someone call a city Big Apple?"*

Portia said:

"That's how Americans call New York.", to what grandma yelled back:

"You better shut up; your days are numbered as the infection will soon eat up your heart and your poisoned blood will contaminate all your organs and your small stupid brain."

A boy came out last. He was holding a phone in his hands and didn't look at anyone. He didn't hug nor did he kiss Portia's father.

They walked into the house.

Portia's mother and grandmother greeted them in the house.

The boy never lifted his gaze, never uttered a word.

His eyes were nailed on to that tiny screen; his brows were touching, lips sealed, there was anticipation on his face, the same expression as Portia's face at ten minutes to noon.

She was called to come in. She came with her hands behind her back and sealed lips. Her eyebrows were touching; a fear of hugging the fat women crawled under her dress.

Portia's father said:

"Believe it or not, this is Portia."

Sounds of excitement and of disbelief filled the room. Their eyes were fixed on Portia, the same way the boy's eyes were fixed on the little screen he was holding in his hand.

"Well, I can't believe how big she has grown."

"Good ten years have passed since you saw her last time."

"More than ten. We were here twelve years ago."

"Is that the girl who used to bite her nails?"

The awkward silence filled the room.

The fat woman said:

"She used to eat her thumbs when she was a little girl. What a bad habit! Dangerous, almost evil."

The awkward silence deepened.

They were all staring at Portia. She hid her hands behind her back. Her thumbs were hurting, her knees shaking.

Grandma said:

"The little devil!"

Her mother said:

"You are an embarrassment!"

Her father said:

"Here, come over here, Portia."

Everyone was staring at her.

Except the boy.

He didn't hear their conversation; he didn't notice Portia; he never knew she had a bad habit.

He missed it all as his undivided concentration was still on the small screen.

The fat woman hugged Portia's mother, and said:

"Some kids have bad habits that are incurable."

The other fat woman whispered, looking at the boy:

"Thank God for Hector, such a fine boy, such an angel."

They nodded their heads; Hector nodded his head as he had just beaten his personal best.

After the bar was raised he didn't allow any excitement or anything to sidetrack him but with a blank stare, he commenced a new game determined to beat his personal best again.

Dance Me

Lillian Liola scooped her hair on the back of her head with a golden clip. She lifted her head up and glanced at the reflection of her image in the mirror from the left. Head held high. The last touch of lipstick: red against her pale skin; yes, red against her pitch-black hair and eyes. She buttoned up a blouse which was almost transparent, so one could easily see the contours of her laced bra. She lifted her chin up again, and looked at her image in the mirror, this time from the right side. She smiled. She almost looked like Eva Ruiz Alonso.

The first time Lillian Liola heard that name was when she was about seven years old. Someone said to her mother:

"This child of yours, I can tell you, she is going to be the spitting image of Eva Ruiz Alonso."

Lillian Liola's mother said:

"Shush! Don't say that. Don't put that nonsense in her head."

"To look like Eva Ruiz Alonso could only be a source of pride, what's wrong with you, woman?"

"Don't put rubbish into her head. Go home and talk rubbish to your own children."

It was obvious from such a statement that Lillian Liola's mother was angry; if one knew Eva Ruiz Alonso, then one could easily conclude Lillian Liola's mother could have even been jealous. Lillian Liola's mother wasn't a woman that someone would call pretty. She was short, stocky, dark-haired and her hair grew everywhere uncontrollably, her eyebrows looked like one long bushy caterpillar stubbornly nested above her eyes. Even from a distance one could notice the excessive hair above her upper lip, and that wasn't a sign of feminine beauty. Her voice was harsh, movements sudden and jerky, therefore she appeared angrier than she really was.

When Lillian Liola turned seven, she had outgrown her mother, which was not really something unexpected or difficult to achieve, for her mother was, as I already said, a short, stocky woman.

At around seven, it was obvious that Lillian Liola was not going to look like her mother. She grew tall, taller than her peers; she was a willowy creature with long, long legs crafted by an invisible yet masterful hand. Her hair was thick, dark but obedient, hence it grew in abundance in the right places. The colour of her eyes matched the finest shade of the colour of her hair. It looked as if she didn't have pupils instead there was a big round black marble in each eye, thick and mysterious, it was obvious that this black pool was going to be a lake that would hold the deepest mysteries usually reserved for a select few. Her neck was slender and long and her earlobes small, measured to create and emphasise perfection. The perfection she was never aware of, no one ever told her she was pretty or that she was going to be beautiful. Her movements were always slow, measured, and she appeared as if she were dancing whilst walking or even doing the dishes or any other mundane chore.

'Hurry up!', 'Stop daydreaming!', 'Come back down to earth!', 'Stop pretending!'

She never managed to hurry up, for she had deep peace within her. She never stopped daydreaming, for she didn't know any other way of existence. She never came back down to earth, for she was absolutely content on her level of existence whatever it could have been called, and she never stopped pretending, for her eyes never saw ugliness … endless beauty resided in her eyes.

"Who is she, Mother?"

"Angelita."

"No, no! The woman she said I look like ... Eva ..."

"Stop asking silly questions and hurry up, we have work to do. Go, child, go!"

Lillian Liola's mother couldn't prevent her from growing up and turning into the image of Eva Ruiz Alonso.

When Lillian Liola was eleven years old, she became aware of the way young boys were ogling her. They would stare with an open mouth frozen in the moment. The reaction she provoked at that early age just deepened every year, and those reactions brought a lot of fun to her. She would internally laugh at the boys or young men who lost their cool upon seeing her.

When Lillian Liola was fourteen years old, she was absolutely aware of the impact she had on people, particularly on young men. She played with their emotions as if they were material things which she could move, freeze, manipulate, transport or break whenever she wanted. At that age, the age of fourteen, once again she heard the remark:

"You look exactly, I mean exactly the same as Eva Ruiz Alonso."

"Seven years ago, our neighbour Angelita said to my mother that I was going to be the spitting image of Eva Ruiz Alonso. Who is she?"

By that age, she was the tallest girl in town; she could easily pick camellias from high branches and tuck them behind her ear.

She would lock herself in the bathroom where, on the mouldy wall, was an old, blurry on edges mirror taped to the wall with two pieces of duct-tape, and she asked the mirror like Snow White would: *"Mirror, mirror on the wall, who is the prettiest of all: Eva Ruiz Alonso or Lillian Liola?"*

On a few occasions after such questions the mirror fell off the wall but it never broke in a million pieces, for it was a cheap mirror made of smeared aluminium. She would just simply pick it up and stick it back onto the wall with a mischievous yet mysterious smile on her cherry-like lips.

She knew the heaviness of the question imposed on the mirror, and as the mirror was made of cheaply smeared aluminium, it didn't know how to handle Lillian Liola's beauty. It appeared that the mirror almost knew Lillian Liola was placed in the wrong bathroom with the wrong mirror, asking the right question. Yes, the right question, for in the past thirty years no girl was born to match Eva Ruiz Alonso's beauty.

One mild April afternoon, she crossed the road on the corner of the florist and the *Gran Teatro* on the other side when a young man approached; he grabbed her by her hand, she turned her face towards him and met his piercing eyes. He said:

"What the hell! Are you an incarnation of Eva Ruiz Alonso, or a mirage! You must be her long-lost daughter."

"No, no. I am the daughter of Ana Mendez, the florist."

"I don't know any florist in this city. Do you look like her?"

"What? Like my mother! Not a bit. She is a stocky, short woman. She has teeth like a horse and her hair grows wildly everywhere, even above her upper lip."

"And your father? You must have inherited these looks from someone?"

"I don't know my father. I have never met him. My mother used to say that he died in a car accident, but I heard that she made up this story like the many others she had made up about him. I don't know who he was. I heard from my grandma, in a heated conversation with my mum, that she

slept with anyone just in the single hope to conceive a child, for no one would ever want to marry her. Isn't that a horrible story?"

"Well, the story certainly is weird. You say no one was related to Eva Ruiz Alonso?"

"I've heard it so many times—that I look like her. But I've never even met her. All I know is that she was pretty."

"Pretty! Don't insult her! She wasn't pretty. She was the beauty of the century. No woman has had such beauty in the last several centuries ... and now, you've come along, my Lord, how much you look like her."

"I don't even know what she looked like."

"Come with me."

He took her by the hand and they crossed the road. Hand in hand they walked towards the *Gran Teatro.* When they passed the main entrance, he led her through a small door upstairs, on the second floor. The entire second floor was turned into a dancing room: with polished parquet floors, mirrors and posters of a woman who looked exactly like Lillian Liola. She said:

"Eva Ruiz Alonso?"

"Eva Ruiz Alonso, the most beautiful woman, and the first proprietor of this school. She was the best dancer, the most celebrated and desirable woman."

"Wow! Almost scary!"

"Why?"

"How could I ever fill her shoes?"

"Well, leave that to me."

"To you?"

"Let me introduce myself: Chauncey Farrin Durand, the Tango doctor."

"You must be French."

"Proudly so."

"Why proudly? Is there something wrong with being from here?"

"Oh, no, no, my sweet Eva Ruiz Alonso."

"Oh, don't call me Eva Ruiz Alonso. No! Call me Lillian, this is my name."

"My dear Lillian, I was born here, but my father was a Parisian; his thirst for Tango and beautiful women brought him here. He met Eva, long before I was born, he fell in love with her, for it was impossible not to fall in love upon meeting her, though she never stayed with anyone, she never belonged to a man, any man."

"A Femme Fatale."

"Oui, oui une Femme Fatale, just like you."

"Oh, no! I am not une Femme Fatale, I am just Lillian Liola, my mother is a poor florist, a short stocky woman, with a visible moustache and masculine arms and a prickly, manly personality."

"But my sweet Lillian Liola, you are not your mother. You are an unseen beauty. Do you think that our meeting today was just chance? Don't be silly! Providence brought us together! I am the one who will bring the world the new Eva Ruiz Alonso."

Whilst they were talking, Lillian observed the posters of the beautiful woman with mysterious eyes. She looked absolutely perfect. Lillian looked at her own reflection in the mirror and she saw in it—Eva Ruiz Alonso. She couldn't do anything else but smile. It was a smile of satisfaction. A smile of young vanity. She said:

"But you have to call me Lillian Liola, I don't wish you to change my name."

"Never!"

"How are you planning to accomplish such a task? I have never danced, when I walk I feel awkward, for I am too tall, because of it I tend to bend my upper back."

"Shush! Let me look at you now."

Chauncey Farrin Durand observed her with his expert eye, in which hidden lust shone. He hoped it was just lust, for he never could afford to feel anything else for a woman but lust. He never wanted to love just one woman in case he missed out on someone more exciting or more beautiful. Or he never wanted to love anyone but himself. He was the best dancer, the *Gorgeous Frenchman* aware that women flocked to his dance studio just because of him. All his life he behaved like a rich and spoilt-rotten child brought to an extravagant and opulent candy shop where he could pick and take whatever he wanted.

Immediately, he booked private classes for Lillian free of charge, never asking her if she was ready to attend. He said:

"The only thing we have to correct is your posture, otherwise you look perfect. You will start with two private lessons: one on one, and you shall attend a group class three times per week, then we'll see how it will progress. I am the best you will find in this city, in this country, to be precise. Look, this studio belonged to my father, who was the best dancer, originally it was Eva's, what more could you wish for?"

"I don't know, I don't wish for more. All I wanted to ask is—Are you going to make me famous?"

"The most famous one can be! You are going to be a star, not only in the Tango world, but you are going to be a movie star, Hollywood is your next destination, believe me."

"I believe you, Chauncey, I really do. All I ever wanted is to be famous, to make something of my beauty; I don't want to stay with my mother and look after her shop, roses are prickly, I dislike my hands. Look at them! Look at all those cuts and scratches, sometimes I am ashamed when people look at my hands."

"You, ashamed? Hey, believe me, from now on you will be proud of each and every part of yourself. You are going to be even bigger than Eva Ruiz Alonso was, because you are in my hands now."

"I like what I am hearing. When do we start, Chauncey?"

"Right now! Put your bag down. What size shoes do you wear?" he asked, and when she told him, he walked into an adjacent room from where he came back holding a pair of high-heel shoes.

"Try them on."

"A perfect fit!"

"Everything about you is just perfect."

She smiled a smile of young vanity.

He smiled a smile of young impertinence.

They shook hands, exchanged telephone numbers and he walked her down to the street. The day was still young, April was mild, the birds were singing their song of spring and Lillian Liola felt something that she had never felt before in her young life. She felt as if the spring with its warm sun, with the birds' song and the buzz of the bees had begun just in order to please her. With a spring in her step she walked down the street wanting to hug each and every person she passed. When she came closer to her mother's flower shop she hurried, passed it without wanting to enter. Her mother never told her who Eva Ruiz Alonso was, never wanted to comment. She would only say, *'Beautiful women are useless women.'*

After that fateful encounter with Chauncey Farrin Durand two things happened.

First was that Lillian Liola had fallen in love with dance and with her body.

The second was, she fell out of love with her mother.

They started training four days a week, soon after five days a week, and by the eighth week of the training they were dancing seven days a week for five hours. Five hours daily she practised her dance, five hours daily she was in the arms of an experienced and talented Tango teacher, Chauncey Farrin Durand, also known as The Tango Doctor. She was improving rapidly, to Chauncey it looked like she was born to dance, that she was the real incarnation of the late Eva Ruiz Alonso. She even had her spirit, perhaps I could say that secretly that fact disturbed the young Chauncey but he never showed any other interest than a purely professional one—his mission was to bring the new Eva Ruiz Alonso to the world.

No one suspected that he could ever be disturbed by any woman, not even by the woman who resembled the legendary Eva, no one ever suspected that her ambition and her lack of open gratitude towards him could move his signature cool look, his calculating mind and his heart made of glass.

Her vanity steadily grew day by day and it grew out of proportion, hence her beauty became ice-cold and her eyes like two black marbles shone bright with pride and reflected pure conceit. But her body became such an instrument made to perfection to reflect God's will for perfection: a dancer without fault. In only eight months she achieved the 'unachievable'. Her dancing was breathtaking; each and every movement would bring astonishment or tears to a spectator. When she looked at the reflection of her body in the mirror, mentally she would ask, *'Mirror, Mirror on the wall, who is the fairest dancer of all? Eva Ruiz Alonso or Lillian Liola?'*

And the Mirror whispered: *'The greatest of all has just been born, Lillian Liola your day has dawned.'*

***

For Lillian Liola, Chauncey Farrin Durand was a mere instrument of learning, a stepping-stone on her stairway to fame. She never cared how many women lusted after him, how many of them wanted him to teach them, and how many of them slept with him in the single hope that there would be a second encounter … but Chauncey was a man who had to experience a woman just once. Yes, only once. He never gave free lessons to anyone; he would take whatever he pleased unable to give anything back. He gave his knowledge, but the price was always too high. He would vindicate that fact claiming he was the best one could ever get in this city. He vindicated the fact he gave free five hour lessons six days a week to a young beauty only because he recognised her talent. He said there was no other reason, but the reason was that she was a talented dancer who looked like the iconic Eva Ruiz Alonso.

Deep down his heart was unsettled when they danced, his step not as steady and his palms warm and sweaty.

Five hours she was in his arms without any complaint, she never mentioned aching feet or calves; she was never thirsty, tired, bored or hungry. She would lean her cheek against his, lips pouted, and she followed his instructions and steps without a word. She just followed his body as they moved around in perfect harmony.

Her heart belonged to a new art. There was nothing else there, just pure *l'art pour l'art.*

That summer was hot! The fans were not enough regardless of their size, power and number, as two additional ones were brought in. The air was sticky and hot for days. Emotions ran hot that summer when Lillian Liola danced, all eyes were on her, the young men smiled with the corner of their lips; there was mist in their eyes, sweat on their palms. Emotions were high and hot under Chauncey Farrin Durand's vest, but the hottest scene happened on August the eighth, precisely at eight o'clock. The sun was still up, though it lost its brightness among the pink clouds on the horizon, it didn't lose its heat just yet.

They were dancing embraced when the door suddenly opened, then closed with a big slam. The glass on the door almost broke. They turned towards an unexpected visitor: a short, stocky woman, dressed in a black dress, with hair pulled up in a small bun, with flaming eyes she screamed whilst tearing down a poster of Eva Ruiz Alonso off the wall:

"Here it is where you spend your useless days! At the whore house! You want to become a whore! How many times have I told you that beautiful women are useless women? In this or that way they ultimately turn into whores, and you did too, but in the most humiliating way."

"Is this the crowning moment of your jealousy? The one that you stored under your hat for many years? Do you think I wasn't aware of your jealousy? You looked at me as if I were an ugly duckling! But you were the one, weren't you? You hated me because I was beautiful, because I am beautiful. You said it was a curse, but what good has your ugliness brought you? Bitterness? Anything else? Out! Get out! I am proud that I am beautiful! Finally, I am proud I look like Eva Ruiz Alonso!"

"She was a whore!"

"She was a dancer!"

"A whore!"

"A dancer! Just like I am—a dancer! You can't stop me! Out! I don't need you anymore! I don't need you, nor do I need your flower shop where I earned so many cuts and wounds that it'll take years to heal them."

"Are you going to heal your imaginary wounds by dancing?"

"Get out!"

"Señora, please leave the studio."

She left the studio in tears (were they tears of furore or of sadness, it was unknown at that time) and she ran without stopping all the way home.

Lillian Liola said to her teacher:

"Let's start again."

"Are you alright?"

"Why wouldn't I be?"

"Who was that?"

"Who do you think it was?"

"Your mother?"

"Let's just continue dancing, that's why we are here."

In a way, her answer scared him.

The coldness of her heart seemed to exceed his own.

That night Lillian Liola asked him:

"May I sleep at your place just for tonight?"

His heart skipped a beat, he said:

"Yes."

The following day, Lillian Liola told Chauncey Farrin Durand that she had a new place where she could stay. He asked where, but she just gave him a look and changed her shoes.

As time passed Lillian Liola became more and more known, she became a burning desire in the mind and eye of all the dancers. As time passed, Chauncey Farrin Durand's new and unwanted feelings steadily grew stronger: he went from bearable pangs of jealousy to pure madness where his sanity was burning on the altar of his possessiveness.

Initially, he thought no one saw his feelings of possessiveness and obsession with his new muse. Everybody knew! They witnessed a quick change: from the self-confident womaniser, he turned into an obsessed, almost frightened man who followed each of her steps regardless of whether she was dancing or walking the street. He became her shadow. He became his shadow. The more he wanted her, the freer she appeared to be.

***

One day a man walked in. A man from Argentina. He walked in with a woman on his arm, with a straight but light step as if he was going to a well-rehearsed wedding ceremony. The woman on his arm he had met in Madrid was a Primadonna from Russia. When Jorge Rubio Rivera, ex-dog-healer-turned-Tango-teacher, and Tatyana Yuryevna Torasovaya, famous Primadonna, walked in the *C.F. Durand Studio*, everything stood still. Like a scene from a distant yet frozen memory. Light music from an invisible instrument spread out and touched the senses.

In that moment rose petals fell down from the sky in abundance, the ceiling opened wide and red petals covered the floor and randomly positioned chairs. The smell filled the air and the hearts of all present dancers. There was a strong feeling that something of big proportions was going to materialise, or there was a strong sense of anticipation of some revelation that would be told in this fragrant room full of rose petals, unearthly music and suspended breaths.

The first person who came to their senses, awoken from this magical moment, was Lillian Liola. She approached lightly, extended her arm and said:

"Lillian Liola."

Jorge Rubio Rivera took her hand and said:

"You look exactly like Eva Ruiz Alonso. You might be her daughter that no one knew existed."

By that time, Lillian Liola rewrote her past. She never talked about her short, stumpy mother again; she would rather tell the story of her adoption, only hinting that she might have been the illegitimate daughter of Eva Ruiz Alonso as there were rumours over many years that Eva gave her new-born baby girl into adoption. No one doubted her, for only Lillian Liola could claim something of that nature and be trusted.

When Jorge Rubio Rivera said, *"You look exactly like Eva Ruiz Alonso..."* Lillian Liola turned her back, and walked to the gramophone in the corner of the room. She put on a new song and called Jorge Rubio Rivera to join her on the dance floor.

After his suspicious and inglorious career as a dog healer ended, Jorge Rubio Rivera took up Tango lessons and his feet and his genes led him to overnight success on the dance floor (his grandfather Miguel was a dancer). In a short period of time he became one of the most sought-after Tango teachers in Madrid.

Tatyana Yuryevna Torasovaya was proud and genuinely happy, for Jorge was not going to be in the position, ever again, to forge his professional persona, to place himself in a situation of mistrust as she was the only person who trusted him without limits. It was obvious that his ancestors danced through his body making the most astonishing movements: yes, it was obvious that he carried their steps in his own feet.

He pressed Lilian Liola onto his chest and her heart skipped a beat. He pulled her tighter and her legs barely visibly shook. He looked straight in her eyes and said:

"Follow me."
"I dance, I don't follow."
"Follow me!"

She nodded her head, for her sentence was wobbly and weak. She felt the flabbiness of her own sentence stopped by its own weakness and the sharp guard of her clenched teeth.

But when they danced, it appeared that they were floating above the polished floorboard. They appeared to be one, total bodily harmony charged by extreme emotions.

Those emotions and movements never skipped Chauncey's ever-observing eye, whilst Tatyana appeared to be absolutely placid, almost indifferent. Now and then, she would close her eyes and sink deep, carried by the music, into her own world. What was stored there no one ever knew, including her long-lasting friend Jorge Rubio Rivera. She opened her eyes when the music stopped and caught Lillian's swift movement when she changed the record. Piazzolla.

Chauncey Farrin Durand cleared his throat loudly, Tatyana Yuryevna Torasovaya closed her eyes and went back to her own melody, and the dancers, chest to chest, cheek to cheek, appeared to be in a world where no one else belonged in that moment, including Piazzolla himself, who opened the secret sacred door.

Feeling his cheek against hers, Lillian Liola, after a long time, felt like crying. She didn't know why she felt like crying, she didn't know why her legs were unsteady and why her breathing was uneven. She disliked those sensations, she was always in control of all her thoughts and feelings, in control of her plans and the way they were unfolding. But in this moment, she stopped thinking and let Jorge lead her as he pleased: she leant her head on his shoulder and wished that Piazzolla had one never-ending song. But the song ended and when it ended Lillian still held her head on his shoulder, Jorge still held his palm on her resting head, Tatyana loudly applauded and Chauncey, once again, cleared his throat, this time almost violently.

"Bravo! Bravo!" cheered Tatyana, but the two dancers stayed embraced. In that moment, they looked like a statue made of the strongest marble which no one could ever break or separate the couple caught in it.

Chauncey walked to the gramophone where on the same table was a semi-full glass of water which he *accidently* knocked down, and when the glass broke touching the hard surface, the spell was broken too. The couple let go of their embrace slowly, unaffected by the sharp sound: in their eyes glass debris was shining.

Jorge said:

"Thank you, Lillian."

"No! Thank you, Jorge! You were absolutely fantastic. How long have you been dancing?"

"Long time, my grandfather taught me, he was ..." before he managed to finish this made-up sentence, this time, Tatyana Yuryevna Torasovaya cleared her throat loudly. He looked at her and shrugged his shoulders almost apologetically, then he quickly turned to Lillian Liola and said:

"You are one of the better dancers I've ever danced with. No doubt whose daughter you are ..."

Now Chauncey Farrin Durand cleared his throat loudly and said:

"She looks like Eva Ruiz Alonso, but they are not related."

In some other circumstances, Lillian Liola would have shot a sharp look at his way, but right now she was disinterested in what other people had to say. She smiled at Jorge Rubio Rivera and he smiled back at her. They couldn't care less whose grandfather really was a teacher, or whose mother was a famous dancer.

As they unpredictably and unannounced came into the Studio, in the same manner they left it: hand in hand, without a word they just walked out.

All the burning words that Chauncey stored in his belly stayed locked in when they closed the door behind. He opened the windows and fresh air filled the room. Lillian Liola changed her shoes and changed the record. They resumed their practice.

Several months had passed, Lillian Liola never saw Jorge Rubio Rivera again, but he lived in her head, she couldn't shake the image of a tall handsome dancer who danced her to the happiness of her heart. Her heart was happy only for a short moment, but that was the sweetest moment that she could ever recall: the moment she longed to relive.

***

It was a rainy Saturday evening, she put a ribbon in her hair to tame it as the dampness in the air made her hair disobedient. She applied a touch of make-up, just to give her eyes a more expressive, dramatic look; she put a shawl on her shoulders and walked into the street where Chauncey was waiting in an already parked car. They were dancing at Milonga El Federal that evening. As they walked in, the noise in the room stopped: all eyes were on them. Chauncey, with his head held high, aware of his looks and his own grandiosity, aware of the beauty he was accompanied by. Lillian Liola, held her head high, as rumour had it by now she was the closest thing to the myth of being the long-lost daughter of Eva Ruiz Alonso.

There were many people: many shook their hands with them, many exchanged hugs and paid compliments.

Like a queen of a small congregation, she sat down on a special chair, designed for her with care as it was a replica of a chair which belonged to Eva Ruiz Alonso. When she sat down, she caught his profile with the corner of her eye. She saw him on the dance floor holding a woman in his arms. She was a short, stumpy woman, that woman wasn't the tall, willowy Russian beauty. Her heart skipped a beat. She cursed her heart. She tried to catch his eye but he kept avoiding her gaze. When she stood up, the eyes of all men were on her except Jorge Rubio Rivera's. He made it seem like he never noticed her.

He never noticed Lillian Liola! It would be the same as if someone said that after heavy rain they didn't notice the sun come out. Despite what people say, the fact he ignored her hurt her deeply. The entire evening he danced with women, he approached each and every one regardless of their looks and sizes, he laughed and charmed them all the same, he talked to everyone but to Lillian Liola. He offered her just icy silence.

At the end of the evening she asked Chauncey what he said to Jorge. She insisted on his answer, but Chauncey said if she insisted, he would call the psychiatric ward to take her for a check-up, as he claimed they never exchanged a word. The whole evening Chauncey internalised all his emotions and victory was obvious on his placid face. His face was calm and placid, for the new turn of events confirmed he was the sovereign ruler of this community where vanity prevailed; he noticed that evening as soon as he walked in that Jorge Rubio Rivera wasn't his real match. Jorge's ego was so inflamed, his silent wish to punish and hurt was displayed for everyone to see at once, for that silence conveyed a thousand words. Jorge's silence screamed in Lillian Liola's face, shaking her legs whilst dancing.

The following Saturday, at Milonga El Federal, Jorge Rubio Rivera came dressed in his finest suit; his shirt was as white as snow on a mountain peak that no one had ever laid their eyes on, pressed just before he buttoned it up to the last button, his tie was just two shades darker, like the colour of old ebony. His hair was sleek, combed backwards, and his big, dark eyes shone as if they were ready to attack his prey. He never laid those dark eyes on Lillian Liola that evening. He never noticed the woman that everyone believed was the reincarnation of famed Eva Ruiz Alonso. It saddened her, but did not know why exactly. Was just her ego hurt? She knew she was a beautiful young woman and didn't need reassurance, he even told her she was breathtakingly beautiful on their first encounter.

Jorge Rubio Rivera came alone again. She wondered what was the Russian beauty to him? Was she his wife, a friend or a lover, for there was a thick aura of intimacy floating around them.

The way she danced that evening was different and only Chauncey Farrin Durand noticed it, because it was noticed only by the eye of an expert. Her heels were disobedient as if they received instructions directly from her shaking heart. Whatever she felt in her heart, whichever thought she turned around in her head, it wasn't shown on her face. There, in the middle of her face stood a wide, warm smile showing those almost perfect pearly-white teeth.

On the third Milonga El Federal, Lillian Liola concluded that Jorge Rubio Rivera was a cruel man. She needed not a cruel man. No, not a cruel one! There is neither laughter nor happiness when a cruel man enters someone's world. She decided to shut the doors and windows through which any thought could come in or escape.

On the third Milonga El Federal, Jorge Rubio Rivera came accompanied by a woman whom Lillian Liola had never seen before. They walked in hand-in-hand. They came quite late. Lillian Liola would never ever admit to herself that she was anxiously waiting for him to come. Waiting to see his tall body, upright and proud entering as if he came to some contest already knowing he was the winner. The eyes of Chauncey Farrin Durand were on Lillian Liola constantly, but he was so versed in his secret way of observing people, especially Lillian Liola, that she was never aware of his look.

When they entered hand-in-hand at 11:45, they came in laughing as if they just shared the silliest joke they ever heard. On Lillian Liola's face, still, that beautiful smile rested and only Chauncey Farrin Durand noticed the little twitch on the corner of her lips. He stood up and took her to the dance floor. She danced like someone else, not like Lillian Liola who took his classes, now for several months. She danced like a little girl, a little girl who put on high-heel shoes for the first time and wasn't sure when she would fall down and cry for breaking her heel. But she didn't fall, nor did she cry. She smiled to her friend and teacher, Chauncey Farrin Durand; she talked to him absentmindedly, only he knew she talked just for the sake of talking.

She tried several times to catch Jorge's eyes, but they were eyes made of ice, hostile and arrogant, the eyes that never again touched her face since they met for the first time.

Whilst dancing with Chauncey Farrin Durand, she asked herself, *'What did I do to him?', 'Have I ever wronged this man?', 'Why does he show me his contempt, what have I ever done to him that makes him behave this way?'*

And the same revelation came again: *He is a cruel man. A cruel, cruel man!*

After such a revelation, her heels straightened, her feet lightened and she sailed on the dance floor holding the hand of her faithful friend Chauncey, whose mood lifted at the same moment: he pressed her closer to his chest and they danced as if they invented the dance. The astonished and admiring dancers started to make room for the two of them, and soon the dance floor was emptied: only Lillian Liola and Chauncey Farrin Durand danced in the most elegant embrace for the rest of the evening. The guests just sat down on their chairs, some were staring with open mouths knowing this was going to be a historical event. It will be written into the thin book of extraordinary Tango dancers or events.

They danced, and danced, and danced, until the last guest had left. Lillian Liola never noticed when Jorge Rubio Rivera left, for she didn't even remember him any longer.

When the last person left the hall, they stopped dancing. Chauncey Farrin Durand lifted Lillian Liola's face and said:

"This evening you have made yourself a living legend of Tango. You have officially become the new Eva Ruiz Alonso."

Mr Leven and the Twins

The incident occurred on a pleasant day. The weather was mild, the light breeze refreshing, it looked as if it were an early summer day, an early morning hour, but it wasn't. Quite the contrary: it was late autumn, the time of year when mornings were already chilly, and the leaves were painted dark-brown, scrunched at the edges, pinned on the bare branches dancing tiredly like puppets on invisible strings. It was late afternoon: that precise moment in the day before the horizon is touched and changed by the young mauve clouds.

We were all seated at the table. A pleasant and generous table. The breeze played with the linen tablecloth. It was embroidered with sunflowers, by Grandma's firm hand. But it danced, regardless of the firmness by which it was embroidered.

Even though it was pleasant, the breeze served as an omen.

Now that we know the setting and the time of year, I will commence the story according to my personal recollection of reality, only hoping that the story will be faithful to the truth.

It looked like God, bored with our lifeless conversation, took charge and turned up the volume of the wind, therefore the light breeze turned into a strong wind which took off Mr Leven's hat. It took it up into the air and twisted and twirled it as if it was a scrunched late autumn leaf. Mr Leven jumped up and knocked down the teapot. The teapot! The one Grandma used to take out only on very special occasions. Mr Leven didn't apologise, so Mrs Leven screamed at him for being clumsy; she almost fainted, for being dramatic was her choice when in social settings. Mr Leven started running, chasing his hat, which after a while landed in front of a random passer-by.

Oh, yes—a random passer-by!

Mrs Leven, now without apologising, knocked down her teacup and swore publicly for the first time in her life, perhaps.

Then she collapsed.

Mr Leven unaware of her fine performance and the puzzled looks from us seated around the table, bent down to pick his hat up. *'Was he bowing down to pick up his hat, or did he bow to a random passer-by?'* That was the puzzling question no one even dared to think of, let alone formulate into a brute sentence. The people at the table, including myself, were guests of dignified air, it was clear that no one would express anything but concern for Mrs Leven's current state.

On Mrs Leven's right sat an uptight Mrs Tornes, who had devoted her longish life to helping women in distress and men in need. If this is still not clear, I shall leave it up to the reader to decide what meaning to deduce from such a sentence, for my wish is not to insinuate or lead towards prejudice.

Mrs Tornes calmly said:

"Mrs Leven, this is not who you think it is. Mrs Leven, you can open your eyes."

I have been a witness to her cunning ways several times, so I wasn't surprised when she opened one eye, still pretending she wasn't fully conscious. When someone suggested to *'pour cold, iced water'*, she opened the other eye, saying:

"Thank you for the lovely afternoon, we'd better be going." Then without saying a word to anyone, she walked off. Without her bag.

Mr Johnston cleared his throat, saying loudly:

"Your bag, Mrs Leven, you left your bag on the table."

When one is upset one can't think about trivial things, and Mrs Leven wasn't an exception.

She kept on walking.

Mrs Tornes, the kind woman who was always ready to help women in distress and men in dire situations, was placed in the biggest dilemma of her life: *What should she do—right here, right now?*

Now, at her forty years of age she knew, first hand, a simple but brutal truth: no one can hurt us as much as the people we love.

When she met Mr Leven, in the seductive city of Barcelona where she studied fine arts, Mrs Tornes was twenty-two years old. Her father was a wealthy man who wished his daughters to study fine art and literature. Back then she wasn't called Mrs Tornes but simply Temida. Her twin sister—Thalia.

Back then, she was not a woman of empathy carried by an unconscious desire to help women in distress and men in need; she was young, her only interest was fine art and foreign literature. Thalia was sent to the other part of the world, to Florence; back then, it looked so far away, it seemed to both sisters they would never see each other again.

When Mrs Tornes met Mr Leven she wasn't concerned by such reality–not seeing her twin sister ever again, for she thought she won the best prize one could win in the world of fine arts! Mr Leven's face was nicely sculptured and his body was the body of Adonis at that time, at an age when all an artist needed was a sculpture of pure, innocent beauty.

Shall I even say that he took her virginity easily and quickly upon their first fatal meeting, that evening when the traffic stopped and Barcelona became the main witness to that drama of grandiose love which ended in pain, threats, hysteria and mental breakdown. The aforementioned madness happened on the exact day when they were destined to celebrate the tenth anniversary of their turbulent and passionate relationship.

They were seated at the table, the guests had already arrived, the tablecloth was white and embroidered with beautiful flowers; the breeze was pleasant as it was meant to be; Mr Leven had a light linen hat, white, informal, emphasising that nonchalant look Temida helped him create. But the cheeky breeze, or bored God, decided to increase the volume, so the hat danced on his head and was taken up in the air … It danced in the air, it looked as if it was playing with the pinkish clouds when it was suddenly lowered down where it landed in front of the feet of a random stranger, a passer-by.

Even though it was a random person, it wasn't a plain or ordinary character. It was a woman of unseen beauty (at least this fatal view was instantly adopted by Mr Leven), not even Russian tales had such an exaggerated kind of beauty. How this description matched reality is irrelevant now, but back then, to Mr Leven, heavenly harps (the ones only he heard) signalled the beginning of a new era.

The creature of unseen beauty was no one else but–the future Mrs Leven. Yes, the one with a strong need for drama and exaggeration, the one who left the table that late autumn afternoon I was just talking about.

When Mr Leven met the beautiful woman destined to be his wife, Temida's hair stood up, and it took her exactly three years to comb it back down. This monumental loss wasn't only apparent in her different but accidental hairdo, it was also displayed on her face—for it became asymmetrical, one brow dropped down at least one centimetre and pressed onto her eyelid heavily; she was forced to stop applying make-up on her eyes and brows, for it only intensified the new asymmetry of her face. It looked almost as if it were slightly paralysed.

Bitterness was easily read on her face, and it took her a rather long time to get over the shock, which came with that light breeze many years ago.

I am not going to talk about her life's ups and downs; I just wanted to introduce some fragments of her past which would serve my further narrations.

It is obvious now, by her new name—Torrnes, that she finally got over this unfortunate episode in her life, that she found the right man and had settled down. At least, it appeared to be that way. There were all sorts of rumours going around, but we have to take into consideration that those rumours were made and spread by a really common crowd—mainly those who envied her for being married into such a wealthy family.

It would take her many years to find that level and extent of complete compassion and empathy towards women in distress, and to integrate it in her daily life. On some deep, unreachable level, she must have craved for the title of—Saint. But, what I've just said, don't take as gospel, for it is my plain speculation based on her behaviour when in social settings.

Taken by her unbearable beauty and elegance, Mr Leven decided to marry the woman he met due to the wind's whims, who became Mrs Leven, the one who faked fainting, which I mentioned earlier. It was told that it was believed they lived a life of bliss, but the rumours that could be heard carried different flavours, as the truth often has many flavours and faces.

A friend of Mr Leven's, whom I decline to identify by name as I'd like to protect him from being labelled as a *'cheap gossiper'*, told me that Mr Leven ached for Temida's caresses (by then, already known as Mrs Torrnes).

One day he ran into her, and she looked rather stunning: her brows were pulled up in a straight line, the left eye wasn't slightly droopy, her eyes shone just like when she was a young student in the seductive city of Barcelona. I don't know the exact words and arrangements which followed, but it was well known they used to meet in a neighbouring village and book a hotel room for a couple of hours. The last one to hear that bitter story, to swallow the bitter pill, was Mrs Leven. Her hair stood up electrified by rage, and she ran to face Mrs Torrnes to *dig out her eye* as she prophesied.

When she ran into the house like a bolt of lightning, she found Mrs Torrnes reading a book to a young child. Mrs Leven screamed, screeched and knocked down several expensive vases, but hearing her accusations Mrs Torrnes told her in a calm voice:

"Why would you believe stories that you never questioned? Your blind rage clouds your reasoning."

Again, in order to shorten the long story, and to avoid the women's pointless argument, I shall just mention that, in the end, Mrs Leven made peace with both of them—her husband, Mr Leven, and their friend Mrs Torrnes, for she dug up the truth that Mrs Torrnes never visited the village in question.

Then the new rumours were heard: the woman Mr Leven was seeing in the neighbouring village was no one else but Mrs Panglese, who was previously known as young Thalia, Mrs Torrnes's twin sister.

When the rumours reached Mrs Leven's consciousness, apparently, Mrs Panglese left the village never to be seen again. No one had seen her since, not even her twin sister Temida, as we know her by now to be Mrs Torrnes.

There was no longer a gradual process involved in the transformation of Mrs Tornes into the most caring, compassionate being when it comes to women's troubles, and men's, apparently. As a consequence of such knowledge (that her twin sister was meeting up in a hotel room with her ex-lover), her other brow dropped down, which wasn't the worse thing to happen as now her brows stood in the same line as they used to back then, when she was a young student in the seductive city of Barcelona.

When it comes to Mrs Leven, Mrs Tornes never even said, *"What goes around; comes around!"* Many times, she sat with her around the same table, and many times she besprinkled her with cold water when she was in the grip of rage or jealousy, exercising her need for dramatic and dire scenes. What she really felt deep down towards Mrs Leven, or even towards her twin sister Thalia, she never expressed verbally, or in sign language, hence Mrs Tornes was enveloped in a cloak of mystery. Even more so, because she never commented or tried to deny or justify her urge to help men in need.

Therefore, when she calmly said:

"Mrs Leven, this is not who you think it is. Mrs Leven, you can open your eyes.", it appeared that she knew more than she was willing to show.

Mr Leven never cared that his wife walked away in the most dramatic manner, as he was mesmerised by the creature standing in front of him.

She looked like Mrs Tornes, back then when she was a young, beautiful student in the seductive city of Barcelona. The woman looked like a mixture of young Temida, of young Thalia and there were very clear signs on her face of himself when he pulled back a memory of looking at himself in the mirror shaving his young face.

I was the only person at that table who knew who the mysterious young-looking Mrs Torrnes-resembling person was. I knew more than the rumours said, for Mrs Panglese's new husband was my father's illegitimate son, a loose-tongued lawyer himself, but I kept the silence sealing my lips waiting for the moment of the truth that I was assigned to announce.

When Mr Leven stood in front of the feet of a random passer-by, a woman that, incredibly but irrefutably, resembled the young Mrs Torrnes and Mrs Panglese, he just looked at her as if she were an apparition.

I stood up and walked her to the table.

There was a silence one could cut with that knife lying on the table waiting to be used to cut the cake. Only the wind ruffled the silence.

That red dot in the far distance was the disappearing back of a person who was, several moments ago, called Mrs Leven.

The eyebrows of Mrs Torrnes were in such distress they didn't show any harmony or mutual understanding.

Mr Leven walked back as a heavily wounded war hero, and the rest of the guests resembled unfinished sculptures left and forgotten by a negligent artist (I've picked the word *'negligent'* rather than drunk!)

The young mysterious woman, with a striking resemblance to the twins and with the visible signs of Mr Leven's features, reached for my hand and squeezed my fingers.

I said (without looking in Mrs or Mr Torrnes' direction):

"Eva Margarita Leven."

Always empathic, Mrs Torrnes showed no emotions even though a sharp eye could notice the twitch that evened out her brows for a moment.

No one said a word, not even Mr Leven.

Eva Margarita reached for my drink and emptied the glass in one gulp. A red circle stayed as an indicator of how much wine she had just swallowed.

Mr Leven cleared his throat but his words were stuck and didn't come out, not even when he lubricated it with red wine.

As the silence was thick, threatening to last, I repeated my words:

"Eva Margarita Leven."

Now Mr Torrnes looked at Mr Leven.

Mr Leven looked at Mrs Torrnes.

Eva Margarita looked at me, and I said:

"Last year, Eva Margarita Rubio came to my office, she wanted to meet her father and change her name. We met with Mr Leven and he learned about Eva Margarita's adoption. He learned how her mother (now I looked in Mrs Torrnes's direction) *gave her to the Rubio family as she couldn't come back home with a child."*

Mrs Torrnes put her hand onto mine and instead of squeezing my fingers, Eva Margarita squeezed Mrs Torrnes's fingers and the latter let her tears fall silently.

Mr Torrnes, in haste, left the table and after a few short minutes, just like Mrs Leven, he looked like a tiny dot on the horizon.

Mr Leven cleared his throat, but once again, his words were stuck and he couldn't squeeze any out.

The wind had increased and it turned over two tall glasses. The wine stained the immaculately white tablecloth and the stain grew bigger.

As I had fulfilled my role, I stood up and walked off without turning my head to see if the last scene had changed.

Maxwell Darby and I, a True Story

I met Maxwell Darby in a bar, in New York, sometime in the early eighties; it could have been exactly 1980, but I am not too sure right now. With the passage of time and my bad habit of drinking too much, and because of too many accumulated wild events during that period of time till the narration of this story, I could have easily forgotten the exact year. But, what difference would it make: give or take a year or two, our friendship has been running along many dirty, winding and dusty roads for almost four decades. Our conversations were flawless, rich and in-depth; he was like my mirror, though I always wanted to take the dust off its surface, wanted to polish it, for when looking at my face reflecting in this so-called mirror, I could easily see a reality that didn't often appeal to me. For him, it was a sheer pleasure to be seen around with me once he learned that my play was almost accepted on Broadway. By the passage of time, this episode took on mythical proportions adding new elements and spice with each passing year.

When Maxwell took me to his first party, only then did I understand the *'hows'* and *'whys'* of his careless lifestyle and spending of money that looked as if it would never run short for him. Once I said to him, *"Let me get that drink!"* to which he replied with almost a tone of offence in his voice, *"You'll pay when I run out of my money."*

All I knew was that Maxwell Darby Senior was a senator in the eighties, and that he had a sugarcane plantation *'somewhere in the middle of nowhere'* as his son, my old pal Max, would say, changing the subject quickly. Apparently, they never got along, they blamed each other for all sorts of things, but I never really listened attentively to any of those stories as it is known that lots of them were fabricated; people like to talk about politicians, about wealthy people, finding fault with them whilst they enjoy their misery in a weird, nasty way.

Max was an aspiring writer in the eighties; alas, he couldn't really write, not even some lines that he called poetry. I was never cruel, never absolutely honest either, when he asked for my opinion or appraisal; I would talk in a broad sense of meaning, in a way that could be interpreted differently. He was an extremely intelligent and sensitive man; early on he understood my ambiguity; only when drunk would he insist on more honest words and clarity, and that was more than I could deliver.

The Broadway Story was partially a true story, I don't even remember now how close I was to being considered seriously, but Max told and retold this story so many times and had added intriguing details that it sounded true and believable.

When Maxwell Darby started to worship my work, I feared he might see me in the wrong light; he might spoil the authenticity of our friendship. Thank God that never really happened, even when he married a woman who was my closest friend (I won't elaborate on the nature of our friendship, right now).

Even though I had published four historical, well-researched novels, even though I received a prize for two of them, I never really made my living as a writer. There was an unspoken agreement between the two of us: he took care of my bills, I took care of his good reputation, promoting him as my best friend and a potential literary success. That was enough, that not only flattered him but justified his easy-going, Bohemian existence.

***

I met Olivia Vanderbilt and almost fell for her, but when I sussed out the whole situation, when I became aware of the whole picture and the vast proportions of her family name and wealth, I knew that all I could ever offer Olivia Vanderbilt was a sincere friendship. She came to my book launch. Maxwell didn't see her that evening, but she left her card telling me, *"Baby, if you like good parties, call Olivia."*

I can't say she took a fancy to me; she was more interested in my name, it was almost as if I was an accessory, a valuable addition to fill an intellectual vacuum on certain days. I kept her away even from Max; I can't remember now, what the real reason was, or maybe I never even thought of the reason, maybe it was plain selfishness. Or fear. I knew, deep down, that our friendship wasn't a friendship of equals. We traded off and compensated our gifts and privileges. I saw it in that light. She was a perfect character for my story, for any story or for anybody's story. She was just perfect. She talked indiscriminately; she talked rubbish sometimes; sometimes she was smart and serious, discovering (for me) new galleries, museums, or plays where I couldn't get in without her.

Everyone liked, loved Olivia Vanderbilt, not only because she was a good-looking girl, not because she was a Vanderbilt, not because she was a girl ready for good times anytime, no! Everybody liked her because she was so confident, carefree, so present in any given moment and sincere like a five-year-old child. When she would touch my hand whilst explaining to me any topic or proposing an outing, I would feel an electric current running down my spine. I would immediately wash down that feeling with alcohol and all would become tolerable, bearable.

"Who is Lizzy?"

"A character."

"It's me! I am your Lizzy Ward."

"You are not."

"You, bastard! I am not that selfish, that spoilt and that arrogant. If you only toned it down a bit, the character would be quite likable."

"You are not Lizzy Ward, she is way too complicated."

But things got complicated when Olivia met Maxwell.

Complicated only in my head. I lost her as my muse, I lost her on a level of which only I was aware. On the outside, everything looked almost the same, only I was aware of the loss, of the new nature of our relationship. Still, I had these electric currents running down my spine when Olivia innocently held my hand whilst walking, between the two of us, barefoot, on the beach.

When they met, it was like a thunderbolt! She asked, *"Maxwell Darby, Junior?"*

"How, the hell, did you figure that out?"

"I know your old man; you are the spitting image of him. My father knows him. I've heard of you; you are some sort of a rebel. A rebel without a cause. How exciting! I am so happy I met you. I've heard about all your strange antics. I also heard you are writing a book. Tell me! Tell me more. Tell me all about it. Do you know that your best friend based the character of Lizzy Ward on me? Yes! It is me! Shallow, stupid and useless! Spoilt and insensitive. Self-absorbed and accidentally manipulative, for the character does not have enough intelligence to be manipulative, so she is accidentally manipulative."

Maxwell tried to defend me, but she laughed it off, she moved ahead, she already talked about Maxwell's new character, she was happy to offer her eccentricity in return for a new role. She loved being the muse for artists, for one writer, and she wouldn't mind lending her personality to a failed one, as I jealously labelled Maxwell in my head. As long as she was the talk of the town, or the centre of someone's attention; someone worthy of seeing her as a central point.

I wasn't, but Maxwell was, the man who could make Olivia Vanderbilt, at least, temporarily happy.

They got married on April 5th, 1988. It was Saturday; the day was mild and she came in her white, sleeveless gown; her back was bare, her skin an alabaster colour; her shoulders looked broader in her wedding gown; she looked taller, she looked happier than ever; she looked gracious and grateful to me and to God that she had met Maxwell Darby on that day when the three of us got drunk and argued about postulates that were (all three of them!) wrong in the heart and impossible to understand or to resolve. Max held the glass she extended to him, she carelessly, slowly, unbuttoned her blouse, and said:

"Blow! I am so hot, damn humidity!"

Instead of blowing into her bare bosom, he leaned over and kissed her. They just kept on kissing, and I packed the rest of my dinner in a container, took the rest of my beer and left them in that small French restaurant where we had our first dinner together. I couldn't say was I sad because I lost my inspiration, my muse and my best female friend, nor was I happy for Max who gained new inspiration, a new muse and a new best female friend.

I was his best man. They decided to get married even though both were fierce advocates against the institution of marriage.

Only when he was fairly drunk would he talk to me about his jealousy of my talent, how desperately he wanted to publish a book, an intelligent, meaningful work that would demand attention and bring the respect of critics and academia. Often, I thought how hard he was trying to please his disinterested and self-obsessed father who never had time for him: not in his early days, not in his formative years, not even when he had married and decided to turn a new page. But he never turned the page.

***

I am well aware I haven't mentioned the letter which I intended to write. The letter in which I could explain in detail *'all my sins'* Maxwell didn't want to hear about. He didn't want any explanation or clarification or, possible redemption. I commenced the letter in my head numerous times, only to scrunch this unmaterialised script with my etheric fist. He didn't need any explanation. Back then I was determined, as I am determined right now, in this moment of writing our story, to explain to Maxwell the whole sequence of events, not only in order to right the wrong, but to prove that, in the first place, there was no wrong at all.

I think I owe you, too, my curious reader, the rest of the story, for Maxwell and I had a long, long history together: the life we shared before Olivia, the life we shared after Olivia and many years of amazing friendship and adventures that lead to the final act.

Maxwell Darby never liked to talk about his family, nor did I about mine. Both of us for very different reasons. I was poor. I grew up in utter poverty, in a part of New York which I never mentioned again. Everybody was poor; my mother was ill, severely ill, and my older brother left her in my care when I was only seven. I can't go any deeper into the story, I dislike delving into it or recovering any thicker plot in my memory, let's leave it there. All I wanted to reveal is that I was born in New York City, poor, insecure, always with death walking behind my back. Yes, my mother passed away young, and I was placed in the care of the government; at the mercy of Social Security Services, but all of that has nothing to do with mine and Maxwell's story.

Maxwell was the only person that I can solemnly claim I genuinely loved. He was an easy person to love. Maybe not to his own father, for he never understood nor did he ever want to understand that Maxwell was someone else, not the person he expected him to be. He was a gifted reader. He knew how to read a book; he understood good literature, but was unable to produce it himself, which made him somehow melancholic and a little bit envious of my achievements sometime later.

I loved Maxwell with brotherly love and was ready to go to extreme lengths to help him develop some skills, but the hardest task for me was to give him my genuine feedback. I never wanted to hurt him in any way, I disliked expressing my hesitation whenever he enthusiastically talked about *'forwarding the manuscript to the publisher.'* He would have been cut to the core, I knew that … deep down he knew it too, so he kept postponing and *'polishing the work'*. Endless polishing, and I wished it would last forever.

Maxwell could attract better looking girls, the posh ones; he had the confidence of a kid who grew up with a rich, powerful father … whilst I was insecure. On the other hand, he used me to impress the girls he attracted, telling them about my extraordinary achievements, and when I tried to tone it down, to tell the truth about my real achievements, he would wave his hand saying, *"He is too modest, but the bastard is a real genius, get his latest book. You should get it; some real stuff has been written there. He is the real deal. My pal, my best friend."*

He drank too much. Very expensive alcohol. I drank with him, but much less even though he bought all our drinks; he took me to expensive restaurants, he knew the owners, all the waitresses, he knew the pianists and many distinguished guests. He talked smoothly, with ease, and when drunk he was argumentative, he talked about his father's faulty character, about his hypocrisy and hidden greed.

I took him twice to rehab. The first time, he paid with his own money, the second time, as I had already accumulated some modest sum of money from my books, I paid for the rehab; it was my modest contribution to our friendship, which I wanted to last until dementia ate our past or rendered us into oblivion.

I had several women, but Maxwell's company and intellect would always win if I were pushed to choose between two extremes. It was the same for Maxwell. He gave me priority regardless of any circumstance.

The only woman I wanted to love was Olivia Vanderbilt. She was his first wife. I already said, I was his best man. She said her heart was broken when he walked away, and I knew that it was probably the last time that I spoke to Olivia in that intimate tone, but it didn't take long before we read in the papers Olivia had married some guy who was almost as equally wealthy as her father. Maxwell never said if he felt anything when we read it together that day; he leaned on the bar with a glass and a cigar … I think all he said, raising his glass, was *"To Lizzy Ward."*

Even though I had never met her again, I had enough material in my head, so I continued taking advantage of knowing her and kept on writing about Lizzy Ward.

Sometime in 2000, we decided that women only brought trouble to our lives. I was writing during the day, and at night we would go out chasing unidentified opportunities, chasing good stories. He had never developed his writing skills, but he had published several short stories in various publications, and he had proudly sewn another title to his name—*Writer.*

When he was tipsy, he would hug me saying, *"You are the only man I would turn gay for"*, to which I would slowly remove his arm and placatingly say, *"Calm down man, calm down!"*

In 2002, he disappeared from the face of the Earth. It scared me like nothing else had before. There was a gap of a good four years that had no explanation. He never talked about it; I don't even know if he was aware of what had happened in those years. Maybe he was on some bad trip from which he returned burnt, his brain was somehow slowed down, he wasn't even interested in my latest book: finally, my real achievement. He appeared to be lost, lukewarm, filled with apathy and nihilism. Only twice did I try to cast some light on those lost years, but he refused to say anything more than, *"Let sleeping dogs lie."*

I was there for him as much as I could; I was writing the new novel, researching and travelling around the country. But when I came back to New York, when I settled again, I found him in a better condition and mood. He was almost the same old Maxwell Darby, he just looked a bit older and the light in his eyes was dimmed, but his spirit was there.

Then we went back to our old lifestyle: writing during the day, dining in good restaurants at night, visiting bars till the small hours. We weren't young any longer, but our hearts and souls yearned for youth and the excitement it offered.

I just want to add something that might already be understood and clear: we had many beautiful women around us, but we couldn't care less, we just wanted a good time and we were real misogynists, sexists, at the time.

I can't claim I was more balanced as a person; I appeared to be, for I had a calmer nature and lacked confidence when in social situations, hence I kept quiet. He was a talker and the organiser.

He had another big crisis in 2007, and he almost drowned himself in alcohol. That battle lasted for a couple of years; thank Heavens, he came back from it as a victor. He gave me credit, saying, *"No other soul would do that for me but you."*

Did I ever grow tired of Maxwell?

I really don't want to ponder upon such a question, for the answer would be too complex, it would ask for a much more structural analysis of our past years.

Without directly answering that question, I can say, I had withdrawn into my world, my shell, towards the end of that decade. In 2011, I received the Booker Prize for my latest work, and Maxwell was happier than I could have ever been. He cried. I couldn't say why he cried exactly, but he wept like a little boy, telling me, *"I am so happy, so touched, we go way, way back, what a crazy road we've travelled. I am so happy, touched and proud, my pal, my best friend."*

Only several weeks after that, he called me, asking me to accompany him to his father's house, as the old man had expressed the wish to see him.

He was trembling like a small child whilst I was driving. I noticed it but never wanted to make him aware of it; I kept on whistling some song which was implanted in my brain early in the morning when I turned the radio on.

When we arrived, he looked pale and unwilling to go ahead with his plans. I grabbed him by his upper arm and walked him into the house.

It looked like a palace and knowing him all those years, it appeared to me as if he never belonged to such a house.

There was a butler, a woman with a white apron, a nurse and some other people. Mr Senator, Maxwell Darby Senior, was seated in a big armchair looking nowhere in particular. His son, my friend Max, came closer with an insecure step, he leaned towards him, and the old gentleman asked:

"Where is Eleanor?"

His mother had passed away during that period when Max had disappeared without a trace.

He looked at Maxwell and asked again:

"Who are you, sir?"

"I am Maxwell. Your son."

"Hah! My son? Did I have a son? I thought I had a daughter. Eleanor, Eleanor, where have you gone, you were right here a moment ago?! Eleanor, tell them I had a daughter, I never had a son."

They brought a chair closer to his father's armchair, and Maxwell stayed seated for a couple of hours holding the old man's hand. His eyes were moist and I saw many emotions playing on the canvas of his face. They offered me a drink. I was drinking and looking into the garden. It was big, well-kept, with beautiful white monuments and small fountains. It looked like that house could belong to anyone else but to my Maxwell. To him, it looked like a home; the home he left many years ago, the home he inherited from his father who couldn't remember he had a son.

***

One late autumn day, he rang with a strange melody in his voice. He caught me packing up my desk and planning my dinner menu.

He sounded elated; immediately, I feared he had drank too much at lunch. But no, he had something to share with me.

I was glad hearing his voice elated, for recently, let's say, for the last two years, his spirit had somehow withered away. He said, he was *'uninspired and tired of life'*. He said, *'nothing happened anyway, life had just gone in vain'*. He talked about how much he wanted to finish this meaningless and boring existence, the existence in which he was only a useless worm who lived at the expense of his wealthy father ... I suspected his depression kicked in heavily again, I suggested several meaningless attempts towards a brighter outcome, I suggested again visiting Henrich, his psychiatrist ... at the end of the day, it was his choice and decision; he spent two years unwilling to look for help. We dined together, attended the theatre and concerts; he talked little during those two years and I was grateful for that, for when he was in a dark mood no one could reason with him. I had to battle my own demons, that was an exhausting task; on some days, I felt like staying in bed, unmotivated to finish the story, unwilling to look through the window. But no one ever suspected I had any demons; I never expressed my feelings but through my characters. All of them were me: men, women, children, even the pets sometimes were me, even the pets had my characteristics, they could bite indiscriminately, randomly, but in my stories, I kept the beasts that wanted to escape and show in my own life on a tight leash.

I often wondered what impact his divorce had had on him. I know he loved Olivia Vanderbilt; he loved her a lot, for the first year of their marriage I witnessed their love. I never thought how I would feel in his shoes; I never thought about Olivia as a woman any more. She became someone's else wife again ... I never wondered if she was happy in that marriage; I never asked myself would I be happy to see her and ask was she happy in her second marriage.

I, myself, was not marriage material, I knew that, I could not offer much to any woman, I was the one who would take without giving in return when it came to a male/female relationship. I was the happiest when I was alone, with my laptop and the thoughts that swarmed in my head without ceasing. The only person I loved and tolerated for the majority of my life was Maxwell Darby, only him. He was more than my brother. I never wanted to tell him how much he meant to me in case he would grow too fond of me, he would adore me even more, but I genuinely considered him to be the closest person to my heart. I never had many friends. The women I'd been with I didn't love, I liked them; the few of them I even thought I might ask to move in … but after short pondering about such a careless idea, I could see the outcome I feared: they might become possessive, clingy or, God forbid, expect me to marry them. I had three, so-called *'serious relationships'*, but none of those women lived with me, I never said I loved any of them, I liked their presence, I liked the softness of Mia's character, the gentleness of her touch … She could bring me to tears when she sang; she played the violin, and in her music, in her voice, I heard the cry of her Jewish ancestors.

***

I promised Maxwell I'd be available that evening. He walked to my house and we took a taxi to "*Bamonte's*". When the light lit his face, it was clear to me what happened to Maxwell. I saw this look in his eyes only once, but straight away I had recognised it. I asked:

"Who is she?"

"No, no! It is not a woman. I fell in love with Tango."

"Now, that is the biggest joke you've ever told me."

"No, seriously, man! I enrolled in classes and it gave me a new life."

"Dancing gave you a new life?"

"Absolutely. It just consumed me like a fire."

"Who do you dance with?"

"With all sorts of women ..." he stopped there, he took a sip of wine, he had an insane look in his eyes, and a dancing smile in the corner of his lips, he couldn't contain or hide his child-like excitement and I asked again the same question knowing him better than anyone ever had known him:

"Who do you dance with?"

He drank his wine and kept silent for some time, I didn't ask again but was waiting patiently knowing him too well. He couldn't keep any secret from me.

"I went back to Henrich because I couldn't cope any more. You know, my old story, nothing had meaning any more, I just felt useless, without purpose, I felt as if no one in this crazy word gave a shit about me, even you. There were moments where I thought that even you were not my friend. I couldn't get up in the morning, I just covered myself over my head, I wished the duvet was the heavy lid of a coffin, shit man! I was in a bad place. Don't ask now why I didn't call you. Because words had deserted me, that's why. I simply wanted to disappear. To vanish. To go forever, who cares where, just to avoid this reality where I felt so shitty."

"Did Henrich come up with that Tango-shit?"

"Sort of ... he said I had to find some passion, some inspiration, again. As if I had a lot of inspiration in my life. I've never really had much inspiration apart from you, who I envied most of the time. I've never had other inspiration, I had enough money, which was, in my case, only an obstacle. I could buy anything, or anyone, why would I be inspired? I found myself caring about women less and less, they all

looked and behaved the same way in my eyes. I was fed up with all of them."

He drank slowly, but he drank with big gulps, he drank a lot of wine in the first part of the evening, only when I said, *"Take it easy, the night is still young"*, he said, *"Yeah, you are right!"*

After a short pause, he said:

"I went out that evening. I had suicidal thoughts in my head. I couldn't get rid of them, it was as if there was a clown in my head telling me ugly things, making me remember ugly people, drunk women, making me remember Olivia's words, you never knew it, she didn't want my child, she said a child would ruin her image, her waist, her nerves ... but the worst, she despised the idea that the child could inherit my addictive personality. You really never knew why we split up. She always wanted a rich man, not only that but a successful one too. I wasn't successful, I was the son of a Senator, a man who had a lot of money. I wasn't capable of making money; I was capable of spending it. She didn't want my child. She said that. She repeated it a number of times in different situations. Maybe you heard her say that. I walked out, but she was the unhappy one."

"Don't talk about her, it was long ago."

"Did you like her? Did you love her before I even knew her?"

"I never loved her. I liked her as a friend at that time."

"So then you didn't sacrifice your love for the sake of being my best friend."

"Don't give yourself such importance. Tell me, recount the latest story, how did you find yourself in that Tango studio?"

"I simply walked in that evening. I said, 'Can I learn the Tango here?' The woman told me to join them that very evening. I couldn't say

what I had made of it, when I came back home. I thought it to be too difficult. You know me, I give up when the first hurdle shows up. I didn't go back the following week. But I went the week after. It was a dark and lonely evening, I didn't want to call you, knowing that you were too busy writing, I didn't want to go to the bar by myself, I wanted to be among people, but not among complete strangers. So, I showed up and the woman's face was lit by a big, sincere smile. I kept on coming back.

One evening a woman walked in. I thought she was a new dancer, but everyone knew her; she just returned from her holiday, I was told. When she walked in, the commotion was as big as if the greatest rock star had just randomly showed up. The men got so excited, started behaving like schoolboys, gleeful, overwrought and spellbound. Initially, I couldn't comprehend what it was all about, as that scene looked childish and pretentious. She looked at me and her eyes burnt through my brain. The very moment that I saw her, a red flag unfolded! I couldn't keep my eyes off her. She looked at me as if asking, "What's your problem?" She danced with everyone, equally kind and friendly to all of us. She smiled at everyone and encouraged everyone to ask her for a dance. She smelt of distant lands' raindrops; when she talked, I stopped breathing, kept my breath in as long as she talked in order not to disturb the perfect order of her words. I thought I was dreaming, I whispered into her ear as we danced, "Right now I am in Heaven"; she just kept on smiling and gliding across the floor. My eyes were searching for her wherever she moved, my eyes couldn't obey my will, my willpower was made of liquid, it ran down my spine, I was soaking wet when she leaned her slim, lean body against mine; I stopped breathing once again when she, casually, put her arm around my shoulders ... I felt as if I was going to cry without a reason, or that I was going to kneel down and tell her to never stop dancing with me. There you go! In my fifties, I never thought I could fall for a woman of any kind. Even if I had met an angel before I encountered her, I still would have stayed disinterested and aloof. She took my breath away; she took everyone's breath away, you should have seen the commotion, the competition who was going to dance with her, who would bring her a glass of water or put a smile on her beautiful face. You are laughing! I see you are laughing inside, internally. I don't care. Just laugh as much as you want, but yes, I fell in love with her the moment I laid my eyes on her, just like all the other men in this studio."

I had mixed feelings listening to his story. I had never heard him talk like that, but he was never that old; never that depressed as he was in these past two years and he was never as lonely … listening and watching him, it was obvious to me that he was never as excited and keen about life, about potential love. He glowed, he stuttered, his voice high-pitched … after a short pause, after taking it all in, I asked:

"Who is she? What do you know about her?"

"She is a Russian opera singer, quite a famous one. I heard about her several years ago, never heard her sing, though. They call her Tattee. I can't say how old she could be, for she can be anything from thirties to fifties, timeless. When I saw her for the first time, I thought she wasn't even in her thirties. They told me she lived with a man, a Spanish or Argentinian man who looked after her dogs, or something like that. He had some problems with the law, yes, he mucked it up big time. I am not sure, no one really is, it was hush-hush, just glimpses of the story, who knows if anything was or is true at all. They said he ended up, the Argentinian man, in jail for some sort of fraud. Apparently, they lived in Madrid ... apparently, she moved to New York when he was imprisoned. She is a fantastic dancer, they said her dog handler was the tanguero who introduced her to dancing."

"Hang on, hang on! Apparently, this; apparently, that. Tell me, is there anything between the two of you?"

"Are you joking? No! She is no one's partner. Dance partner, or any kind of partner. She comes alone, she leaves alone. She is too kind to everyone; friends with everyone, but disinterested in any of us. Believe me! Like in some cheap Hollywood movie about the untouchable beauty who lost her one and only love. She signs autographs and invites people to her performances if they ask, 'when and where', but no one knows much about her; no one dares to ask her anything too personal. She has those kind of eyes that tell you to stay at a distance forever, even though she leans her slim body against yours. Hey, man, you have to meet her, otherwise you'll never believe me, you'll think I've gone totally crazy. You'll think I went back to my drinking days and am in the midst of delirium tremens. You got to see her to believe my words, in my sanity."

"How long have you known her?"

"It's now been six months that we've been dancing together. Every Thursday and Saturday I visit my hairdresser and the beautician, I spend the afternoon at the Beauty Parlour and after that I head to the Studio."

"Six months has passed since I saw you last time. Gee, time flies! Look, whatever has happened I can't be anything but happy. I am glad you got your passion back! It's a fantastic pastime, I mean, dancing. It is fantastic that you met the woman of your dreams. I suppose all that's left now is my approval! Yes, I will come along to see your mysterious beauty."

Before we parted our ways, we set up a date: he would pick me up next Tuesday at seven. Before we parted our ways, I asked if he knew her full name. He said: *"Tatyana Yuryevna Torasovaya, but we call her Tattee."*

"I shall Google her name, it sounds very familiar."

"I already have, but you won't find anything about her private life. Only that she was born in Moscow into an aristocratic family. You'll see her photos, but they don't do her justice! In reality, she is like live poetry, you'll believe me when you meet her."

I did not really know what to make of his story, but regardless of the story making any sense or not, I was happy to see Maxwell in such a good mood. I didn't want to worry myself much with harder questions, like—*'how much was he exaggerating?'* and *'did he fall into a hopeless kind of love?'*.

Truly, there wasn't much on Google to be found about her apart from her education and performances. She did look pretty: petite, blonde, with a charming, yet shy, smile; she was too pale for my liking, I'd say almost etheric in appearance … but knowing Max, I wondered how long that infatuation would last anyway.

***

The doorbell rang and I sincerely asked myself, *'Who could it be now?'* I wasn't expecting anyone. Maxwell walked in, he looked good, too good, so I laughed:

"You've never made such an effort. Never!"

"C'mon man, you're still in your dressing gown. Hurry up, we'll be late, I cherish every minute I spend in that Studio."

Quickly, I put on an old pair of jeans, a white cotton shirt and a pair of moccasins.

"Get yourself dressed in some better clothes."

"What? Like I am going to your wedding? C'mon! It doesn't matter what I wear, it is you who matters. You look smart. If I put anything better, I can snatch your girl from you."

"I am not afraid of that. No one is going to snatch that girl. She is happy to dance, to smile, and off she goes. None of us are in her league, believe me."

"Shut up, and drive. I will debunk your myth this evening. Or ... I need a character, someone different ... she might be an inspiration if she has a fraction of the traits you mentioned."

***

The evening started slowly. A few people showed up, some were as clumsy as I was, others were a bit swifter in their movements. There were two teachers: a female and a male. The lady's name was Margot; the man's Gabriel. She had a wide, sincere smile, warm eyes and a steady, commanding voice. Gabriel was quieter, though his jokes were original and his feet quick, steps effortless, elegant; when he danced, it looked like there was no easier task to perform, but trying them out was pure pain. A few men wore two-piece suits, some women were beautifully dressed. The music which was playing I recognised from a film … I couldn't remember the title.

Maxwell was nervous, looking at the door most of the time. He couldn't concentrate and follow instructions; his mind and his heart followed the steps in the corridor.

She never showed up that evening and he was bitterly disappointed. He acted like a hurt child. The disappointment was clearly shown on his face, right there, in the middle of his forehead it was written: *I am sad and devastated.*

We walked to the car in silence. When he buckled his seatbelt, he shrugged his shoulders and said:

"So strange! She always comes on Tuesdays. Maybe she had something more important, I can't say, but this is so strange."

"There could be many reasons why she didn't show up. Maybe she caught a cold ... or had a rehearsal ... maybe she had visitors ... who knows what prevented her."

"But she always comes on Tuesdays when she is in New York. Only when she travels, she doesn't come. But then, she tells Margot, Margot tells us, we all know when Tattee is abroad."

"Let's have a drink!"

"But you have to come next time."

"Yeah! I'll come next Tuesday. Now, I am really intrigued to meet your Tattee."

For the rest of the evening he was in a low mood; he said he was tired, but I noticed the lack of concentration; he looked as if he was waiting for someone to walk through the door regardless of the deep conviction that the person he was waiting for never intended to come.

He was so distracted that he never asked about the latest book I was writing. He always asked about my new book, the plot, the protagonists … even when I was unwilling to share any details. He was forgetful, absentminded and disinterested in any conversation. I called it a night and promised, once again, I would follow up.

***

We were faced with exactly the same scene and the same people when we walked in the following Tuesday, full of anticipation—she would show up this time!

Women and men alike were very friendly to one another, I gathered they were friends or acquaintances for a while. Maxwell behaved like a person who belonged to a religious cult. He hugged every person, he kissed Margot, he poured water for the ladies, he cracked jokes and gave compliments. As always: I felt like an outsider. An observer. Someone who doesn't belong, especially to this group of randomly selected people. I begged Maxwell not to tell anyone who I was, for he liked to advertise my work, my books, he liked to tell stories how we met and endured our forty years of friendship.

The dance room was full of people by eight o'clock. There were more than thirty dancers, almost an equal number of men and women.

The music never stopped, nothing had changed, but all of a sudden, the room became livelier, men happier and brighter, their steps lighter and more extravagant. I turned my head around—nothing had changed! I turned my head around again, then my eyes spotted a woman sitting in a chair, leaning forward tying her shoes. At once I knew—it was Tattee. When she joined us, saying a short, courteous *'Hello everyone'* it appeared as those words were like the magic mantra that changed the mood, the colours in the room, the steps of the dancers ,and it changed the music from an ordinary *Milonga* into heavenly sounds.

Only I was unchanged. I kept on repeating my steps as my disobedient feet made a fool of me. At least, that was how I felt.

I glanced at Maxwell whose radiant face looked ten years younger.

A thought escaped—*This is dangerous!*

I feared for him.

Then I studied her: She was prettier than in the photos. She had a willowy figure, long and lean limbs and a very slender and long neck. Her hair was scooped up on top of her head. Yes, she had regular features, pronounced high cheek-bones, a small chin, big, big blue eyes, pale skin, sensual lips and healthy, big teeth. She even had a small-sized birthmark above her upper lip. Her nose wasn't small, neither was it large. It was longish, which gave her face the appearance of a face from a fresco of invaluable rarity: a fresco made by a gifted, patient and dedicated old master.

She was dressed immaculately and had a dark ribbon running parallel with her eyebrows. A small bow was tied at the back of her head.

This was what I surmised, when it came to her physical appearance.

Her bearing was elegant, chin up and a little undefined smile was constantly present on her lips. She smiled at everyone; she greeted everyone with equal kindness and she gave the same attention to every person.

Max went almost down on his knees when he approached to greet her. He came a little bit too close to her and she backed off slightly, tilting her head backwards barely visibly. He wasn't able to notice anything, or anyone. He just stared at her so much so that I was embarrassed by his indecent attack on her integrity.

There was an obvious competition between the men, who was going to dance with Tattee; who would be the first one rushing to get her attention.

Max won the first dance! They danced cheek-to-cheek; he held her as he would the most precious porcelain doll that she truly resembled. I could notice a slight discomfort in her, maybe in the way she held her head, or her arm … on some parts of her body, I noticed clear signs of unease. Maxwell was transported into another world; he danced like an inexperienced dancer, but his will to dance made his feet float above the dance floor. I was sitting, curiously observing this colourful group of people, trying to remember each and every person and detail of the evening. I felt like a sponge, soaking up the atmosphere.

When they finished dancing, he led her to the table; a smile on his elated face, I noticed some tiredness on Tattee's. She looked kind, but unimpressed. With each person she danced, she had the same expression—the expression of a kind annoyance.

We were introduced just as we were about to leave. Maxwell, all of a sudden, became aware of my presence and led Tattee towards me:

"Tattee, meet my friend Bart ... Bartolomeo de ..."

I stopped him, unwilling to be presented by my full name (or, God forbid, defined by my profession).

I said, *'Bart'*, she said *'Tatyana'*, I nodded my head, she looked at me with almost a child-like expression and curiously asked:

"Have we met before?"

"I don't think so. I would remember it, believe me."

"Hmmm ..." said Tatyana, then followed with, *"Sorry!"*

Maxwell hugged her tight, I noticed she pulled back, we left the Studio and on the street, excitedly, he asked:

"So, what do you think? Isn't she fantastic?"

"You are in love."

"Oh, I am not."

"Oh, you are."

"Is it obvious?"

"Yep!"

***

From his stories, I imagined her somehow different.

That evening, when I came home, I found myself thinking of Tattee. I wanted to know more about this woman. I searched Google, but couldn't find more than I had already found before. Nothing personal about her.

Before I fell asleep, I remembered her asking me, *'Have we met before?'* I said that I would remember if we had; I said, *'Believe me'*; I know I would remember Tatyana if I had ever met her.

Without waiting for his invite again, I called Maxwell the following Tuesday asking him if he was going to his Tango lesson, to which he happily answered positively. I casually asked if I could join him one more time.

That evening Tatyana came a bit earlier. She was dressed in white: a white dress, white stockings and shoes, even the ribbon in her hair was white. She looked like a willow tree, one that could resist any wind. Even the strongest hurricane, yet she was so fragile, supple and mysterious, that I found myself looking at her more often than I wanted to.

Again, she danced with everyone; she had her fine and gentle smile on her lips; she talked to everyone showing interest, but in her eyes, I noticed distance and some kind of absence, as if she belonged to someone else or somewhere else.

After a while, she asked me to dance with her. I was taken aback. I said:

"This is my second ... my third class, I am not ..."

"No, don't count your classes. Let's dance."

I felt extreme discomfort in hugging her; discomfort when she leaned her willowy body against mine. She pressed her bosom against my chest; she embraced my shoulder and placed her slim hand on my bare neck.

My feet were glued to the parquet floor. She encouraged me to move with her body, I didn't know what to do, how to dance or what to say, so I just kept on repeating *'Oh, sorry!'* each time I took the wrong step or almost stepped on her foot. Towards the end of our dance she said, *"You don't have to apologise, it takes a long time to learn the Tango."* I asked, *"How long is long?"* to which she replied, *"In two years' time, you'll be a good dancer."*

I never wanted to dance the Tango nor did I want to frequent Margot's classes for two years in order to be a good Tango dancer. All I wanted, after that evening, was to get the answer to her question, which she posed again:

"Do you really think we've never met before?"

I kept on coming and dancing, witnessing Maxwell's strange behaviour more and more often. His jealousy couldn't be hidden any longer; whenever Tatyana danced with any other man, including myself, he expressed a variety of extreme reactions.

Once, he stormed out, red in the face, when Tatyana danced with Hector. Hector was one of the best dancers, swift feet, the body of an athlete, a personal trainer by profession, and a semi-professional dancer. When he danced with Tatyana, it was sheer pleasure for all the senses, a celebration of steps in harmony, total unison. They looked like lovers, though they never were. Hector was, at least twenty years her junior, which in fact didn't really make any difference to this picture of harmony, but the way she behaved towards him, was the way a kind mother was proud of the achievements of her handsome and gifted son. In my eyes, I didn't notice any erotica between the two of them, I only noticed total unity.

I never felt the pang of jealousy, what I felt I'll keep to myself.

After five lessons, maybe, I gathered some courage to ask her to dance with me. I wasn't in awe of her beauty or anything like that; I just wasn't confident in my skill. My dancing was still poor and raw, whilst she danced and looked like an elegant swan.

She leaned her willowy body against mine; she pressed her bosom on my chest and I started breathing heavily, praying to my own God that she would never notice my breathing. I felt embarrassed by it, as if it was some sign of … something that was obvious. After a short while, she moved away just a little; she looked me in the eyes and smiled. At that moment, in my head, I heard the voice, *'This is ... her.'*

She barely visibly nodded her head and placed it on my shoulder.

I could not understand what had just happened. What was that silly voice, why did she look at me with such softness, and why did I feel as if her head belonged on my shoulder. I cleared my throat and said to Tatyana:

"Pardon me, but I desperately need some water." I let go of her and in a brisk walk headed to the table where the big jugs of water were placed for the thirsty dancers.

She followed me, took the glass I filled with water; I started pouring water into the other one, and she just stood there looking at me with that little smile on her lips. All she said, with the faint smile still on her face, was:

"They should turn the aircon higher."

I took a gulp of water and she was already taken; Maxwell took her to the dance floor, pressing her like a precious flower to his chest. She had almost disappeared in his strong embrace. I kept on drinking water and observing the odd couple: the swan and the old drunkard.

On our way, back home, he was unusually quiet. To my questions he answered with a short, *'Yes'*, *'No'*, and *'Sort of'*.

That same evening, Margot asked for my telephone number. She sent me a message two days later, letting me know about the social dance, the Milonga in our neighbourhood. She said they would be happy to see me there.

My real problem was: I couldn't write for an entire week for some uncertain reason. I would sit with my laptop in front of me and stare at the blank page. I wouldn't call it writer's block, for I never believed in it. There is no such thing as writer's block. I could always write, just give me a topic, a feeling, a sentence, a scene, a verse, a memory … suddenly, I couldn't write, for I thought that nothing was good enough to be written down. That's the reason why I kept on dancing—whilst my brain wasn't cooperating with my ideas and imagination to produce stories of my liking, I thought I might get inspired by the happenings at Margot's Studio.

It was my first Milonga, ever.

The men came all dressed up and the scene resembled a scene from a movie set in the twenties, naturally, somewhere in Buenos Aires, or, maybe even Paris in the thirties.

Lots of women looked stunning.

Tattee came, once again, all in white. Such a sharp, yet strangely soft, contrast to all the woman traditionally dressed in black and red colours.

She wore a white tiara. It looked like it was made of white gold and it shimmered as if the diamonds were real ones. Her dress was made of unusual fabric; the dress hugged her body in a way that I thought— *'How on earth did you squeeze yourself into that dress?'*; she had on silverfish stockings and silver shoes. She carried a small purse, made of crystals.

All eyes were on her: men, and women alike, couldn't take their eyes off Tatyana Yuryevna Torasovaya, or Tattee, as they called her.

I was standing next to the bar, when Maxwell walked in.

He was surprised he found me there. I can't tell now if he was pleasantly or unpleasantly surprised, but his voice came out higher than usual when he greeted me:

"Look who is here! How come?"

"At the moment, I am struggling to find the course of my story."

"Therefore, you came here believing you'll find the course right here?"

"You wanna a beer?"

"Sure!"

The first dance Tattee danced with Hector. Maxwell frowned; he said Hector was a *'cocky young shit'*; I abstained from any comment. But they danced as if they had invented the Tango themselves. I just smiled and enjoyed drinking my beer as my mouth was dry.

The second dance, Tattee danced with Gabriel.

For the third dance, all the men geared up: who was going to be the third partner to dance with Tattee?

This competition was won by my old friend Maxwell! He almost ran, but before the race even started, he positioned himself in the right place.

As they danced, he wore an expression of a man who just heard he had secured himself a place in Heaven.

I wasn't able to dance with her, for I was too slow, somehow shy, embarrassed for the sake of others for such rowdy behaviour. I decided to go back home in the faint hope that I would come up with some words worthy of writing down, but on my way towards the doors, Tattee gently approached.

"Leaving?"

"Yes. It's time to go."

"Do you have to be elsewhere?"

"No, not really ..."

"Then, would you like to stay just for one dance with me?"

We stood opposite each other and I looked at her eyes where I saw an abyss and in it, I saw myself, standing and searching … She asked:

"Have you found what you have been searching for?"

"No."

"Not an easy task," she said, still smiling.

This time, whilst her bosom was pressed against my chest, I heard my heart telling me:

"It is—her!"

When the music stopped, I said, *'Thank you!'* and hurriedly, without saying a word to anyone, I left the hall.

***

I kept on researching more about Tatyana. I wanted to know more about her—*What did she know that I didn't? What was she insinuating? Was she genuine? Was she a fraud? Was she playing with me? With all of us? Does she ask every man the same question?*

Ingrid knew Tatyana the best. I invited her to have a drink with me, and without any delay, I asked her what she knew about Tatyana's background. She said she used to be (deliberately minimising her importance talking about her career in the past tense) a famous opera singer, she was born in Moscow into an aristocratic family; she said her mother's family had blood relations with the Romanovs. She said she lived in Madrid with an Argentinian man; she said he was jailed for some sort of fraud. Ingrid was a chatterbox, someone who knew everything about another person. She said she knew who I was and asked if I was going to write about her telling me Tatyana's story. I heard the Argentinian man wasn't a noble man; I heard he was a conman, a low-life; I heard they were lovers … but that bit, I couldn't believe it.

The next time I met her, she smiled again, and said:

"I heard you were asking around about me. You could have asked me, I would have told you whatever you wanted to know. You wanted to know more about Jorge Rubio Rivera?"

"Tatyana, don't get me wrong."

"I am not. You asked about my private life, didn't you? Looks like we never change our ways," she said, keeping her mysterious smile on her lips. Then she continued:

"Jorge Rubio Rivera was a conman. I knew it from the very first day I met him. You might ask—why did I keep him under my roof? You know, there is more to life than the eye can see. Every aristocratic family in Imperial Russia had one Rasputin ... I know you can't get the whole picture, but let me tell you this: Jorge Rubio Rivera was a good man. He was poor and saw me as a vehicle to somewhere, wherever he wanted to arrive, but, on the other hand, he taught me many things that I would have never known existed. He taught me to dance the Tango properly. He used to be, many, many years ago, a famous Tango dancer, the most sought-after artist. We danced together. Then he came again into my life many, many years after that, the man who taught me dancing again and

kept on dancing with me ... Bartolomeo, we were not given the awareness to see everything that is around us, as I said before, every aristocratic family, back in the times of Imperial Russia, had one Rasputin. Let's dance, we danced beautifully before."

I didn't know what she was referring to when she said, *'We danced beautifully before.'* Did she mean *before*, like several days ago, or did it have a different meaning? Was she one of those New Age hocus-pocus-reincarnation freaks? Oh, no!

Even though I was ready to write that evening, words deserted me again. I fell asleep in my armchair, with a lit cigarette between my fingers. I had the most peculiar dream:

All I was aware of, at that moment, was that there were just the three of us: a woman, myself and a priest. We were in a church. It was a magnificent edifice: tall, frescos everywhere, magnificent chandeliers ... the priest wore the most unusual attire ... It was the day of my own wedding. I looked at myself as I would look at an actor on a screen. I was nervous. I was young; a handsome man; in the dream, I looked just as I look right now, only some thirty years younger. Just like in my youth. When she pulled up her veil, I saw her face: the woman had the face of Tatyana Yuryevna Torasovaya; she smiled at me showing the little dimples in her cheeks and the crystal tears in her eyes. When the priest pronounced us 'husband and wife', I became aware of many people who filled the church ...

Suddenly, I woke up and found myself in the armchair with a cigarette butt slowly burning the insides of my fingers. I jumped up, then sat down.

"Who is she?"

Then I remembered, the priest called me *Conte Braghi ... Braggi ... Brogli ...* He called me *Conte*, he called Tatyana … I mean, the woman I was marrying in the dream, he called her *Contessa ...*

What a dream! What a silly dream! *Conte Braghi, Braggi or Brogli and Contessa*! I laughed it off, and went to my bedroom. But I couldn't sleep. I had a story. The story started to unfold in front of my eyes.

I just wanted to sleep. Usually, I would do anything for a good story, that is exactly what I do: I search for good stories, I provoke good stories in order to write. I am always ready for a good story but I felt dry and exhausted for a good six weeks.

Now I had a story and was yet reluctant to commence writing it.

I felt like she was playing with my mind. Tatyana, with her mysterious little smile; she, who smiled with her eyes to everyone, the smile of superiority as if she knew something others never had an inkling of. *Did she know more than the rest of us? Who was she? What did she mean when she said, 'Every aristocratic family had one Rasputin'?*

I couldn't sleep that night nor could I write. Not a word. Words were just swirling in my head and I felt as if I was on some mad merry-go-round that would never stop and let me off.

The morning found me exhausted.

I Googled her name again. I read the history of the Romanovs, again. I read various blogs and stories about Rasputin. I looked at her pictures on the internet.

"Who was she?"

***

Now, I couldn't give up! I went to the class, without my best friend. We met there. When Tatyana walked in, as usual, the atmosphere changed. Everyone became somehow livelier, happier. She just smiled as the one who knew what effect they had on others. When she greeted me, she said:

"Allora, Conte Bartolomeo, come sta?"

I looked sternly into her eyes, but their expression never changed: they were kind and soft, though penetrating. The smile on her lips was like the Mona Lisa's smile: somehow shy, somehow mocking!

There I was: standing without a word, unable to articulate any of my questions which tormented me the day and the night before.

She said:

"Aren't you going to ask me for a dance?"

We danced without a word; I could only hear my heavy breathing—to me, it was louder than the music which was playing.

I saw Maxwell with his arms crossed looking at us, no expression on his face: just a stern, curious look.

"You said that every aristocratic family in Imperial Russia had one Rasputin. Who's the Rasputin of your family?"

"Oh, I can't share that story. A prominent male in our family claims that our DNA and Rasputin's are almost identical," she said, followed by soft laughter.

"The power in your eyes is something that one doesn't see every day ..."

"No. Your assumptions are wrong. I am just an ordinary person."

"With extraordinary talents."

"No. I am an average singer."

"Hmm. OK. Call it average."

"Just like you—you are an average writer."

"Am I?"

"I read some of your stories. They lack authenticity. Not convincing."

"I don't think I am trying to convince my readers."

"Do you write from your heart or from your mind?"

"Mind, I'd say."

"Obvious."

That evening, when I was leaving, once again, she crossed my path. She held my arm, saying:

"Don't get me wrong, your writing isn't bad, but it doesn't speak to the soul."

"Do you think you have a suggestion?"

"Suggestion no, but there is a story worth writing although, it could be shared with, and written by, only a person who has a deep, mystical soul."

"I am not the one."

"You used to be."

"Are you saying something I can't grasp?"

"You can grasp it, but you are blocking your subconscious mind."

"How do you know? Where do you read it?"

"It is late. You have to go, and I have to go, too. Have a good, productive rest of the night."

"You, too." I said, and walked out.

When I was about to sit down in my car, I heard Maxwell calling me. I turned to him and he smiled. Through his forced smile, he asked:

"Has it come, finally?"

"Who? What?"

"You have been waiting for your revenge since Olivia-times."

"Maxwell!"

He turned his back and walked towards his car.

With a fist, I angrily punched the windscreen. Blood everywhere. *'I won't be able to commence the story,'* was the only thought in my head.

***

That evening, I decided not to attend the Tango lessons any more. I was not in love with Tatyana, nor was I her fan. I never wanted to compromise my friendship. I loved Maxwell like a real brother, and his insecurities were more severe than mine. I never had father issues. I had never even heard of him. In my early imagination, he was some sort of Rasputin: a mad monk, an expert in dark magic and dishonest deeds; someone that you should keep a distance from, forever.

When I said, the next time I met Tatyana, that Rasputin was *'a mad monk, an expert in dark magic and dishonest deeds'*, after a longer silence in which she analysed my words, she asked:

"But was Rasputin just that? Or was it the way many wanted to portray him? As an evil, dark force? To call him evil, is it just proof of ignorance, for if you do more detailed research you could find him portrayed as a man of peace who worked strongly against war. Wasn't that the reason why the generals poisoned him, and after poisoning him shot him on the ice of the Neva river. He tried to teach others how to live a moderate life, to live in peace and search for answers within yourself, not in the material world, for that creates envy and hate."

She said if I wanted the real story about this mysterious man, I had to look for it in the right places.

"The world in which you live, the truth has been twisted."

"And in your world?"

"Well, I can't make you see the world through my eyes. You have to search for the truth, alone. We are all lone travellers."

"But, you said we've met before; obviously, we were not lone travellers if we travelled together. Even now, we are sharing some of the journey, aren't we?"

"Bartolomeo, you are not a good writer. You write with your mind. You need to learn to speak from, and to, your soul. You have forgotten that language."

"Do you want to say, I used to speak the Soul's language."

She looked deep into my eyes, smiled, touched my cheek with her fingers and walked away—straight into Maxwell's embrace and danced away, leaving me with an unanswered question.

Maxwell was in love with Tatyana, I was not. Yes, just the way he was in love with Olivia, and I was not.

But observing Maxwell now, seeing him open, fragile and responsive, and at the same time paralysed and unresponsive, I started doubting that he had ever loved Olivia Vanderbilt sincerely, deeply.

He looked at Tatyana as if she was a creature from some other world, a world he was never let into: one of eternal lust, of deep, disturbing emotions, of painful love and unquenchable thirst. A mystical world, where everything was possible, where one could meet any kind of angel, archangel, nymph, or maybe a dark Medusa or even Rasputin himself.

***

That night I had visitors. They came randomly, telling me stories that didn't make any sense: *I was in an army where I lost my arm, said the dark Medusa: I was on the merchant boat sailing the wide seas, said a nymph; I was in Venice, Piazza San Bortolo, a woman greeted me, tears in her eyes, laughter of ultimate happiness ... said my archangel; I was in the arms of a woman, a beautiful woman who called me Conte ... I called her 'mia Contessa' ... there was a picture on the dining room wall, I couldn't remember which saint it was; was it San Bortolo or ... was it even a saint at all: he had insightful, transparent blue eyes, penetrating deep into my soul, he read my past and my future speaking to me telepathically, I heard names Tiziana and Tatyana ... the voice said I'll meet them both, she would follow me wherever I went, the voice of San Bortolo said that I had to obey and to follow, I broke into a sweat in front of his eyes, I cried, I begged not to take her away, he laughed, stood down from his frame, I screamed when I recognised his face: the face of Grigori Yefimovich Rasputin.*

I switched on the lamp, checked the time: 2:20, early morning.

Quickly, I put on some clothes, lit a cigarette, without combing my hair or locking my door, I found myself on the street. Regardless of the time, there were still many people outside, my neighbourhood was always lively, populated by night owls.

I believed that a brisk walk would loosen those pictures the dream had crammed into my confused head. I had a story, but didn't know how to commence it, I lacked the first sentence, the opening.

Whilst walking and talking to myself, I almost bumped into a couple: a tall, strong man, taller than I, stronger than I, and a woman who looked like a ballerina, made of Murano glass. I looked at her, she looked at me, her face frozen, I said:

"Tiziana!"

She looked at me, her eyes looked like pale-blue icebergs, cold, cutting through me like daggers, she said:

"How can I help you?"

The tall man said, *"Keep on walking, Tatyana"*, and they walked off into the mist. It was a misty morning; all I could see were his shoulders getting bigger, whilst Tatyana's figure was getting smaller and smaller. I needed a stiff drink. *'How bizarre!'*, I thought; *"How bizarre"*, I said and walked into a still crowded bar.

I couldn't go back home, particularly to my bed, I kept on spending money on beer, later on I walked around without a plan … with a single leading thought, *'I might stumble upon her again ... Yes, Tatyana, Tiziana, whoever she was ...'*

***

I guess, by now, my reader knows me well enough to assume that I went back to the Studio that following Tuesday. I had, actually, two people that bothered me greatly by now: one was Tatyana, *Tiziana*, the woman I met on the street the other night, the woman who danced with me; and the other one was Maxwell Darby, my best friend—his attitude had fundamentally changed and it hurt more than anything I had experienced before. His aloofness, the distance he put between us, the shadows in his eyes, the bitterness in his sentences; whatever I tried he stayed trapped in that mood, in that world from where he looked at me through a glass door. The door was thick, impenetrable.

I terribly missed those days when he would just pop in unannounced; a pot of coffee on the table; we chain-smoked and listened to music without the need for any conversation. After a couple of hours, two pots of coffee and almost a packet of cigarettes we shared, he would just simply get up and touch his temples with his index finger. I missed our silence and our lively conversations on other occasions. He was, usually, the initiator of any topic or of any particular mood. Whichever mood he would walk in with, I would adopt it, welcome it.

I missed Maxwell Darby, my best friend, but the glass door to his inner world was tightly closed. I didn't want to be a burglar, I knew I had to be patient and wait until Maxwell Darby opened the door ready to let me in again.

His heart was in the dark grip of jealousy.

Several times I attempted to write him a letter, telling him that he doesn't have to be jealous, for there was no reason for it. I never fancied Tatyana Yuryevna Torasovaya, not the way he did. Just like I never fancied Olivia Vanderbilt in the way Maxwell did.

Maxwell was a man who would provoke jealousy in other men, not me. He was The Maxwell Darby … you know, I grew up in an orphanage … he didn't need to be jealous of me.

I wasn't a conman, I was a writer, a novelist.

I knew Tatyana Yuryevna Torasovaya belonged to a world I never even heard of except in Tolstoy's novels; he wrote about that class where he himself belonged and Tatyana Yuryevna Torasovaya's ancestors as well.

I had to face one question I kept on avoiding: *'Why was I thinking about Tatyana all the time?'*

"Who was the tall man I met you with, on Christopher Street, last Friday?"

"Christopher Street? Where's Christopher Street?" She said she never walked on Christopher Street with a tall man, especially not last Friday, for, she said she wasn't in New York that weekend. She said she left on Friday afternoon. I did not believe her.

I asked:

"Who is Contessa Tiziana?"

"You are a writer, you should know."

"Do you think writers know everything that has ever been written. I have never heard of Contessa Tiziana."

"Yet, you are asking about her."

"You mentioned her earlier."

"Wasn't it a dream?"

She pressed her body closer to mine, Max's eyes shone in the dimmed room, my breathing got heavier, my brow shone, hot and sweaty, she whispered, *"Close your eyes"*, I did and a scene opened where I saw us dancing: right there, I, *Conte Braghi, Braggi or Brogli e mia Contessa Tiziana.* I whispered:

"Contessa Tiziana", she said nothing, she kept her eyes on something invisible but pleasant to the eye, for she had the most pleasing smile on her face.

We kept on dancing even when the music in the room stopped; as we continued dancing, the music came from the past, from other eons, or from some parallel world where we danced every evening.

Still, I kept on holding her, and came to my senses only when she said:

"Bartolomeo, open your eyes, the music has stopped."

I felt like running away, through the closed door, I had an urgent need to get out and get some fresh air, I needed the evening freshness, it was stuffy in that room, all eyes were on us: me and Tattee; she was walking, in her measured step, towards her table, head held high, with a mysterious smile of victory. She sat elegantly and poured herself some water, then she closed her eyes and gently rocked her head to the music. Once again, she escaped, right there, into her own world where no one belonged: not Maxwell Darby, not I, or any other person in this room.

I stumbled to my car as if I was intoxicated; twice, I almost bumped into the tin rubbish bins; I took out a key, it was the wrong one; I checked again my set of keys, looked up and met his face: Maxwell stood in front of my car.

He said:

"It took you a good thirty years to reveal who you really are."

"Maxwell!"

"You son of a bitch!" he said and walked away as if he was chased by his past.

I almost punched the windscreen, again. I couldn't determine the exact reason why: was he, Maxwell Darby the reason, was she the reason, Tatyana Yuryevna Torasovaya, or was I the reason, being aware of the proportions and impact she had on the both of us?

'Who is she?' I asked myself. When I sat behind the steering wheel, I leaned my head on my palms and remained there sitting for many hours: everybody had left long ago, even Margot and Gabriel, who always stay last to tidy up and to prepare the Studio for another day.

I never saw Tatyana leaving.

'What does she want from me?'

'What was she insinuating?'

Yet another night I couldn't sleep, nor could I write. I was staring into a blank screen: nothing was there, no words, no miracles, no stories of any kind. Just spooky silence staring back.

'Was she manipulating my mind?'

No!

I just needed a good night's sleep, then everything would look different, everything would look fine, just as it looked before. Way before. Before we even met Tatyana Yuryevna Torasovaya.

But a new question formed in my mind: *'Did everything look just fine? Before? Way before I met Tatyana?'*

Maxwell Darby lived in my shadow, that is exactly what he believed, how he felt. Like an obscure wannabe writer, an untalented man who fed off my ideas and occasionally stole some of them, presenting them as original ones. I would turn a blind eye to such doings and attempts of his, I turned a blind eye to his unrealistic glorification of his mumblings that now and then were published in some third-rate literary magazine. I let him believe in his childish and unrealistic view about himself, knowing that it was of short sight, for it was always followed by some sort of depression and self-hatred. I could never harm him.

I lived in Maxwell Darby's shadow, that is exactly what I believed and how I felt. An obscure lover, untalented romantic who fed off his adventures and occasionally stole some of his encounters and wrote about them in disguise, presenting them as original stories. He would turn a blind eye, pretending not to recognise the characters I was so skilfully writing about, even disguised to perfection, he knew they belonged to him. He let me believe that he wasn't aware of who those women were, he let me believe that those adventures were my own, for shortly after publishing the book, I would retreat, reluctant to see him for a longer period. He could never harm me.

I knew I loved Olivia Vanderbilt, regardless of my countless denials and attempts to portray her as a shallow and superficial protagonist. I think he thought my sacrifice was the most noble thing that came from one orphan. I was never a noble man, I wasn't polite but quiet; I wasn't kind but insecure. He was a noble man, he was loud but always polite; he was self-assured but always kind to everyone, including me. He was of good stock, of good upbringing, which was evident in each and every deed of his, even when he was drunk, he was a gentleman. At least, in my envious eyes.

I was talented.

I would never want to lose Maxwell for the sake of a woman. Any woman. Not even Olivia Vanderbilt! Not even because of Tatyana Yuryevna Torasovaya.

In his anger, he called me a *'son of a bitch'*. I thought I might write him a letter in which I could explain that non-existent relationship between me and his muse. I wanted to tell him that I couldn't care less about that woman … but I couldn't bring myself to lie.

She stirred something dark within me, some story buried deep down in my subconscious mind, a story that never had its end, and was asking to be told, asking to be ended.

I felt like a helpless victim.

Not a victim of Tatyana, not a victim of my subconscious mind. I felt like the victim of a mistake. Some divine joke!

I lost my willpower and always did the opposite of what I had decided to do. I stopped writing even though I firmly decided that I would commit every morning to writing from 4 am till midday. I never wrote a single word, for words deserted me. It was like the Sahara of my mind.

The only oasis in this dry land was a single thought about Tatyana Yuryevna Torasovaya. When I thought about her I could see pictures of some other times; when I danced with her I knew every step whilst she was taking me, retracing our steps, to the times when we danced together. Even though I saw the pictures and read the script she was speechlessly revealing to me, I couldn't write it down, as if it was forbidden! As if my mind was weak, exhausted and frightened, therefore it couldn't tell the story Tatyana was telling me with her eyes, her energy and her movements. I knew her, she knew I remembered. I, who never believed in anything else but the five senses, I, who laughed at anything that had a hint of supernatural or beyond this reality, was convinced that Tatyana Yuryevna Torasovaya was a woman I had loved before. Every time when I had such a thought whilst holding her in my arms and dancing, she would, as if she read my mind, move her body slightly away from me, look me in the eyes, smile and nod her head, barely noticeably.

At that time, Maxwell stopped attending classes, stopped coming to Milongas and stopped knocking on my door. It did hurt, but I needed to get to the heart of this story. I was obsessed with *'our past'*, I was under the spell of this beautiful woman, I was ready for the first time in my life to lose a friend, to lose my publisher who was pressing me, to lose my mind.

It was almost as if I lived in a parallel reality: I saw pictures, Venice, balls, the Carnevale, *mia Contessa* and I, dancing, laughing, making love, drinking wine from the same cup and drinking God's divine nectar so generously offered to young lovers.

I couldn't move, couldn't pass through that darkness that would encompass my memory after several scenes which were regularly revealed.

One evening, whilst dancing with Tatyana who had a tiara on her head, a tiara that brought some memories again, I suddenly asked:

"How did it end?"

"What?"

"The story of Contessa Tiziana and her ... husband or lover?"

She shrugged her shoulders, yes, with a smile on her lips.

"It is up to you to figure it out."

"I don't have the means to find out. You have to help me."

"I can't help you. I can dance with you."

"Is that all that you are offering?"

"What else?"

"You started it, didn't you?"

"Started what, Bartolomeo?"

"This dance of ours."

"You should improve your steps, concentrate on dancing, you should be the leader. The man, is the leader; the woman follows."

"I need to tell you something ..."

"Don't! I know it already. Keep it to yourself and keep on dancing, that's how you'll improve."

"Who was that tall man I saw you with ..."

She looked into my eyes. Her deep look penetrated my soul. She kept on looking and looking and I couldn't bear it anymore, so I said:

"You are not going to tell me."

"Tell you, what, Bartolomeo?"

"Who was that man?"

"It was—you!"

***

It was a rainy evening, I went out, I needed fresh air, it was a cold evening and there were too many unanswered questions in my head. In the distance, I saw a man. His step was wobbly, twice he stumbled, twice he grabbed a street lamp. My walk was brisk, I caught up with him just at the moment when he faltered again, I hurried, caught him firmly, he turned his head and the drunkard smiled at me with a mellow and tired smile. It was my former friend Maxwell Darby. Holding him in my arms, I felt like crying after many, many years. He looked so old, worn out, he looked like a homeless man, an old bum who had never had a proper home.

I said, *"Maxwell"*, he just burped and wriggled out of my grip. It was a cold evening, he was in a single shirt, without a jacket, with only flip-flops on his feet, and a pair of jeans that were too large. He had lost so much weight.

I took him home.

I fed him with a soup that I made earlier that evening. I put him in my bed. All this time, Maxwell Darby didn't utter a single word. Neither did I.

I slept on the couch. I got up several times during that night to check out if he was covered, if he needed anything. He slept like a little child.

'Who is this woman?' I asked myself countless times.

'Who is she, and what did she do to me? To Maxwell and me?'

I fell asleep early in the morning. All night, I was taking care of Maxwell and thinking heavy thoughts, asking questions that couldn't be answered. Time and again, I thought that she was a great manipulator who manipulated my mind. And, probably the minds of many, including Maxwell's.

I fell asleep early in the morning and woke up when the sun was high up in the sky. I went to check on Maxwell, but when I got to my bed—it was empty. He had left. He didn't eat, didn't take any food; the only thing he took was my old winter jacket.

The next day I found out that Maxwell had moved out. No one knew where he went. I asked several people who could have known, but they shrugged their shoulders. Carol, the barmaid, told me he had been drinking heavily lately. She said he would come without his jokes, he just sat there and drank. She walked him home several times. She told him not to drink that much, but he told her *'mind your own business'*.

It took me a month to find out where he had gone. His attorney told me Max sold his father's estate.

I found him at a ranch in Montana.

He said he was old and tired. Ready to go.

He told me he knew he wasn't a writer. He was *'plain shit'*. He told me he loved me like he would love a real brother. He told me I was a great writer, but as a friend, as a man, *'plain shit'*.

I said nothing.

I didn't have a meaningful story to tell.

We didn't even shake hands.

I left.

That evening, when I came back to New York, walking back home from the taxi, I saw a woman holding a tall man under his arm. She looked like a porcelain doll, dressed in a white dress and silver fur, and he was so tall that he looked unreal, his shoulders broad, his hair in a long pony-tail, wearing a tuxedo, as one would in my modest neighbourhood.

Anger rose in me, violent anger. I ran after them. I grabbed her by the arm, she turned around and an older woman looked at me in amazement, the tall man pushed me with all his might, assuming I was a pickpocket, I almost flew several meters and ended up hitting a parked car. He came closer and punched me in the face, my nose bled and I felt like fainting.

***

After six weeks of absence, after losing Maxwell, most probably forever, after I was beaten in the street, I went to the Studio, where I was warmly greeted by the ever-smiling Margot.

"Bartolomeo, you are back. So nice to see you."

"I want to have a word with Tatyana, is she here already?"

"Oh, you don't know?"

"I don't know what?"

"She went back. To Madrid."

"She went back? To Madrid? Is that the end of the story?"

"What story, Bart?"

"Err ... what story ..."

"If you wanna know ... I heard, her friend was let out of jail ... apparently. You know, there's been a little bit of mystery surrounding her since she walked in. I think, mostly it was gossip. People gossip about beautiful, talented people. I loved Tattee, she was such a character. She attracted so many men, to be honest, I miss her ..."

"When did she go."

"Six weeks ago."

"Six weeks ago?"

"Yes."

"What exactly did she say?"

"She said, 'Jorge called. I am going back to Madrid'. That was all ... Err ... I only asked if she was coming back, she smiled and said: 'Oh, no!' Just that, 'Oh, no!'."

"Just 'Oh, no!'?"

"Yes." said Margot, quietly.

"Will you join us this evening?"

"Oh, no! Not this evening."

"I understand." said Margot and shrugged her shoulders as if in resignation.

I felt nothing.

Nothing, I felt!

Only the cold wind blew its icy arrows; my mind was still frozen, empty, without any answers or any conclusions. I felt nothing but the icy wind in my heart.

La Famosa Tanguera

If you ask people, women and men alike, in that Tango scene about me, they might tell you all sorts of things, thus I'd better tell you my story in my own words. There are lots of rumours, lies, I would say. Women are jealous of me; yes, they are, it isn't the mere imagination of my creative mind, I can feel their envious eyes on me all the time. Men, they dream of me!

I have been changing my name and my career often, I like to play characters, hide-and-seek games with men, I like to exercise my power over men: those desperate losers, needy of my presence, small and insignificant when I penetrate their miserable privacy. When I discover who they really are, I leave.

Everything was as it should be before that woman appeared; she called herself Tattee, an arrogant, pale, washed-out Russian doll, without brains, without class. Oh, yes, I can say that, my ancestors were French, my sister was a fine artist born in Paris ... I was born and bred in Australia, and came to New York in 1991. Quickly, I found myself in my rightful place among the New York artists as I had numerous talents which I was ready to showcase. I wanted to conquer the Big Apple by all means.

They say I lack empathy! They say I use men, or even, some say I am a slut just because I could have had any man I wanted; I slept with a lot of them just to make them remember for the rest of their lives—that they spent the night with the most beautiful and talented woman. What a gift to them! You see, I am a generous person!

Being a *femme fatale* runs in my blood: my French grandmother was a theatre actress, men loved her more than opium, back then; I still keep all of her black and white photographs in the top drawer of my desk.

I met Aldous Black in the summer of 1991, and by the end of the autumn, that same year, he proposed and we went together to his native New York. We almost ended up getting married, but the trouble was he told me a *small* lie: he wasn't a wealthy man at all; he had an average job, a bank-clerk, or something … he was renting an apartment, I never lived in an apartment myself; he couldn't promise to bring my pets all the way from Sydney, he couldn't even promise to get me two dogs and a cat, he couldn't promise to buy me a new car, nor could he organise events where I could showcase my work. I left!

I left when I met Jacques in a busy bar. He had a well-tailored three-piece suit, a snow-white shirt and quite a big leather briefcase, so my first thought was *'he is probably a lawyer'*; I have had so many men, therefore I don't make a single mistake when assessing a man. It is not just my natural beauty that attracts men to me; I am a charmer, my eyes know that unique language and when I connect with a man, the first eye-contact is often fatal. I smile in a way that a man can't define: am I shy, cheeky or am I promising some great adventure? I think, there are elements of all of it, but the ultimate goal is to catch that fly in my web and see how it'll survive. A nice game, sophisticated; a game in which I was the master player.

I forced myself to cry a bit on that evening, told him about a man who abused me, used to beat and mistreat me; I told him I ran away and had no place to stay. I ended up in his house *'for a short while'*: we drank the most exquisite wine, we dined in expensive restaurants, he loved taking me out showing me to his friends, he generously shared everything with me, helped me to establish my own boutique and when the business took off, I left him. It wasn't a clean-cut break up, he just kept on complicating my life, in the end he even threatened to sue me … but women's tears are a mighty weapon. Several weeks after that I met another man whose name I had forgotten a long time ago. All I remember was that he was a tall man, a body-builder some fifteen years my junior, who had fallen madly in love with me and was ready to break the lawyer's jaw if he wouldn't leave me alone. He was a strong guy, gifted in many ways. Nature was kind to him, endowed him with many physical gifts, hence he served for several months as the perfect lover, as a delivery person for my exquisite boutique, as a guard … but as time passed by, I understood we didn't have much in common apart from extraordinary antics in the bedroom … when I left him, he said I would pay for that. I changed all the locks on my door; after a short while he stopped pestering me, especially when a colleague of mine took up the chance and accompanied me wherever I had to go. We went to exhibitions together, the theatre, parties and picnics in Central Park. I loved New York back then: such a great vibrant place, so many flamboyant characters, a place where a woman like me could flourish and explore.

If someone told me, back then, that time would fly so mercilessly, so pathetically quick, I would have enjoyed my life even more, but those twenty years passed like in a dream: I had the fantastic company of many interesting men, I had the greatest customers (some of them were my occasional lovers, no one could resist my charms!), I organised the greatest exhibitions, wore the greatest clothes, put up the greatest shows and I had a troop of jealous women gossiping behind my back. Yes, they couldn't put up with me: my extraordinary looks, my talents, my popularity with men and my wits! It was I who dominated this scene, it was I—

the darling of any party, the most desirable and the most sought-after socialite. My fashion boutique was an iconic place where rich men were drawn to like moths to a lamp in the dark of night.

I had mirrors everywhere, tens of mirrors in my boutique—they reflected my beauty back to me and to the customers alike. Initially, it was a fine men's fashion boutique with exquisite accessories and leather goods. I was their fashion icon, their goddess. Me, Julie de Rosette, as I was known way back then. I expanded the field of my interests, my talents multiplied: I had a fashion boutique, a jewellery store where I designed my own jewellery, I was a nude model for several influential and well-known artists and I played guitar in a trendy café on Saturday evenings for a select clientele. I changed my name with every new career change from Julie de Rosette to Janice Rosien and a few more.

Well, people talked ill about me, and I knew why: they couldn't have the same success that I had, the same connections and the same ease with which I danced to life's rhythm. I was like a butterfly, free and flying high.

Had I ever fallen in love? This is a question without an easy answer. I had fallen in love many times, but I would sober up very quickly seeing that there was not much for me in the given relationship. I couldn't give more than I would receive, I couldn't commit emotionally, I couldn't stand when someone, anyone would catch hold of me … if I needed, or better to say, when I needed a man it was for a purpose: for physical pleasure or for material status. There was no man who could hold onto me, like a baby, like a parasite, like a vampire sucking up my energy. Oh, no! I wasn't a one-man woman!

When my cousin, Juanita, (her real name was Sally McKinsey) passed away in Buenos Aires, I flew there at once. I feared someone could pick or steal the jewellery she bought in my boutique back when she visited New York. She rang me one day saying she wanted to buy some jewellery (assuming I would sell it to her for a cheaper price!!). I never sold my jewellery cheaper to her, but she had a friend with her, a gentleman from Buenos Aires who paid the bill. A large bill.

When I heard she passed away, immediately, I booked my flight and arrived in Buenos Aires. She was buried already and her jewels were nowhere to be found. In her apartment, I had found numerous photographs on the walls.

She was a dancer. A famous Tango dancer. They called her Bonita Juanita. There were numerous photos of her dancing with young, attractive men. A number of photos and a number of men. It took me several hours to go through all of her photos, in the end I was allowed to take them with me if I wanted. The astonishing thing I heard: she died of Tango.

How could that be possible? —to die of Tango?

Ah, what a silly statement!

What a childish myth!

No one died of Tango.

It was exhaustion. She had numerous lovers; countless young men she taught to dance. What a lucky bitch! She dated older men, the wealthy ones, but she slept with the young ones, well built, with good endurance and free-spirited, those that never wanted commitment, only endless fun and sweetness, just like her.

I thought, because I lived in New York, that I had a much richer life than my cousin Sally in poverty-stricken Buenos Aires. Alas, I was wrong! Her life was richer in a different way to mine—her life was a constant dance party with young good-looking men, whilst mine was a struggle to find younger lovers as I was approaching the age when a woman needs a lot of time and tricks to keep up with the merciless signs of ageing. I left Buenos Aires without my jewels but with hundreds of photos of Bonita Juanita and the determination to find the best Tango studio in New York.

I dislike putting myself into an age-box, but when I found that Studio, I shall admit only now that I was in my early fifties, but no one would have guessed it. No one! I looked at least fifteen years younger and when I walked in, I knew I was going to be the envied queen of the dance floor, the talk of the town, the dream of men who couldn't take their eyes of me! I knew it and I felt as if I had found a long-lost home, or meaning, or a seductive lover. Yes, Tango was my seductive lover!

It was like a candy-bar for me, a playful child that needed to bite into every sweet temptation, without the intention of finishing the feast.

I called each and every man to my home to fix my curtains, to change the light bulbs, to teach me the new steps or to paint my bedroom red. I danced and played with them in various ways, games that gave me immeasurable pleasure. I pinned up all of Juanita's photographs on my wall with the intention to be reminded daily where I wanted to be: a better dancer than she ever was, a more desirable dream than she could have ever been. I was so pretty when I dyed my hair black, applied my make-up and put my skin-tight see-through dress.

I felt pretty at that age, though I never felt pretty when I was young, Sally was the pretty one, Bonita Juanita won all the prizes.

Men were mesmerised by me. I would call them to Milongas or simultaneously send text-messages to six different men telling them to meet me at certain place and I wouldn't show up. Or, I would hide and watch what would happen: would they sort out the misunderstanding, would they fight with words, would they search for me, ring me or send messages? Yes, there were so many different scenarios, and I enjoyed each of them equally, even when my safety was compromised. I was the Queen of the Tango scene, I was the woman everyone talked about, and I would never allow any other woman to win that title. Those, a bit pretty, a bit daring, always lost the fight with me, I knew how to put them in their rightful place: I would gossip about them, ridicule them publicly, telling men silly stories about them or ridicule their clumsy beginnings.

Ten years had passed, and I was indubitably the inviolable Queen of the Tango scene, I was the dream of every *tanguero* … women hated me, envied me, and that was the perfect fuel for my victorious, domineering feeling that gave me enormous power, not only over men, but over women, over my past, present and future. I could pick any man and dance with him all night long, or I could cut deep into any man's heart just by refusing to dance with him.

Women gossiped. Just because they were jealous, there was nothing to be gossiped about! They said I lacked empathy, I was self-centred, I lacked maturity or human warmness. Rubbish! They were simply jealous.

In my own opinion, and the opinion of the majority of the men, I was the prettiest woman there, the most desirable dancer, and I knew how to stay on that throne for a long time. The younger women, those perkier, I knew how to throw out of the game: I would spread gossip, or whisper in their ear something horrible or snatch away a man if I assumed they might want to dance with, or God forbid, they might fancy. All of them were my admirers!

When I discarded a man, I let him bleed, I let him leave the Tango community forever, or if he wanted to stay, I would tease him for being a weakling. Some of them desperately wanted to stay friends. I had many friends.

Ten years passed, and things started to change. I wasn't in demand like years ago. Even though I was the best dancer, many men didn't come to ask me for a dance. I asked *them*, instead. I would pull a man by the sleeve and jokingly, joyfully say:

"Don't be scared of me; I won't bite!"

Ten years passed, and things started to change, though not too obviously, but I felt the difference. My body had changed, my hair needed more care, my cheeks had sunk and it took me the entire day to recover after a night of dancing. As fewer men were willing to accompany me home after the Milonga, I signed up for several dating websites which was a great move! Once again, I had an inexhaustible source of supply. I would arrange a blind date and invite men to the dance, or to the Milonga and they would appear and look for me. If they were good looking, I would approach, if not I pretended to be someone else. An endless source of fun and entertainment!

Women gossiped, they were envious for they couldn't do the same, or because they didn't have my strength, energy and beauty, or they didn't know how to be on the top of the game.

That year, I was engaged three times but broke up with each of them because I feared I had made the wrong decision. I changed my address often because when I met a man, I liked to move in with him in order to experience what life would look like with that person. Yes, I always escaped quickly, unable to cope with people's habits, temperaments or needs.

***

One evening in February 2016, a seemingly self-confident woman walked in. She wasn't tall but looked tall because she was slim, wearing very high heels. She was blonde, her long hair just hung down to her shoulders. She had blue eyes, a small nose, therefore she looked like a boring picture of a pointless, unwanted doll. She had pale skin and an unappealing accent. I dislike people with strong accents, they bring something disturbing … making me feel and think: *I really don't want to get to know you*. She wasn't pretty nor was she ugly. An average looking blonde pale woman. Maybe she was younger than me … maybe, I said. Maybe she could have been in her late forties, early fifties … maybe some ten years younger than I … maybe fifteen, I couldn't judge that from a distance, but at once, I concluded that there was something superficial, fake and unapproachable in her demeanour, I knew I would never talk to her if she stayed.

For some unknown reason, I couldn't take my eyes off her just like most of the men who were in the Studio that evening. She walked slowly, with a certain step as if she knew precisely where she was heading. She changed her shoes, tied her hair up into a loose pony tail and straightened her back. She never looked my way, and for me that was like a neon sign was switched on saying, *"War has been declared"*.

Ah, what else but a Russian! With that accent, with her pale complexion, with her aqua eyes and that small, silly nose!

The strangest thing was: almost all the men were instantly attracted to her. She said her name was Tatyana (of course!), but the men quickly gave her a pet name, *Tattee.*

Apparently, she was an opera singer. I doubted it. Probably some third-rate singer somewhere in some Russian provincial place … What was she doing in New York, I wanted to know. The most likely scenario was that she married a wealthy man, she probably found someone on a dating site: that's what they do!

She held herself as if she was a queen: her back straight, head up, nose up, a little fake smile on her lips; cordial but vivacious, almost flirtatious.

I knew she would be leaving this place in no time. I'd show her how we operated here, who's who and how not to cross paths with the real dancers, those who dominated the dance floor and men's hearts and moods.

Another strange thing was: in a short time, so-called Tattee won not only the men's hearts but even Margot's and some other silly woman's.

Soon after she joined, Maxwell Darby came. Soon after Maxwell Darby came, Bartolomeo del Duca, yes—*the del Duca*, the famous writer, came.

Maxwell couldn't hide his obsession with that woman whilst del Duca was more decent in his outpourings, but after a short time they couldn't hide the fact they were competing for her attention and who would dance with her first.

I did everything that was in my power and knowledge to attract Maxwell's attention; sometimes we would dance together, I would pull him by the arms on the dance floor and I would whisper sweetness into his ears, or I would passionately groan, to no avail: his eyes followed only her body, they resembled a faithful dog's eyes, or they were green with passionate jealousy. Especially, when Tattee danced with Bartolomeo, Maxwell's steps were clumsy, his palms sweaty and voice croaky. He couldn't say much, he kept his lips sealed, teeth clenched.

Was she worthy of their attention? No way! Men, they are blind! What did they see in her, I would never be able to answer.

The more I tried to put her off, to snatch the men, to spread gossip, the less effect I had on her. She appeared as if she never noticed me, or envied my most sophisticated dance moves; I was dancing as if I was floating on the floor; she would need another hundred years to have my softness, ease and skill. I couldn't understand that unreal ease she had when it came to men: she wasn't trying to get attention, she looked away, she checked her phone, she played with her hair looking at the table … but she never looked at any man to give him the indication to take her onto the dance floor. The less she cared, the longer the queue was. I once heard Bart comment, *"To get to you one has to queue up, just like queueing up in the seventies to get a ticket for a Rolling Stones concert. A five-mile-long queue."*

She laughed a fake laugh. I laughed louder when I danced with any of the other men. I laughed so that every woman could hear me. And every man!

I said before, I had to sign up dating sites to get new men, new lovers, for newcomers to the Tango were few, old pals were not interested any longer, even those that were my most fateful friends gravitated to the unexplainable pull of the fake charm of Tattee.

I wouldn't let her sit at my table, I never said a word to her, never bid her *'good-bye'* when she was leaving and hugging everyone, I would rather leave for the bathroom to comb my hair. If she were joining the group of men I was talking to, I would leave, I wanted to show her that she never interested me; I wanted her to know that she could have what I wasn't desiring.

At the Milonga everyone wanted to dance with her, not a single man could see through her, how fake and common she was. I thought her to be a Russian peasant who came here in search of a better life, in search of a rich man. What did Maxwell Darby, the Senator's son, find in her, or Bartolomeo de Duca? What did they talk about with such a common woman?

I wished I knew where she lived, I swear, I could have easily poisoned her dog if she had one!

The last time I saw her was in March.

I think she finally understood how little I liked her and how little she was welcomed to this community.

She passed me by and I pushed her. Yes, I did. I pushed her with my shoulder as she passed me by, and she lost her balance. She hit the corner of the table with her hip, she grabbed the chair and managed to stay on her feet, then she sat and lifted up her foot. I think she twisted her ankle. I never said anything, I picked up a short and stumpy man, hugged him warmly and whispered in his ear, *"Show me what you can do."*

I saw Margot approach her at alarming speed; she knelt next to her, examining her foot as if something serious had happened. She was seeking attention, nothing else, I was dancing and laughing, my laughter was louder when I noticed Maxwell sat next to her squeezing her hand.

Margot took her out into the fresh air; after a while she came back alone and she gave me a look that I'll never forget. Little fainthearted Margot, she thought only about money, nothing else but money.

That was the last time that I saw her, so-called Tattee, the so-called opera singer. When she disappeared, the two best friends disappeared too: I have never seen Maxwell again, nor have I seen Bart since the mysterious departure of the *famous Russian.*

I never asked about her, why would I? But I heard a rumour that she went back to Madrid. Why Madrid, that's what I couldn't figure out, as far as my knowledge goes Madrid isn't in Russia.

Strange.

Very strange!

I am who I am. Happy to be myself again: Queen of the dance floor, the famous *tanguera*, the prettiest, the wittiest, the most extravagant and the most desirable!

That's the end of my story, and I want to emphasise: the story is absolutely true; I haven't made up any detail of it; I haven't added or deducted any event or any person in it.

Tattee

My name is Tatyana Yuryevna Torasovaya, but I like when people simply call me Tatyana, even better—Tattee. I was born in Moscow into a very well-known family. They called us *'aristocracy'*, I disliked that word, that description or title. It caused distance between me and other people. I loved my paternal grandmother, the *Duchess,* as everyone called her, and how silly, for a long time I was convinced that it was my grandmother's first name.

I can't even bring myself to talk about my mother's death many years ago. She passed away young, beautiful and full of melancholy in her heart and her movements. She was like music: pleasant, present, decent and heart-filling but elusive, almost etheric, with a touch of unexplained melancholy. My heart was broken, my tears couldn't stop flowing, my purpose was lost and only music sustained me as though through music I could get in contact with her soul: soothe it, and soothing hers I would find a refuge of my own. Her name was Ekaterina Yuryevna Torasovaya. Ekaterina. My father called her Kitty; my grandmother, the *Duchess*, called her Katie. I simply called her *Mummy*, that was the sweetest name I could come up with, the only name I had ever pronounced with love and adoration. That enormous loss carved a big bottomless hole in my soul, and her own melancholy nestled in my chest and stayed there permanently. That gift from my mother's soul wasn't a burden to me, on the contrary, I indulged myself in such feelings treating them as though they were rare and privileged guests. Welcomed guests who came to stay for good. I accepted and embraced these gifts, for they were the vehicles through which I communicated with my mother. I could get all sorts of 'knowledge' just by asking questions and waiting for the answer. I could ask about anything and in the right time I would get the right answer. I could look someone in the eye and read their past and their future, but I wasn't aware of that gift for a long time. I never saw anything special in it—it was just another way of communicating with all sorts of information that was all around us. I don't even know if that was a *'gift'*, or was it *'picked up'* as I was growing up. My grandmother, the *Duchess*, was a close friend of Matryona Rasputin, Grigori Rasputin's eldest daughter, who later changed her name to Maria to fit easier into the circles of high society. My grandmother, actually, was a friend of Nikolai Soloviev, the treasurer of the Holy Synod, whose son, Boris, married Matryona Maria Rasputin. That's how my grandmother met Maria, through Boris. What was interesting and intriguing about Boris himself was that he quickly emerged as Rasputin's successor after his murder. Boris was a graduate of the school of mysticism, he studied Madame Blavatsky's Theosophy and hypnotism. All together they would attend meetings and séances at which Rasputin's followers attempted to communicate with the deceased through prayers and trance.

It was rumoured (the story everybody whispered throughout my childhood) that the *Duchess*, my grandmother, had exceptional powers, magnetism and the gift of seeing the undisclosed and the hidden. She never talked about it; no one ever dared to ask her about those gifts. But I know, she knew about events that were going to happen. She read people like one reads a naïve child, but she did it all with elegance, poise; she did it without any effort, in passing, without raising an eyebrow or her voice, or lowering it.

When my mother got ill, the *Duchess* prepared the household for a tremendous change. A year passed before anybody knew Mother was ill. She took me to the Netherlands to visit Mother's sister who was married to Baron Van Heerdt and lived in a beautiful country estate where I could ride horses all day long. One day, whilst riding on the back of a black horse, a big bird landed next to me. It just stayed there even when the horse jumped. The bird told me to go home, and I came home crying. Grandmother looked me in the eyes and said it was time to go back home. On our return, we learned Mother was ill. Never before that day, never after it had I seen such sadness in my father's blue eyes.

After Mother passed, Grandmother made all the decisions, even those for which my father believed were his. Just like me, he knew who his mother was, what powers she possessed; he surrendered his will, believing in her better judgement.

Before the Revolution our family was rich with properties, houses and money; after the Revolution everything was taken, but my grandmother would say, *"They can take our money and possessions, but they can't take the nobility out of our souls."* She insisted on classical art, literature and education; father and his three brothers were highly educated, and in the new circumstances which left them without their vast wealth and properties, the-ex *Duchess*, adopted only one value: the best education and manners. In our household, we still lived by her rules and code of conduct. I was, predominantly, home-schooled; I had teachers coming to our house five times per week, Grandmother taught me how to play the piano, she taught me French, Italian, and Igor Petroniev started teaching me Latin, Greek and Spanish at the age of seven. His brother Vanya was the first to suggest to my grandmother that I should start with singing lessons as soon as possible; without a doubt he knew, by only the speaking voice, if a child would have *'the voice'*.

***

When I became the so-called *famous Opera singer*, I didn't know how to deal with my inborn timidity. On stage, I was someone else; when the lights went on, I would blush and try to hide, tried to run away, far away from the cameras and curiosity. But the inborn poise and my grandmother's way of teaching me how to conduct myself in high society, in any society for that matter, helped me to hide my timidity, or to keep it in check.

There were a few men that I liked, but never really loved anyone. The thing is: I could read them so easily, I became bored, sometimes offended, knowing how shallow their intentions were, sometimes I was just so self-sufficient that I would forget about any man. I loved playing the piano and going to my rehearsals, I loved reading, taking Grandmother to the theatre or to the opera when I wasn't performing or when I was in town.

Upon my arrival in Madrid, I met a very unusual man. He claimed he had healed my dog, I never believed such a story, but … I simply remembered him. Yes, I remembered him!

I know he said so many wrong things, he did many things I would never agree with, but he was someone else once upon a time; he used to be my beloved friend, someone who saved my life many, many years ago. Yes, Jorge Rubio Rivera, used to be Simon de Cubiry, my beloved Simon de Cubiry who almost lost his leg, his life to save my own. When I peered into his eyes, when the story unfolded, I asked him:

"Do you remember Simon de Cubiry?"

He quickly rushed into falsehood:

"Certainly, I do. He sends his regards."

I had chosen, back then, to interpret it in this way: Jorge Rubio Rivera said, *'Simon de Cubiry sends his regards'* because he, on the deepest level, got in contact with traces of Simon de Cubiry, he was aware how much de Cubiry was fond of me.

Even though Jorge Rubio Rivera was a conman, there were still many habits and noble remains of Simon de Cubiry that only I could determine and understand why he was such a controversial person.

Sometimes, he used to tell me the tales which a simple man like Jorge Rubio Rivera wouldn't know living only one life, only a life of a man from a small village in the relative vicinity of Buenos Aires. When we would listen to some pieces of classical music, his fingers played the right keys. When I played to him, he would close his eyes and listen attentively, surrendered completely to the music, his lips moving as if he was singing along … I was waiting the moment when Simon de Cubiry would take over and start singing in his deep baritone … but, it never happened, Jorge Rubio Rivera just kept his eyes closed even when I finished, then, upon opening them moist from utter enjoyment, he would say:

"I would give my life for you if you ever needed it. Such an extraordinary talent."

Once, he almost did it. He was ready to do it again. I could not determine easily what he wanted from me: my presence, my wealth, my status, did he fancy me, or, was all that he wanted buried deep inside his rough exterior, was it just the memory of the two of us: so close—inseparable, with his heart ready to die for me?

I decided not to chase the answer, for the answer wouldn't change anything anyway. When he was jailed, I told him to learn his lesson and to remember well what that lesson taught him.

I told him I'd go to New York City for the period of his imprisonment as my work required me to be there. I knew that my beloved maid Olga and her cousin, my devoted chauffeur Oleg, were the people who unmasked him and helped him face justice. I couldn't blame poor Olga, she did it out of her uttermost concern and love; she couldn't see behind the veil; whatever she did for me only confirmed her kind and biased heart. One thing I know: she never lied, she never stole, she never gossiped, but in her attempt to *'protect me'* she made several not-so-innocent mistakes. She wrote a letter to my grandmother. After I talked to Grandmother, together with my agent, I decided to take up the offer and go to New York City for *'an indefinite period'*; the *Duchess* knew when I would be back, for the book of Future was never closed to her. We understood each other to the core, we were the mirror of each other, the shadow of each other's thought and the beam that could penetrate into the most secluded place. She knew what was in my heart.

I omitted one important piece of the puzzle in the tapestry of this tale. Though, I believe by now, this is so obvious. Let me put it into plain words. My grandmother, the *Duchess,* wasn't only my dearest relative and confidant, she was my teacher, the person who initiated me into the art of communicating with different worlds, or frequencies, if that is easily accepted as a term. She started training and preparing me without me even being aware that we were passing information and knowledge that wasn't available to *'common souls'*. Every person I had a previous connection to I could recognise easily. Was it a burden? Hard to say!

The first lesson that was engraved into my young mind was that I am infinite and can achieve anything I set my mind to. She convinced me early in my life that I was immortal, unlimited, an inexhaustible source of energy that could achieve any task, regardless of its grandiosity or complexity. I believed her, for she was such a shining example of unfathomable and strange success.

The other lesson was to be exceptionally kind and utterly good willed, having always in mind a higher plan, to please the One who gave us our gifts.

And one more important lesson was: not to interfere. I could recognise people, even events, I could see outcomes, the *'mistakes'* my friends would do, but I was told *'to watch, observe and to guide only when possible'*.

Men liked me more than I wanted to be liked. I never liked too much attention, though by destiny I was chosen for the work I was doing—being on stage, on front pages, in the news, practically in every country in the world. I was given the gift of physical attractiveness and an exquisite taste and style. I read in men's eyes what they thought of me. There were only a few of men I couldn't read and they were a real challenge for me.

Women? They often—disliked me. Even prior to meeting me in person, many of them had already decided to dislike me. What I read in their eyes, I won't say now, for my way of telling stories keeps me from being too judgemental. Margot, when I met her, said to me, *'Don't worry about those few that show coldness and disdain towards you. They are plainly envious.'* I said to Margot, *'Oh, don't say that, Margot! They are not.'*

I knew the art of how to turn *'enemies'* into friends. Only with my kindness and touching, almost healing words, for I knew what kind of pain some people harboured in their hearts. I went right there with an open heart and warm feelings. This particular way of dealing with people and their emotions was where the *Duchess's* mastery lay. She could penetrate into almost everyone's soul and communicate directly with it in some sort of a divine, inarticulate language. The *Duchess* had many admirers, people who genuinely loved her, but she had a few enemies too.

To be in contact with my creativity, with my source, with my soul, I needed solitude. Only in solitude was I myself: a creator, a witness, a vessel and a quiet celebrant of love.

***

When I joined a Tango school in Manhattan, I didn't expect to find so much drama there. But that was exactly what I encountered, and it made me to be both—a curious, passive observer and a keen participant, often a provocative teaser to the right measure. Just to see how far the game of imagination could lead. Always to the measure, to the limit that I had drawn.

I met all sorts of characters and all of them not worthy of a story. I liked to concentrate on the most extravagant, the extreme ones, those who tried so hard to impress me with all sorts of extravagant deeds, or those who tried even harder to ignore me completely, to send a blatant message: *No, you are not noticeable, you are not attractive, you are not exceptional in any way, just an indistinguishable, plain woman that I would never pay attention to.*

That was Oscar's attitude. When I met him, I said *'Hello'* the way I say it to everybody. His eyes, half-mast, looked at me as if he was observing a rare insect, his lips went downwards, he lifted his chin high, looked once again at me, turned around on his heels, took a woman by her upper arm and walked her onto the dance floor. Since then, every time he walked in with his head high, his hair slicked back, combed across his head, he would glance at me, without saying a word, keen to show me that he never noticed me. He kept that attitude for the entire evening. Never looked my way, never said a word, never asked for a dance … I was familiar with that kind of man—in his grandiosity he was petrified to show his vulnerability. If he ever caught my eye I sent a big, friendly smile towards him. That gesture of mine made him uptight, made him scornful, almost offended, *'Oh, how dare you, you, Russian woman, how dare you smile at me!'*

One day, a lonely, sad-looking man walked in. He looked confused and lost, like someone who drank alone, mourning a loss that had never really occurred. He looked like a learned man, someone who had a good upbringing, bearing himself with dignity even though he appeared to the trained eye a bit tipsy.

I danced with him that evening, he had pleasant energy, he said his name was Maxwell. We established a good rapport easily, I hoped we could make good friends, but among the hope I had feared that he would take me *'seriously'*, that he would mix my friendly, warm attitude for something else. But I didn't know any other attitude, and long ago, I learnt that in making a friendship with a man, a heart could be broken. I didn't have any deeper connection to Maxwell, anything from our past, but he had been a gentle soul, wounded because of the softness he had; I liked his energy and subtle sense of humour. He really made me laugh without even trying. Each and every word of his was well chosen and intonated.

I knew him for several months and couldn't help but notice a monumental improvement in his attitude and his physical appearance. He looked healthier, as if he stopped drinking alone, as if he stopped drinking altogether. The choice of his shirts and ties, the barely noticeable print on his vests, the fit of his suits and the quality of his shoes told a story of someone who was well informed about the latest trends and who had an impeccable sense of dressing. He would adorn his sentences with quotes from Shakespeare to Churchill, Roosevelt or Dostoyevsky … or anyone else important at that particular moment. Witty! That's what Maxwell was. His manners were the manners of a nobleman. He never talked about himself, he cared to entertain me whilst we danced and now and then to pay a discrete compliment. His best achievement was, *'Tattee, I am in heaven right now!'* and to that line we both would burst into laughter.

One evening, whilst we were standing in a circle with some other friends, who else but Maxwell, asked:

"Tattee, you are indeed the Tatyana Yuryevna Torasovaya?"

And that was how everyone learned who I was. I disliked when people changed their attitude upon getting to know my profession: some would warm up and become too friendly too quickly, usually those who were distant and superior, and some would withdraw a few steps further with a few less words.

***

Then, one evening, Maxwell brought a friend along. A quiet introverted man. He had a pair of poignant, piercing eyes, and only because of his eyes my mind started quickly changing the slides, something my mind would do upon meeting someone of *'significant'* meaning.

It turned out that the introverted man with piercing eyes was no one else but Bartolomeo de Duca. When I asked about de Duca family, he changed the subject. I read his books, he was a good stylist, his mockery of everything and everyone, including himself, extended to the beyond the written word itself. The randomness of details left hanging and my personal feeling that his literature lacked connection to his soul, made me comment, to which he replied:

"Yes, literature is an act of profound criticism, particularly the best literature, but the finest criticism is literature in the highest form. Thank you for your wise but not useful observations."

"Are you vain?"

"Are you vain, Ms Tatyana Yuryevna?"

"Tattee. Call me Tattee."

The first time I danced with Bart, when I leaned my chest against his, I saw the picture: we had danced before. I knew who he was. I asked him if he remembered when we danced together, he smiled, and just said, *'The Beauty and the Beast.'* Did he mean he wanted to emphasise that he remembered my subtle beauty back then and his clumsy appearance? But he was exactly the same, just a bit smaller, a bit quieter, pensive and withdrawn. We would dance and the film would run in front of my closed eyes; when I opened them, I'd see us embraced just like many years ago, just in a slightly different setting … I knew who he was. He knew it as well, but his mind wouldn't allow him to remember. He believed in logic even though he had a great imagination, he believed only in logic.

I never said more than that, I wasn't allowed; it was up to him to remember and to act upon it.

I met him one evening, confused, worried and somehow lost. I was walking with a friend, he approached us, grabbed my hand, and when I asked where he was going in such a confused state, he left quickly, saying, *"He was the devil, I don't know how I can fit him into the story."* He left quickly calling my friend, *'Rasputin'*; we looked at his back getting lost in the mist of the evening and my friend commented, *"What did you do to this poor lost soul?"*

I had the feeling that he started to collect glimpses of our past, he roamed the streets in order to meet me in the twilight; he wrote a short story set in Venice in 1899, and he called the female protagonist Tiziana, *Contessa Tiziana*. He called it all *'fiction'*, unwilling to embrace the story unfolding in front of his eyes.

But there was another battle his soul was involved in: he struggled to maintain his close friendship with Maxwell Darby, his best friend of the last forty years. Maybe, the only sincere friend the introverted writer had ever had.

By that time, Oscar had exhausted all of his extravagant but unnecessary outbursts of weak character and ego, and danced with me often, always ready to *'blame'* me for my imperfections as a dancer, or he let himself to go even further—to point out the flaws of my character. He said:

"I see in your eyes that you've brought hell to many men."

"Really? And how are you so sure of that? Where exactly do you read that?"

"You have a beautiful pair of eyes, but they are evil."

"So, I have evil eyes and I bring misery to men, is that what you want to say?"

"I am glad you are not my type. It would be a curse to fall in love with a woman like you."

"Then you are lucky, protected by a lucky star."

"God sends women like you not to be a blessing but a curse to men."

I couldn't do anything but sadly witness a widening rift between the two best friends. It was like an abyss made by tearing dry land in two parts, leaving each of them to stand on the edge of the opposite side staring into the abyss. I wasn't the abyss. No, I wasn't! That was their story that had to be written by their own will; I was just a spark of a tiny light brought into their lives to point out their weaknesses in order to overcome them.

But when human emotions are too strong and run uncontrolled, when the ego is too weak and vulnerable, no amount of light can bring enlightenment.

When I said, *'I was just a spark of a tiny light brought into their lives to point out their weaknesses in order to overcome them'*, I am not sure right now if that was my sole reason why I appeared in their lives at that time. It could have been that I had to end up there myself. I didn't know that back then, nor do I know it right now, as plenty of what had always been revealed bares its opposite: lots had been undisclosed in order for me to discover it myself. I could participate in my own story the best way I could, to finish unfinished stories in the best possible way. When it comes to others, I could see things much clearer than when I'd reflect upon my own situation. I couldn't see, but I had to act!

My choice was to run back to Madrid. To rescue Jorge Rubio Rivera from himself. I still felt it in my bones that I owed him something. On my way back from New York to Madrid, on that flight, I understood—I never owed him anything. Particularly not now. I had paid my debt to Jorge.

I knew yet another thing: I couldn't go back to New York to talk to Bartolomeo. He had enough information, enough hints, dreams and stories he had written to understand it all. I was explicitly told not to interfere, and I never would, my Grandmother taught me all the lessons.

When I came to Madrid, I was hesitant to let him know I was back. Let him read it in the morning papers.

I switched off my mobile, went to bed and said to Olga:

"Tomorrow don't answer any calls, don't open the door regardless of who's there."

Dear Tatyana, a letter

Dear Tatyana,

It has been a month since you left abruptly. You left New York without warning, without saying 'goodbye' to Maxwell or to me. I heard your lover was released from prison. It could have been plain gossip. This Tango scene is an unreal arena: gossip, strong, poorly handled emotions and lots of unfounded assumptions. A clash of egos. And men being bigger gossips, bigger cry-babies and drama kings. Tatyana, Tatyana ... you just disappeared and left them hanging onto their unfinished, unfulfilled dreams ...

What have you done, Tatyana?

Yes, I am teasing you a little bit, but I can sincerely say that since you left there isn't that unique energy that only you could project. To many of us it simply looks as if a light has been switched off; the star got tired of her role and retreated.

You might wish to ask about Maxwell, am I right? He went to Montana and refused to see me, as he worded it—'ever again'. He broke my heart, Tatyana. What broke my heart was the fact that he cared more about you than our long-lasting friendship. We were friends for over four decades; he was my only sincere friend. How can I replace Maxwell? Or, how shall he ever replace me? Tatyana, Tatyana ... you, and your ever-present smile. Mysterious? Malicious? How could I ever know? Who are you? The answer to this question is going to stay a mystery as you showed many faces to me, to us. Yet, there was one I was aware of, but was never able to grasp who was the exact personality you were trying to present. In my opinion, you should have been an actress, though being an opera singer is not far from that perfect guess of mine. I had the impres-

sion that every time you walked into the Studio you would adopt your 'Tango persona', that famous 'Tattee Girl' who was darling to all of us. Then, I found a deep mystic under your doll-like façade, someone who studied metaphysics or the occult. In your well-hidden need to be admired by each and every man who crossed your path, I saw a woman, somehow afraid of love, afraid of deep feelings, or afraid of losing control. But there was more to it, Tatyana. That melancholy which was, also, buried under your smile, told me you longed for times that were gone forever, it might have been that you longed for a person who had gone forever, hence you, in your vivid imagination, created parallel lives, created past lives where you found the place for the protagonists you wanted to keep around you. Yet, you didn't have the need to keep anyone, I was aware of it, I saw it in your eyes, I heard it in your voice, for whilst you were in New York, I went to the Met every time you were performing. I would close my eyes and listen to your voice. It was given to be admired by the masses, to melt the hearts of the masses, but the gift of the 'golden voice' placed you into some sort of solitary confinement where you couldn't reach other human beings when the stage lights went off. You couldn't relate to anyone, you just smiled politely; you gave compliments generously, you made vague promises and went home alone. And what did you do at home? You practised. You sang, you wanted to reach the unreachable in each and every performance. In every instance of your life but love, I'd say. Forgive me for my frankness, you read me like an open book, yet your book was tightly closed for my curious mind. I don't have such penetrating eyes and developed intuition, but I am a well-read man who has lived many lives in this existence, the only life I believe was ever given to me. I believe we were given only one life and we don't repeat ourselves, we don't meet again, we don't pay debts, and don't redeem our souls. Even though, I might ask you—'How will you redeem your soul for what you have done to Maxwell?' I found him crying one day, he would never admit to anyone that he was crying just because of a woman, but he was crying bitterly as you danced with me that night and wouldn't look his way. Yes, he was fifty-five years old, but you have to know that the older we get, the mellower some of us become, that was just what happened to Maxwell when he met you, he thought he met his other half—finally.

And there was I. A curious, indifferent observer! Or, was I? Or, wasn't it sufficient to you, a man who was just a curious observer?

You came that evening all in white, his eyes were moist of his dreams, I saw that look in his eyes, only once: on the day when he met Olivia Vanderbilt, his first wife, a woman that was my friend. I walked Olivia by her hand straight into his life. He loved Olivia, but with you—he was smitten. He admired you like a child who has an authoritative, beautiful, kind, loving and generous mother. He admired you! But you just kept on smiling at everyone; you danced with everyone, showing the same amount of kindness and interest as if we were all one and the same person. That was exactly what was hurtful, for Maxwell wanted to be special to you. I think we all wanted to be special to you; when I only remember Oscar, how much effort he put into ignoring you, never asking to dance with you, never calling you by your name ... and all of a sudden, he turned into a man who would wait the entire evening just to have the last dance with you.

Then, it was my turn to be charmed. You told me you were remembering me, suggesting we met in some other time, in some other place, in another life. I almost bought your stories, I wandered the streets of New York dreaming of meeting you, dressed as Contessa, with your piercing-blue eyes ... Tatyana, Tatyana ... I almost wrote more than twenty pages which I dedicated to a story of Tatyana. I almost wrote a novel, a love story about ... that was how close I was to being manipulated by your sweet voice, by your stories of eternity, of other lives, of mysticism and your family connection with royals and the evil spirit of Rasputin.

I did my research and the people you talked about never existed, your stories carefully planned that you could attract those little mad flies into the web of your deceit. Yet, everybody liked you, Tattee. We all liked you; we all waited for a dance with you; and dreamed of driving you back home after midnight. You never took anyone home, where did you go? Alone again, you wrote letters to a man who was imprisoned for forgery. I heard he was a conman. I even found an article about his case, your name was withdrawn from the story. Because of one article, I knew it was you, as it said, 'his companion, well-known opera singer', but the name wasn't mentioned. I never found anything online, not a word about you or him, except what was related to your career and education. Not a single sentence about your personal life.

In your presence, I felt as if I had to re-learn something about myself, as if I had to make myself somehow better in order to spend half an hour with you. You knew the magic of words, they were arranged in a way that any writer could envy you: selected carefully, to flatter subtly, to give hope, to add excitement to the present and sweetness to the possibility of tomorrow.

Your magnetism was so strong and the web you weaved was made of such resilient strings that I couldn't escape in that moment; I was waiting to see you on the particular evening just to be in your vicinity and be intoxicated by your words and their melody.

You started messing with my head to the extent that I started dreaming the most unusual dreams. Dreams about you. Dreams about us. All of your subtle suggestions you'd serve whilst dancing I carried into my restless nights. I heard unusual voices, strange accents and languages, I saw fragments of some stories that were written a long time ago ... I heard choirs singing, your voice above my bedhead, I almost felt your arms hugging me. I would get up, barely dressed, I'd leave my apartment and walk the streets of Manhattan, hoping to find 'something significant', something that would point towards you, an omen, a merciful sign of my destiny unfolding.

All I would find was deep seated sadness and contempt in Maxwell's eyes.

He was a good man, I wasn't. He had a kind heart, I was an orphan. I never knew which heartless bitch gave birth to me and left me on the doorstep of the orphanage. I was a boat without an anchor, an arrow shot from a broken bow. He taught me kindness and some manners. I hid behind the façade of a learned quiet man. I was, and I am, a learned quiet man, but I would now be someone else if there wasn't so much shared history with my best friend and me. Maxwell Darby and me.

I would do anything for Maxwell. The only thing I should have done for him was to stay out of his way when he introduced us. I know, I know, Tatyana, you would never have ended up with Maxwell Darby, but had he swallowed that bitter pill, I would have been there for him: drinking together, taking him to the theatre, walking the streets in the late evenings, sitting in bars till the early hours. That should have been my role in this story. But, no! I got involved in a way that was fatal to both of us: Maxwell and me. We lost each other. I never counted on you anyway. Did he? Did he ever count on you, Tatyana? We will never know the answer to that question, but in my heart, I know that his was broken like a ball made of thin glass.

I have written a story about you and your conman, that was my only revenge: 'The Twain Shall Never Meet'. Now you judge when you read it, is this story made up, or was I a witness to something that happened on some different level? Was I a psychic when I was writing it, someone who penetrated the mysteries of people's destinies, present and past? You judge my story and feel free to correct it. Feel free to give me feedback letting me know which parts of the story were 'absolutely correct' and where I took creative liberty to adorn the story with details which you couldn't recall. Are there such details at all, my dear, Tatyana Yuryevna?

You said, 'Every aristocratic family in Imperial Russia had one Rasputin', but the little I know about my mother I will share with you now: She was a Gypsy. Yes. A Gypsy. She came from Russia, hidden in a container full of grain. I found a man, a high-ranking police officer whose palm I greased well, to do the research. He loved my novels, we met at my book launch and conversation sparked. A highly intelligent man. We kept on seeing each other occasionally, for he was 'pleased to keep the acquaintance of a gifted writer'. In those feeble details about my birth mother's background I learnt she was a Gypsy and a 'very gifted fortune teller.'

You see, Tatyana, in my family there was a 'clairvoyant', a psychic. She left me, for she knew it would be better for me to make my own struggle through the maze of life and become whatever I have become without her influence.

She was a weak person, a weak psychic. A woman should never leave her child. There is no clairvoyance in it, Tatyana. Only selfishness.

Were you selfish when you left without a word? Without saying goodbye to Maxwell Darby, who was patiently waiting for Tuesday to take you on to that dance floor and hold you in his arms? You knew he liked you a lot. You looked into his eyes and smiled. That sweet, innocent smile. The warmth in your eyes when greeting him. Him and all the others.

I knew that would be the end of Maxwell Darby if you decided to go. I only can't forgive myself that I was charmed and sucked into the plot.

Yes, plot, Tatyana!

Here it is—my story to you, Tatyana; read it and laugh!

Part Two

Synchronicities

Caselli's Youngest Daughter

On that fine winter day, I went to Caselli's boutique with a well-tailored plan. At Caselli's they sold the best quality furs and the finest leather goods. My, my, how it smelled inside when I entered! It smelled of the youngest Caselli daughter, I could never remember her name, but when she noticed me she approached in a fast pace:

"It is you, Mr De Sanctis, please, do come in..." spreading her little white arms with a gesture as if she were laying something out in front of my feet. I liked that gesture; it was friendly and somehow meek. And in the exact same manner, she commenced her talk—friendly and meekly:

"Oh, we are so honoured by your visit. What could this fine house do for Mr De Sanctis? We will try our best to give you the best ..." she spoke, extending her hands with delicate and manicured fingers towards me.

I thought *'that's good'*, yes, that was the welcome I really liked.

She took a lock of her fine dark hair between two fingers and started to play with it, twisting it slowly. She smiled at me and there was a mischievous sparkle in her eyes. I didn't know how old she was, but I assumed she couldn't be older than twenty-two. Oh, such a fine age! She was a good ten years younger than Annamaria, my ex-fiancé, with whom I just broke off my engagement a week ago. She was even younger than Bea, the woman everyone blamed for ending my engagement. We were never an exclusive couple; I have always denied a relationship with Bea, all those years. No one's business!

Even though she wore shockingly high heels, Mrs Caselli walked up briskly:

"What can we do for Mr De Sanctis?"

Whilst asking me the question, she fixed her eyes into her daughter's and they talked in some sort of unspoken sign language that only the two of them understood. The girl said:

"I have already taken care of Mr De Sanctis, Mamma."

Mamma said only:

"You are in good hands, Mr De Sanctis."

Well, at once I understood her ambiguity. She always used to subtly give ambiguous comments, since the first time I came in, which was more than fifteen years ago. I was an old and loyal customer.

Mamma had a very fine waistline and breasts strapped in a tight bra pushed up high, her cheekbones were high too, and her opinion of herself and her three girls was also very high. There were three of them; all three so different they didn't look like sisters at all. I always fancied the youngest one, way back when I used to come in with Annamaria. When Annamaria was buying fur, it lasted for days and weeks. I had to accompany her, to give her my opinion in which fur she looked better, which one was of better quality. Annamaria wasn't a determined woman. Her insecurity was verbalised in such sentences: *"I can't make up my mind"* or *"What do you think, sweetheart?"* What do I think! Make up your mind; you are the one who is going to wear it!

Stealthily, I would observe the youngest. I kept a record of her changing whilst she was growing up and turning into a young graceful lady. Every time I visited, she gazed at me with those big eyes full of dancing sparkles, smiling thievishly showing her teeth and batting her eyelashes as if she were performing in some fine theatre, deliberately emphasising certain parts of her sentence, or giving them special meaning.

And there she was: standing in front of me, again, smiling thievishly, showing her white teeth, the sparkles in her eyes dancing, and her eyelashes dancing in similar rhythm.

She should have heard already that I'd broken up with Annamaria as that was the latest hot topic in town.

I didn't walk in with the intention of buying any of her fine articles. I just came to scout around, not knowing for what exactly, just a random visit, to check out the climate at Caselli's, or to see how the youngest Caselli daughter would treat me now that I was free again.

But I had to get my act together, I started checking out some leather bags as she was taking them out and placing them on the high table on the left side of the leather sofa. She was laying them on the high table one after another, bags of different shapes and sizes, different colours and qualities, different smells and textures grazing under fingers, and whilst she was putting them down, she was looking in my eyes without blinking.

All the time I kept my back straight, chin up, like a real aristocrat does, but in a split second a little smile twitched the corner of my lip and I said casually:

"Poor thing, I didn't want to make you work hard."

"Oh, don't pity me, you didn't make me work hard! No, no, you didn't, it is my pleasure."

"What is your pleasure?"

"Well..."

"Well?"

"To be at the disposal of my customers."

Customers? She takes me for a customer! For her I am just a customer she serves! Which means, she plays with the lock of her hair for every customer who enters; she smiles and bats her eyelashes ... out of sheer enjoyment! Oh, no, I didn't like that! But she hurried to explain:

"What I wanted to say ... is ... I like to be at the disposal of ... a very special customer."

That was what I liked to hear. She kept on looking straight into my eyes grabbing at that mischievous dark lock of her hair, which rebelliously curved into the opposite direction because of the habit of twirling it around her fingers.

"A very special customer?" said I, seemingly stricter. But she wasn't the type to get confused easily:

"Aren't you our very special customer, sir? You have that exquisite taste, you often spend generously, and beautiful Annamaria is our very special customer, too."

Why? Why was she now mentioning Annamaria and pushing her into our story? Was this some sort of gimmick? Did she want to know if we are still in a relationship as she might have heard just the opposite? Hmm, she appeared very suspicious, I never showed my suspicion, but in a steady voice I said:

"Well, we can say that ... That we are your very special customers ... but isn't the boutique itself a very special place as well?"

Upon my saying that, she started to laugh—childishly and naturally and through her laughter she spat out:

"Yes ... you are right ... ha-ha-ha ... everything is, actually, so special ... ha-ha-ha ... so special ... ha-ha-ha ... so special ..."

I couldn't tell why she was laughing. She laughed as if she were empty-headed, that's how she laughed. But she had infected me with her childish laughter; she almost choked laughing. I came closer attempting to hold her, for she could have fallen down from the intensity of her laughter. I held her tiny waist, I felt the blood coursing through her young body; she smelt of her boutique, of fine leather, of fur, like a young tiger-cub, so in a slightly quieter voice, I said:

"Stop laughing ... If you don't stop, I'll kiss you."

At once she stopped and looked straight into my eyes. She placed her hand over her open mouth. She wiped the tears off from the corners of her eyes, and after only a short silence she burst into a side-splitting laughter again. I didn't know why she was laughing again, but as if I were bitten by some mad mosquito who jumped from her onto me, I started to laughing loudly myself. We laughed and held hands, and I felt like a child again whilst holding hands with a woman that still resembled a child. Once again, her mother cheerfully came to us with a bright expression on her face:

"Your laughter is so contagious. It is selfish if you don't tell me why you are laughing so heartily."

But we kept on laughing, and laughing, and laughing, it seemed we would never stop laughing, and affected by our laughter, Mrs Caselli burst into laughter herself, as if she also bit into that crazy mushroom wc partook of earlier and swallowed a tiny piece.

So crazily and heartily we laughed for good several minutes, we simply couldn't stop that mad train, which carried us, and every attempt to stop it caused a new attack of laughter.

Then the laughter slowly ceased; whilst looking at each other, we let out a sporadic *'ha'*, lifting our shoulders upwards.

When all three of us calmed down, the first to talk was Mrs Caselli. Still with a wide smile on her face, she asked:

"What was the reason behind your laughter?"

"I don't know. Ask your daughter. She started it first, I was caught in it, like in some sort of web ... then you were caught too."

The youngest Caselli's daughter said, *'It doesn't matter'* why she laughed and offered to bring some coffee for the three of us. As her mother had to leave the boutique, she came back with two cups, which we placed onto the marble table and sat on the expensive sofa, upholstered with soft fur of a spotted animal. She crossed her long legs. She had beautifully shaped legs, the reason why she wore such a short dress; that was the reason too why she kept on crossing and uncrossing them all the time whilst sipping coffee in my company.

I told her I ran out of time; I couldn't search for a bag any longer, but I mentioned that I might pass by tomorrow or some other day this week. She said she would be very pleased to see me again.

Of course, she would be pleased to see me again! How could she not be! Now that I wasn't with Annamaria anymore, I must have been the most desirable bachelor in town.

Bea.

Why would I talk about Bea? She was happy being anonymous. I know that. No, she never told me, but if a woman always shrugs her shoulders, it is a clear sign of wishing remain anonymous.

Simona.

Who would ever connect us? She was an odd duck anyway!

But this fine bird, the youngest Caselli daughter, was on my menu now.

Synchronicity

I sat in a train on platform eighteen, the train to Milan.

As soon as I had comfortably reclined in the chair, all the memories rushed in through the open window. Every time I travelled to Milan I asked myself, *'Does this train take me to De Sanctis?'*, as I used to call him. Even though I was well aware it didn't take me back to him, I liked to daydream and secretly hoped that I might catch a glimpse of him waving at me. Who knows, maybe he would like to accompany me and wave, once again, whilst the train was leaving the station?

But I kept on daydreaming about meeting him in the train, knowing well that he never travelled by train, he was a De Sanctis—they don't travel by trains. If I ever was to see him travelling to Milan, it could only be in one of his fancy cars, with the roof rolled down waving at me casually, carelessly. That fancy car, his casual waving, his carefree smile, all of it spoke of our vast unbridged differences.

With the train's rolling wheels, memories were rolling and the wheels were unable to grind them into dust, my memories were unable to run away with the rolling wheels to leave me liberated.

There was no other train in my memory, just this one, which was rolling in my memories, whilst I was not willing to create new ones.

A sudden unbearable smell made me change carriages; the sudden urge to leave as if such a decision were a matter of life and death.

***

The carriage was full of people; there was only one empty seat next to a man who was looking out of the window. There were newspapers folded on his knees, and an open book beside him. I knew it was De Sanctis; I knew it by the way he was holding himself; I knew it, for my heart recognised him and started to race faster. Prior to that, it seemed as if my heart had stopped beating, like the heart of an old tired woman telling me with its almost non-existent rhythm and faint feelings that it didn't know me any longer. But, at that first glance, my heart had livened up, and started beating faster as if it was mine again. I knew my heart had recognised him; I sat next to De Sanctis, I recognised his bodily scent, which overpowered the smell of his lotion, and those mixed smells of his body and the lotion confirmed that it was him, and that my heart was racing because of such cognition. A tide of strange excitement rose up in my body and caused mental confusion, therefore I started fixing my hair, scratching my nose, crossing and uncrossing my legs and opening and closing the book I had just taken out of my bag. I couldn't sit motionlessly, peacefully.

I felt him guessing my identity—he sensed me.

I felt his discomfort.

C. G. Jung coined the term synchronicity referring to those remarkable moments when outer happenings reflect our inner states.

I opened the book I was holding and let my hair loose to hide my eyes from him.

In the glass window I saw his profile; he bowed slightly in an attempt to touch my features with his eyes, hidden by my hair, the hair which like a thick waterfall was hiding my restless face.

Jung's psychology is understood only when it is a lived experience.

Six years had passed since I saw him for the last time. Six silent years, and now he was sitting next to me pretending to observe the scenery whilst in the window he was watching my every move. Nothing exemplifies this experience more than the mystery of synchronicity.

What was he thinking sitting there next to me? Was he really aware of my presence? Was he going to strike up a conversation? Was he aware it was me … or was he just keen to look at an unknown young woman hidden behind a waterfall of thick hair? What if he was aware it was I—his, apparently, first and biggest love? What was he feeling if he was aware? Did he still remember me? Did my presence awaken old memories and feelings? Did he see this coincidence as meaningful interplay which was alive in our reality? The notion that there is a deeper principle operating in the world? But, De Sanctis had always believed there was only the conscious force guiding him and nothing else.

He spread out his newspaper and commenced reading it.

Still, I had the feeling he was looking at me with the corner of his eye. It seemed to me that I could read his thoughts; it seemed as if his emotional tide overflowed from his body into mine; it seemed the emotional crescendo was at its peak when he asked:

"You wouldn't mind if I opened the window, would you? Just a tiny bit."

I never lifted my eyes up pretending to read my book. I just uttered, *'I wouldn't'*. Yes, it was his voice. The voice reassured me that next to me De Sanctis was seated. I was almost confident that he knew who I was, even though my short *'I wouldn't'* didn't reveal much. It didn't reveal the softness of my tone, my excitement or my identity. But still, maybe he suspected …

I kept on reading my book; he kept on reading a newspaper. It wasn't too hot in the carriage nor was it stuffy, but he had opened the window, for he needed fresh air. My breathing was heavy just as his … yeah, maybe he suspected …

Maybe he was over-flooded by the tide of memories (I don't dare to say over-flooded by the tide of emotions!)

Incorporating the meaning of this synchronicity required something authentic from us—let's say a different attitude if not real inner change.

All of a sudden, as if he had awakened from a deep meditative state by a pin pushed into his rear, or as if some particular thought brought unease, he stood up and walked into the corridor. He opened the window and lit a cigarette; I saw the reflection of his face in the dark window. I couldn't sit still any longer, I couldn't pretend to read any more, I couldn't even breathe, I needed fresh air, to get out of this stuffy carriage and whilst I was slowly approaching, I took out a cigarette and quietly asked him to light it as I had lost my lighter.

When our eyes met, he simply said:

"Bea" and I, with a faint smile on my face, uttered his name after six long years:

"De Sanctis?"

There was nothing I could read on his face. Not a single visible emotion was written on that mask, so I showed a gentle smile hiding my real emotions behind it.

We led a tedious and unnecessary conversation. It was polite but nothing else. He asked me how I was doing and if I had completed my degree. He asked me about the weather in my home town (*'Does it still rain that often?'*), did I travel frequently to Milan, he asked me who I was going to visit and in the end, he asked a question I thought he wouldn't ask me—*'Are you married now?'* He asked me all those questions just for the sake of a conversation, not that he was genuinely interested, but just to keep on talking. He kept on asking did I still ski, did I still drive that little red car, did I still adore Pavarotti … and whilst asking questions, he looked above my head, into the distance, through the window, disinterested in my answers. He kept on asking trivial questions because he thought a real gentleman conducted himself in such a manner, and I kept on answering in the same manner showing respect to his politeness and protecting my confused and tender self.

Synchronicity is addressing life in the present, cleansing and healing an old wound.

Right there I saw in his eyes, I understood in this shallow conversation how different we were, I understood that our separation hadn't left any mark or scar on him, he was in charge of his emotions and his conduct.

In the past years, I still dreamt of us suddenly meeting, a random encounter, somewhere on some lonely street, in some quiet train carriage … I dreamt we might tell one another something we had forgotten to say or we might reveal a hidden secret, we might open our souls to each other … I hoped that such a coincidental encounter would reveal an important secret, maybe a fallacy or a cardinal mistake …

Yes, I hoped, but it wasn't the encounter I dreamt about; it was just an encounter with Mr De Sanctis full of formalities and politeness, absolutely devoid of any emotion, therefore a new thought popped up:

"Did you get married?"

"No, no!" he answered quickly, and it seemed to me rather too quick an answer; it seemed as if he hadn't spoken the truth.

After the past has been explored, additional enquiry into it does not lead to further healing, but a change of attitude should be the result of synchronicity.

Alas, I gave him my telephone number as a result of his quick and nervous *'No, no!'*, and I failed nature's honest attempt to teach me the valuable lesson of synchronicity.

Synchronicity II

I sat in a train on platform eighteen, the train to Milan.

It was a foggy morning; I felt more secure travelling by train, though I never liked public transport, but I thought I could take advantage of travelling by train and re-read my speech several times.

I'd caught the reflection of myself in the mirror: what a handsome man I was! Impeccably dressed. I dislike trains, full of second-class people, but Annamaria said it would be better to take the train as the fog was thick and looked determined to lie low the whole day. I obeyed; Annamaria always knew what was better for me, she always patronised everyone. The better choice was to obey her wishes than cause her a *'splitting headache'*.

The train started its easy sail and at that moment I felt unusual ease, similar to the one when I would leave my mother, who never hugged me at my departure. Annamaria also never hugged me at my departure; she just said, *'See you!'* and turned her head to the other side unable to get up, fearing she would get a splitting headache if she got up.

***

I read the newspaper.

She sat next to me and took out her book. I couldn't see her face. Only her hair I could see. That hair reminded me of a woman I used to love. I remembered her name—*Bea.* Six years had passed since I saw her for the last time.

Ah, emotions! Silly emotions, why would I remember Bea … she cried … as if the world had fallen apart … as if she hadn't found someone else the following week. Who knows, maybe all those years that we had spent together she had someone else?

Who cares anyway!

I read the newspaper.

I couldn't see her face, for it was hidden behind thick sandy-blond hair. I saw her hands. Her hands, just like her sandy-blond thick hair, resembled Bea's. She had beautiful hands; they looked as if they were made for caresses, her fingers long and tender, warm fingers, she used to tickle me with those fingers as she loved hearing me laugh; she, herself, loved laughing loudly, spontaneously, delightedly like a child, and a child she was when I met her… she was only seventeen.

But why am I reviving such silly memories right now!

I read the newspaper.

Her hair hid her face, her fingers played with book pages; she lifted the book in order to cross her legs. She wore a pair of jeans; she had long slim legs that reminded me of Bea's legs … I started to suppress emotions that were creeping in. *'Do I really still remember that girl who passed through my life without leaving almost any trace? I am De Sanctis, after all, or am I not?!'*

Still, I couldn't see her face and all I could do was to pretend to read the paper. She didn't give anything away, she kept on reading her book, I asked:

"You wouldn't mind if I opened the window, would you? Just a tiny bit."

She kept her eyes on her book and said:

"I wouldn't."

I kept on reading the newspaper.

The letters disobediently danced in front of my eyes, they didn't form any meaning, just as those scenes which were changing on the window of the running train. Nothing made sense; the only thing that made sense in this moment was the hair of the woman seated next to me, and her hands and the way she held her body.

I wanted to peep under that thick blanket of hair and see her face, but I wasn't that kind of man, I was raised to be a gentleman.

I wanted to ask more, something meaningful, but an unusual restlessness found refuge in my chest, my hands couldn't rest peacefully on my knees and it seemed as if all of a sudden some very strange, but carefully suppressed feelings surfaced out of nowhere. I panicked and screamed inside—*I don't want feelings!* and I hurriedly walked out to light a cigarette.

I am a man! A strong man. I need no past or silly feelings. I am De Sanctis! I lit a cigarette and looked through the window, the changing images liberated me from flooding thoughts and feelings evoked by the hair colour of some woman who sat next to me …

I looked through the window inhaling deeply and she approached from behind asking me to light her cigarette.

Our eyes met and I said:

"Bea."

"De Sanctis." She said.

What was that feeling in the pit of my stomach?

Feelings. Feelings. I didn't want any feelings. I inhaled deeply and gathered my strength, regained my soberness and fixed my eyes into the distance, on the passing fields. Irrelevant questions flew in through the window and I asked her about the weather in her hometown, about her friends and did she complete her degree? She appeared calm, somehow withdrawn, her answers were short and stingy. Abruptly, I asked:

"Are you married now?" and when she swung her head twice I felt as if the heaviest stone was lifted off my chest. Somehow excited, I kept on asking irrelevant questions about her car, whether she was still skiing, if she still loved Pavarotti … but all the time I kept on looking outside the window, into the changing pictures, having no strength of will, or character, to look at her directly into her beautiful eyes. Was I a coward? Too scared to look her in the eyes and commence an honest conversation, express my honest feelings. *A coward? Me? I am, after all professor De Sanctis. Afraid of nothing!*

I kept on being smart, cool and collected. Above all, I kept on being polite, a real gentleman, showing no feelings.

I thought, for a moment, that she would not ask if I got married, but she calmly asked:

"Did you get married?"

I never possessed that calmness of hers which I always envied, and in this particular moment, I disliked her collected self, asking that question as if I were a complete stranger, or someone she met a long time ago, only once.

Even if I wanted I couldn't prolong my silence, I wanted to answer that question but there was a hot, burning coal in my chest, and as if I wanted to spit it out, I hurriedly said:

"No, no, I did not!"

It wasn't a lie after all. I live with Annamaria, but we are not married.

I noticed a gentle smile twitched in the corner of her lips; once again I hurried my burning words:

"It would be great if you could give me a contact number whilst in Milan."

She smiled.

They all smile!

She smiled, but I couldn't grasp what kind of smile was on my face.

Bitter or sweet?

The Swapped Dream of Carlos Garcia de Veres

On the same day of April 7th two tiny, undernourished boys, both named Carlos, were brought to the Sisters of Mercy Orphanage.

The saddest fact was, the sisters of mercy never showed any mercy, they exercised cruel discipline governing their gloomy kingdom with strict rules and corporal punishment, displaying a lack of any emotion or warmth towards *'no one's kids'*, or *'little devils'* as they used to call them.

As they were brought in on the same day, they were placed in the same room. They couldn't tell them apart, and, why would they? To make a slight divergence, they called them Carlos One and Carlos Two, or even simpler—just One and Two. They were just two small numbers. Tiny and undernourished.

As they grew up they turned into two mischievous boys under the roof of the sisters of mercy, who would turn into shrew-sisters, no mercy, for they would punish according to the boys' merit.

They were born in the same year, even though no one knew the exact date of their births as they came without birth certificates. Carlos One was brought by a local priest, whilst Carlos Two was left on the Orphanage doorsteps.

Carlos One showed himself to be a strong and resilient child, whilst Carlos Two showed little strength and was prone to illnesses and extreme melancholy. His melancholy was so thick and intense one could see how it painted pictures on the bare walls of the tiny room they shared.

When in such an intense grip of melancholy, which was laced with sadness, he would claim he remembered his mother from his own dreams. He claimed she visited every night covering his cold body with a blanket, she whispered in his ear that she would come and take him back home in her beautiful sunny house overlooking the wide-open sea, where white boats sailed, where white women's arms waved *'good-bye'* to their departing sailors, to their arriving sailors … He said he remembered her from his dreams, but it was always the same dream he dreamt—she would come, dress him in a white little suit, an immaculately pressed captain's suit (as in that dream she claimed they came from an old naval family), she would buckle his shoes, so shiny and soft, comb his silken hair, sprinkling it with fragrant water, she would wash his hands …

He always washed his hands several times per day, that tiny sickly Carlos, he longed for clean, fresh-smelling clothes, he combed his hair carefully, he was orderly … as if he were meant to be a gentleman, a *señor*, as if he were placed here by a cruel mistake, deeply convinced that his mother would come to take him home, he knew she would come …

He didn't have any recollection of his arrival; he assumed it had to happen on the first day he was born. He believed his mother had an urgent task to do, hence she placed him here, for a moment, she had never forgotten him, she would come to take him back, very soon … she would come … *A mother would never leave her child; that couldn't happen just like that; she couldn't leave a child for too long, my Lord, not in an orphanage! No, not in such a place! Not her own child, her only child*, he thought.

(And little by little, Carlos Two was convinced that the dream was reality in the making.)

Whilst she was covering him at night, her long hair would touch his forehead and he described the beauty of her face to Carlos One with words:

"She is as beautiful as the picture of the Lady on the wall, (it was a picture of a saint, I never managed to find out what her name was) *she has big moist eyes, moist with longing for me, moist with yearning to see me again, big from expectancy of that promised day, the day God Almighty promised to come, and Santa Maria della Salute had promised the day will come, Santa Maria Stella Maris made a promise, I heard them talking in my dreams thoroughly planning her blessed arrival. She is going to bring a brand new white suit for me, shiny shoes, she will bring the presents she collected for me all those years we were apart ... She'll come in a chariot, pulled by winged horses, everyone will be called to attention by their mighty whinnying, they will know who has arrived and will say: 'Here, Carlos' mother has arrived, with her golden jewellery, dressed in the nicest clothes, with diamond rings on her fingers, with a winning, shining smile on her face' ... Yes, she comes at night telling me this is how it'll happen, she promises that every night. She says: 'Carlos, be a good boy, I will come to take you home, I'll come accompanied by Santa Maria della Salute and Santa Maria Stella Maris ...'"*

Soon after he told that story again, they came to take him. But only two of them came. Just Santa Maria della Salute and Santa Maria Stella Maris.

Could it be that Carlos's mother was waiting somewhere else for her little darling, for when those two women came to take him with them, Carlos One witnessed shining light filling the room.

The light woke him up. When he rubbed his sleepy eyes, he saw the two women woven of light. He asked them:

"Who are you?"

In one voice, they answered:

"Santa Maria della Salute and Santa Maria Stella Maris."

With eyes big, full of wonderment and with a voice trembling with elation, Carlos One asked:

"Where are you taking him?"

Santa Maria della Salute said:

"His time to get healed has arrived."

Santa Maria Stella Maris said:

"His time to see the open sea and the white boats, the white hands waving to the arriving sailors, waving to the departing sailors, has arrived..."

"But, where is his mother?" asked Carlos One.

In one voice, they said:

"She'll send someone today to take him home, but they won't find him waiting. They'll take you, instead."

When they said that, Carlos One saw the soul of his little friend, Carlos Two, departing with the two women, two saints bearing the same name—Maria. Whilst leaving with them his little pal waved; the angelic smile on his innocent face wide and sincere, only his little body was left lying on the bed. It was cold and stiff in the morning, his eyes were opened wide, full of wonderment as if they had witnessed something extraordinary in that last moment of his short life. As if he had met Santa Maria Stella Maris in person.

About his nightly vision of two saints, he never uttered a word to anyone, for long ago he had learned that silence was holy wisdom or redemption itself.

The funeral was as any other burial of an orphaned child: no one expressed any feelings: no sorrow, no mercy—almost not a word was uttered.

The rainy day, the grey building, and the emptied room. Only sad reminiscences of the same, plain days: boring, filled with whining, with accusations, with angry remarks from disappointed sisters … with the smell of bad-tasting food, the smell of poverty, of mould, dampness and stale air … with the sound of a ringing bell, the sound of hoarse voices, the solitude and the howling of the wind coming through the cracks, the sound of squeaking mice under the bed, the sound of loneliness …

And he had no more friends.

He had got used to the flogging, to threats and to blasphemy, he had got used to it all.

Carlos Two had the ability to dream the strangest dreams—as if they were woven from cotton wool, as if they were made of clouds, they floated through the room colouring it in rainbow colours … and when he departed he took with him his dreams, or shall I say he became one of his dreams, he met the two saint women named Maria who took him to his mother's place …

Now he, Carlos One, found himself all alone, without dreams, for he didn't have any and didn't know how to dream unusual dreams; all he felt in his heart was endless contempt towards the women without compassion and kindness in their hearts, contempt for his own life that imprisoned him between those cold walls so early in his life. He was without any hope as if he knew that no one would ever come; he never waited like Carlos Two did for his mother and the two saints, he never waited for anyone, for his imagination was dry and his dreams were like a barren land.

***

As he didn't have any dreams or visions, he believed he would stay imprisoned by those women within those walls forever; he believed that even his own soul had deserted him, for he didn't have the rainbow soul of Carlos Two; a soul that floated above the offing, saluting the white boats which were sailing across the seven seas.

***

Then the most unusual event took place.

The most unusual thing: Carlos One woke up in someone else's dream. In Carlos Two's dream.

This is how it all happened:

The director of the orphanage was a woman with a harsh voice, and a harsh expression permanently stood on her frozen face. He rarely met her; he never saw her talking to other people outside the orphanage. He didn't know that in such encounters she would sweeten her voice and try to give her expression a mellower touch, though her face then looked like an unnatural or grotesque mask.

A sister walked into his room and barked:

"You, little rat, might have a lucky day today. Get up and get dressed."

Without a word he started putting his clothes on: dressing his skinny body slowly and wearily, his movements resembling an old man trapped in the body of a young boy.

"Hurry up, you rascal, they are waiting for you!"

Who could be waiting for him? She said, *"the Mistress is waiting"*. What does she want from him? He didn't do anything wrong … but, he learned one thing—even if he hadn't done anything wrong, he could still be punished or accused just for anything. He didn't put any effort into finding an excuse, for he would be punished regardless of any excuse.

He walked in front of her. When they reached the door, the sister cleared her throat and knocked at the door. A hoarse voice called them in. They entered. There, in a large room the Mistress was seated in her wooden chair. Around the table there were three men—the two of them wore black robes. They looked to him like two bishops. The third man was a man with mellow eyes and a faint but warm smile. He knew the man didn't belong to the clergy, as he possessed the kindness of a secular man who practises kindness. He read in the man's eyes that he respected all people equally.

He felt a shiver down his spine—*'What do they want from me?'*

The Mistress commenced her speech with a voice hardened by indifference.

"Sit down, child!" signalling to sister to leave the room.

Carlos sat down looking at the floorboards. Looking at his sandals that were falling apart. He thought, *'I would most probably be ashamed of my sandals if I were somewhere else with this kind man who is wearing a beautifully tailored suit and a pastel-coloured tie'*. The Mistress said:

"They brought you here when you were a tiny baby."

He nodded keeping his gaze nailed on his sandals.

"Your mother left the country, went to Italy where she met this fine man, doctor Ulliese Monte and married him. She was searching for you,

and now that she has found you, wants you to come and live with her. We had a long procedure to follow; you shouldn't feel concerned with the details. This gentleman is your mother's husband, doctor Ullisse Monte. Your mother's name is Portia de Huante. All the paperwork has been finalised and you are free to go with mister Monte, you are free to go and live with your mother ... You see ... you were the lucky one, you found your family and your home. I wish you all the best. God bless you."

As they were still signing some papers, from his dream-like state her voice brought him back:

"Go now, pack your things; don't let doctor Monte wait too long."

Slowly he got up, his gaze still nailed to his sandals that were falling apart. Was he really going to go away with these worn-out sandals, with this fine gentleman who was wearing a perfectly tailored suit and a pastel-coloured tie?

A tide of shame rose up touching his cheeks.

Silently he repeated her name—*Portia de Huante*, he heard her name for the first time.

That was Carlos Two's dream. He dreamt that his mother was looking for him, searching everywhere, he dreamt she had a name, a real name, he dreamt that she promised to find him and take him *'far, far away'* …

The night before he died, in his dream, he met the two women, the saints, who cured his frail body, and then they took him to oversee and lead boats through stormy seas …

But now, here came a man called *Signor dottore* who had a wife, Portia de Huante, who they claimed to be his mother, a mother he had never waited for, a mother he never knew existed or that she longed to find him, that she would send a fine *Signor dottore* to bring him back to her … in those sandals that were falling apart, whilst a grim autumn was present in the bare trees, a grim, cold, late autumn.

Benedict Leaving

"Benedict, where are you off to?"

"Umm, nowhere... just collecting my stuff..."

"You mean, you are tidying up?"

"Sure, call it 'tidying up'."

"Benedict, what are you going to do later in the evening?"

"Watch some TV... or listen to music..."

"You mean, you are not going to prepare the table?"

"I'll do all of that after I prepare the table."

"Benedict, you can't do whatever pleases you after you prepare the table. We are having a dinner."

"I meant, after the dinner."

"Benedict, don't you remember, my mother is coming."

"Oh, yes, your mother!"

"Oh, yes, my mother! Is there something wrong, Benedict?"

"No, no, darling, nothing's wrong with your mother coming."

"You are a darling, Benedict!"

"Yeah!"

"What's that supposed to mean—Yeah? Are you teasing me, Benedict?"

"No, I am not teasing you."

"You'd better not be."

Benedict kept on tidying his desk, humming, focused on one thought. A single thought. Leaving.

Nothing new. He had been thinking about it for a long time. Many years. He wanted to leave without a trace. He wanted to vanish. Like he had never existed.

"Benedict, stop daydreaming, hurry up! You will never finish your tidying up. You have to take me to the bottle shop."

He nodded his head while looking at the postcard. The postcard Millie sent seven years ago. He kept it next to his computer.

"Say something! A single word! Did you hear what I said at all?"
"Yes. I heard you."
"Why do you pretend you haven't?"

Millie travelled a lot, but her last postcard came seven years ago. She sent it from Madrid. He had never been there, but it was Millie's dearest destination. She sent her last postcard from her dearest destination as if she were telling him—*'I will settle here where my heart belongs.'*

No, Millie didn't settle there, he knew it, knowing that she had sent many more postcards to other people from other destinations, but to him she sent a silent message between the lines *'From Madrid, my favourite place.'*

He could have married her. But he didn't. He never asked her and she never showed any regret. She took off and never looked back.

"Benedict, are you still staring at that postcard?"

He placed it down and looked through the window.

"She doesn't care about you anymore, she never sent another postcard. And you, poor fool, you are keeping the last one still in your sight. Hurry up, Benedict!"

He changed his shirt, buttoned it up and took his car keys.

It was raining.

'I wonder—how often does it rain in Madrid?' he thought.

"Stop staring into the rain, take an umbrella and hurry up!"

Millie's bags were always packed. She travelled from one destination to another with such ease; only Millie could travel in such style. She's been everywhere. When she was a little girl her father took her to an exotic country… he had forgotten the name… it was long ago, long, long ago… It is strange that he had forgotten it, for he had never forgotten anything that had to do with Millie, her life and her travels. But that little fact he had forgotten because he felt such an intense fear when she said, *'I will never settle down, I'll keep on travelling and travelling and travelling ... I have to be on the cutting edge where life can be most fearsome and also most exhilarating.'*

"Watch out, Benedict! You almost ran into that car! What is the matter with you today!"

He could have said *'Stay! Settle down with me.'* After several years, after he finally understood that it was all he wanted. If he had only verbalised it, she might have stayed, or at least, might have understood what he wanted.

He never spat out that word: *Stay.*

"Stop! Stop here, Benedict! What is wrong with you today? Focus on life, not on your dreams... what is in your silly head, Benedict? Let us not get caught up in the excitement of someone's resurrection."

"Pardon?"

"I said—Stop here!"

He stopped.

Just opened the door and walked off, down the street.

She screamed:
"Benedict, Benedict, stop! Stop at once or I will..."

He stopped and turned his head. He asked:
"What?"
"You are not listening!"
"No!"
"No! How dare you!"
"I do dare!"
"Have you lost your mind?"
"On the very day I married you."
"But she never loved you, Benedict, I pulled you out of your rut, I did everything for you. Is this the way you are paying me back?"
"Actually, no! This is not the way—just to walk off."

He walked back, she showed a little confused smile as if she wondered in disbelief *'who was this person'*, for he wasn't acting like Benedict.
He came near her, she said:
"Oh, Benedict, don't be a fool."

He pulled her dress from the shoulders down; when it stubbornly stopped at her hips he ripped it off; he ripped off her bra and heard someone calling the two policemen who were standing in the distance. Benedict said:
"Do you feel ashamed? Bare and ashamed?"

She said nothing.
He took the keys, threw them in her direction and said:

"Hurry up, your mother is coming and you've got to get her some wine. Be on time, she is mad if things are not the way she wants them to be."

As the two policemen were approaching fast, Benedict ran into his freedom with the liberating thought, *'If they jail me, I will be free!'*

A Hat, a Violin and a Pipe

Anastasia took her hat.

It was a lovely hat, knitted, made in an old-fashioned style. Her grandmother used to knit similar hats and mittens, although this particular hat she hadn't made; it was bought in one of those vintage shops Anastasia frequented.

Anastasia took her violin.

It had a beautifully crafted wooden case with three letters engraved in the left corner—*ABT*. The case was engraved a year after it was given to her. Her father arranged that just two days before her birthday as if he knew the engraving would be his last, and rather peculiar gift.

When she locked the violin in its case, she locked the memory of her father together with the violin, some spare strings and a piece of paper with some sharp musical notes.

Anastasia took her pipe.

Yes, she secretly smoked a pipe. A pipe that smelled like a forest of cedar trees, a smell which grew thicker daily, under that knitted hat, made in an old-fashioned style. She grew lots of memories under that little hat regardless of whether it was she who was wearing it or if it was the hat wearing her out. Anastasia liked her pipe, for she inherited it from her half-brother, even though the inheritance was never announced or written in any form, even though the brother wasn't aware of such an act of extravagance. He was, apparently, her mother's adopted son. Anastasia never challenged that story. Her grandmother, while knitting hats and mittens, used to mumble under her breath *'adopted, adopted'*, always twice. The second *'adopted'* was always a little bit louder in case Mother hadn't heard it. Hearing Grandmother's comments, Anastasia's mother, Allina, always swung her head. Allina didn't have any eyebrows or eyelashes, for they left her face to find solace in her paint brushes. Therefore, Allina's strokes were graceful but firm and convincing, her pictures literally talked; Anastasia heard them whispering so many times into her upwards turned hat, telling her to break free, to leave the door open, to give the whispering paintings a chance to be seen by a wider audience.

Anastasia took the pipe only in order to hold onto some solid evidence of her half-brother's existence, so that he would not be carried as a myth into the future.

Poseidon was his name: a solid, reliable name with which she intended to decorate her future tales.

Once, some random, nameless person told Anastasia that her half-brother was an original gypsy-boy found in a gutter down the road. He was dark in his appearance and darker in his soul. Nothing bright came from that child. To make the story more bizarre, it was told that he came together with that pipe, tied to his left arm.

The story was told by some older family member that Anastasia came into this world together with her violin. It was tied around her waist.

Grandma knitted so many stories!
Who could ever believe in all her stories?

Then, she was never challenged; she could say whatever she wanted as if she was a seer protected by a universal law which each and every person in this land had to unquestionably obey. She could and would read people's destinies imprinted on their palms, or sometimes written by leaves in a cup of tea; or she would, with a thundering voice, curse innocent cats, dogs and little kids alike if they showed disinterest or disobedience.

Then, one mute morning Grandmother simply died.

No one believed that she was destined to die; no one took it seriously, therefore her corpse was decomposing for two long, stinky, weeks in their home, indicating the definite end of an infinite game of chance. Two weeks after her passing, policemen knocked on their door and Allina was taken to the station to answer numerous questions.

On that very day, whilst they were investigating her mother, Anastasia played her violin while her half-brother ran away at exactly six o'clock that evening. In a hurry, he forgot to take his pipe, which only showed how desperately he needed to be liberated from the tight grip of the three women he had lived with.

And for Anastasia there was nothing to hold onto in this house any longer. No more Grandmother knitting her stories, no more Mother painting half-naked, no more half-brother with his dark-coloured soul and secrets knitted into his undershirt.

It was time to move on.

Without voicing any complaint or showing any grimace, which would indicate her inner turmoil, Anastasia took her hat, her violin and, by now, her pipe; then she left the house door wide open for new gifted inhabitants to move in to admire the artwork her half-naked mother passionately painted over the past thirty years.

Madness Inherited

Act One

Everyone has a story to tell, but I was told mine wasn't an interesting one, so I kept it hidden from my acquaintances and random people alike, fearing they might laugh at me. I thought everyone I knew was interesting and exciting, but I, somehow, was always pushed away and overlooked. No, I have never found the exact reason for such utterly unfair treatment but I have to admit—I have never possessed any valid tools or an insightful mind to work it all out.

Now I will commence my story and shall present it from several different angles.

My mother would say, *"You are clumsy, short-sighted, ugly and too slow, you will never amount to anything."*

That wasn't a sentence which could lay the groundwork for great achievements, neither to build the self-esteem needed for success of any kind.

'OK', I thought (on some deep but unknown level to me) *'you'll get what you want!'* and I started to be clumsier, pretended not to see things in front of my nose, avoided a shower whenever possible and dragged my feet and my sentences to painful ends.

Consequence: I was often beaten by my mother and her sister, who lived with us during that period of time. The year her sister moved in all I could understand was that her husband was a *'monster'* and a *'brute'*, but these epithets were never explained clearly, hence I feared meeting him in the street.

He was a drunkard!

My first conscious resolve to overcome fear was born on the day when Aunt Clair had beaten me with an electric cord.

Most probably she was drunk too on that day, but calling me *'forever ugly and stupid'* brought more pain than the electric cord which left fat blue marks across my legs.

Out of spite, I never cried.

On that day, in the late afternoon, just before the sun touched the ocean, I put my shoes on and went out of the house. I didn't have a well worked-out plan, but, as I walked, some thoughts were formed. They formed quickly; they were sticky, so they glued a story in my mind.

I rang the bell. He was standing there: tall and handsome, unusually sober; he lifted his brows.

"What do you want, child?"

"She said she'd take you back."

"What are you talking about?"

"She said that you are the best man she has ever met, just a little bit crazy when drunk. But she is willing to take you back, she said anytime, she said her heart aches for you, I hear her crying herself to sleep and Mummy sings lullabies to her ..."

Standing there, he was looking at me in disbelief, scratching his unshaven chin longer than I wanted, for my heart was racing like a crazy, wild cat. But I appeared to be calm and collected.

I can't say how long I had been standing there with my knees shaking barely visibly and my eyes looking unfocused, but I had never been more aware of a situation in my entire life. After a while, I felt as if I were a protagonist in a movie which in ten years time they would call—a *cult classic.*

There I was: in my light summer dress, with red cheeks, a ponytail, and multiple lies and tricks under my hat. There I stood with a cheeky smile on my lips; even though my knees cluttered, I could hear fine music coming from my insides—my intestines played better music than an orchestra of mismatched pipes. He walked out and looked down the road. He looked up the road. He looked behind the house and then quickly said:

"Come in, girl."

I walked into the strangest room I had ever seen, but I pretended everything was just plain and ordinary.

He gave me a pillow, and we sat on the floor.

"Are you lying to me?"

A hot dumpling in my throat!

"No, sir ... why ... why would I?"

"Yeah, why would you?"

"Yeah, why would I?"

"Yeah, you wouldn't, would you?"

"I would never!"

"Yeah, you never would."

After that short but meaningful conversation I stood up, took that pillow I was sitting on and handed it back to him.

"Thank you for the pillow."

"Well, thank you, girl."

"Clementa."

"Thank you, Clementa girl."

"Fine."

***

My Aunt Clair hated her husband, for he was a drunkard with a sadistic streak which blossomed when drunk, and often Aunt Clair was seen with the visible signs of his temper on her face or her slim body.

She used to be pretty, just like my mum: lovely slim figure, fine facial features, blue-eyed, and thick blond hair. She was a singer in a local band just like Mum before she had me. She said I ruined her career and her life; she blamed me for being the child of a man who never had any decency and left when he found out Mum was pregnant. I never met my father, he moved somewhere to the North with his guitar and his backpack (and a part of Mother's soul).

The next day, after my visit to my so-called Uncle, all hell broke loose (as I expected!).

He came to pay us a visit! Seeing him from my window approaching the door, I hid under the bed; while my mum was ironing, I heard Aunt Clair open the door. Judging by the slur in his voice I assumed he might be a tiny bit drunk.

She said something that I couldn't hear, but I heard her screeching as he grabbed her by her long hair; I saw it as I jumped up and looked at the scene from my bedroom window. I heard her screaming:

"I hate you! I hate you! I hate you!"

Just the opposite of what I told him yesterday!

No one dared to come to her rescue but an anonymous neighbour called the police. I managed to run out through the window and two policemen found me at the shopping mall and brought me home. I found Mother alone but she never told me what happened to Aunt Clair that day. On the fourth day after his visit, Aunt Clair came back from hospital—I never uttered a word.

Never again did I walk down the street where my so-called Uncle lived. I avoided his house in big circles for the entire year.

So much for being *'clumsy, short-sighted, ugly and too slow'* and for, *'you will never amount to anything'*.

Act Two

By the age of sixteen I wasn't ugly anymore as I looked like my mum, but in school everybody avoided me, for I *'brought bad luck'*.

'Wacky-Girl', or *'Crackpot'*, or *'Mental'* were my nicknames behind my back. I still lived with my mother and Aunt Clair but we rarely met in our house. We barely spoke since that incident when Aunt Clair was beaten and came back with a broken jaw and wrist. They never blamed me, for they never heard the conversation I held with my so-called Uncle, but nevertheless, they just sensed that somehow this incident had something to do with me. They thought my presence alone brought bad luck.

The English teacher said I was illiterate.

With a smirk on her face she would call my name in one elongated sentence:

"Cle-men-ta, you, smart girl, do you think you'll manage to learn the English alphabet by the end of year twelve? Get up and read this sentence, quickly and clearly."

People laughed, I heard them saying:
"Yeah, quickly and clearly ..."

I had that conversation ready for Ms Walters. The sentences in my head were perfectly arranged—every comma inserted in its rightful place, the exclamation marks ready to bring her to shame. I repeated the prepared speech a number of times in my head and when I walked into the teacher's room after school finished, I was ready to confront her in my own way. But as I slowly opened the door I heard voices, even though they were very quiet.

The two voices were whispering.

They were whispering very naughty words.

Very, very naughty!

Explicit and vulgar, indeed.

There, on the kitchenette bench, our fine Ms Walters was lying half undressed, her panties around her ankles, and her lips smudged with red lipstick, shamelessly uttering naughty words.

We always wondered, *'Why did Mr Pitt marry Mrs Pitt a few years ago?'*, but now seeing him and hearing his hot vocabulary, I was certain the reason why he married his wife wasn't—love, nor was it lust. She was a stern woman, unattractive and short, with a rather bitter outlook on life. And no one, no one ever liked her.

When I witnessed Ms Walters and Mr Pitt in a passionate clinch, I gave up my speech for good. Instead of speaking up myself, I decided to give my phone a chance to *'talk'*.

'Click ... click ... click.'

They couldn't hear me, no one saw me.

***

The next day I travelled to the neighbouring town. As I took three photos of the couple in love, I made sure their faces were visible.

I printed out three photos in three copies: one for Ms Walters, one for Mr Pitt and one for the school principle—Mrs Pitt.

There we go!

"Stupid and slow", she called me countless times!

Looks as if, with age, I matured, I was less and less stupid. Slow? Maybe, but justice as we know it, is slow, too.

Act Three

I met Stephen Van Veer in 2011 at a random gig, and I think what happened to me at that moment could have been love at first sight. I know nothing about love for no one ever loved me, but at that moment something strange happened to me.

I was seventeen years old and I really never had a friend. I knew many people, but there was not a single soul I could call a friend, so I went everywhere alone.

Even though this is a small town, I had never met him before.

I already said that from an ugly and insecure child, I turned out to look just like my mum, but still, I was insecure, for that ugly little child was still locked in my heart. Stephen Van Veer placed his beer on the bar and called out to me:

"Why don't you join me?"

I turned my head around in disbelief that he had addressed me. He said:

"Yes, you, pretty blonde!"

I am not a *pretty blonde*! No one ever told me, never called me, that. What was I supposed to do with this statement? To go and join him? To smile? To say something? Just anything? I stood there pretending to be disinterested. He took his beer and when he came closer, he extended it to me.

I took the glass and emptied it in one gulp, he said:

"Wow! Congratulations!"

I shrugged my shoulders, but I have to admit that soon after the effect of that beer gave me some sort of silky feeling.

"Stephen Van Veer, you can call me Veerie."

"Clementa. You can call me Mental."

"Mental?"

"Mental."

"Is it short for Clementa?"

"Just Mental."

He brought two more beers and we sat at a small table; our knees were touching, and as they touched each time my intestines involuntarily played badly tuned tones. For the first time in my life I prayed, asking that person I was addressing to talk nicely to my intestines, and tell them on my behalf to calm down and stop playing embarrassing music. But as they played to the tune of my nerves they obeyed only one master, therefore my prayers were declined.

Even though the music was loud and his speech was loud, at one moment he asked me:

"Is that your stomach?"

"Yes. Sometimes beer does that to me."

"Let's switch to whiskey!"

"Whatever!"

We drank whiskey and after maybe the fifth round, my intestines gave up—they stopped playing disharmonious tones.

I can freely say that it was the most beautiful evening of my entire life. I even laughed at his remarks.

Then we kissed and it was my first kiss, for no one ever wanted to kiss that *'Wacky Girl'*.

I liked his kisses, and I let myself explore that uncharted territory with uttermost delight.

Kissing him, somehow at that moment, I thought of Ms Walters and for the first time I understood that urgency and panic in her voice.

After a while he said, *'Let's go for a drive'*, and we left the bar.

Whilst leaving, hand in hand, a boy came and whispered something into his ear. He laughed and said, *'No worries, mate'*, slapping him on the back.

He drove the car drunk and we hit a tree, we laughed and he kept on driving until we came to the end of a long road. There he said, *'Take off your bra'*, and I did. I would probably have done the same even if I hadn't been drunk, for I now believe that I was intoxicated by his kisses more than any whiskey, which brought the same outcome, anyway.

We slept in his car two nights, and three days we just sat there, talked and kissed. On the third day, a policeman knocked on the window, so we had to move.

We went to a small café. It was late afternoon; the café was almost empty; we ate sandwiches and drank coffee and beer; we kissed and stared into each other's eyes as if seeing them for the first time.

I didn't know what that feeling was, but I could swear it was the best feeling I had ever experienced. Maybe it was love.

"Where are we off to now?"

I replied, *"Wherever you wanna go, I'll go."*

"I have to go home, I think my mother will kill me; I have to make a really good and believable story this time."

"Good for you, my mother won't be bothered! She never asks about my whereabouts."

"That's strange."

"Don't get me started."

I didn't want to tell him about my early life marked by emotions which isolated me from the rest of the world and helped forge my so-called *'unique persona'*.

We agreed we'd meet up tomorrow underneath the bridge, on the left side of the riverbank. Lovers used to meet there in the olden times, in times when my mother was young, perhaps.

We agreed we'd meet up underneath the bridge at five.

We walked out in an embrace, I felt as if I were floating, I couldn't feel my legs, couldn't feel any part of my body except my heart that was singing like a just awoken joyous bird. We walked out through the door barely aware of anyone, but a boy stopped Veerie and said:

"Let go of her, I just want to tell you something."

They went back in, and I was left standing close to the café's door. I recognised the boy, for it was the same boy we encountered two days ago; once again he whispered something in his ear, he made gestures as if in urgency, he furrowed his eyebrows and nodded his head.

Veerie looked pissed off; he looked up and down, then left and right, he looked at me, I smiled, he said something I couldn't hear, and when he was about to turn his back on the boy, a tall, lanky and, from the distance, young-looking man touched his right shoulder. Veerie gave him a hug with a suppressed smile on his lips. They hugged and talked in a quiet voice, never looked at me, and to me it all looked strange … like they were talking about something important, so important that he had completely forgotten about me, standing next to the door, puzzled, confused, almost ashamed. At that moment, I understood I wasn't blessed with a great deal of willpower, just with a right dose of weirdness, so I kept on waiting and quietly singing a long-forgotten song about lovers who never met underneath the bridge which connected the two towns separated by a large, murky river.

As the sun was getting down, it touched the window, the glare of the sun fell on the face of the tall, lanky, and from the distance, young-looking man whose indulgent expression and most scruffy deportment were the first things I noticed upon laying my eyes on him, and I said almost loudly, *"You, bastard!"* and ran away fast as if he might change his mind and talk to me instead of talking to Veerie.

***

The next day I put on a dress, and walked to the bridge where we were to meet at five; my heart was pounding, my knees were shaking, palms sweating, and I thought I could read from the book of events that hadn't happened yet.

I waited for two hours. I sat on the riverbank and sang songs to the birds and ants and random passers-by, I sang to my heart, I sang to the trembling leaves and to my past and to my frightening future.

What I felt I couldn't put into sentences; my so-far-denied weirdness blossomed in those two hours and from a plain, almost quiet, singing I started to sing louder and louder whilst slowly taking my clothes off. When I was completely naked, random onlookers freely took photos of me; some talked on the phone as if in urgency, and I wondered later did they call the police? When police came, they talked to me as if I were a criminal, as if I were some sort of a loose woman or a total crackpot. *'Crackpot'*, that was just my nickname. I told them that! I told them *'Crackpot'* was just my nickname, not my trait. They laughed. Yep, they laughed, they poked me with a baton right under my ribs. They were rude.

They called my mother; when I came home they beat me: both of them. I didn't say a word. Nothing to anyone! To whom, in the end?

But I had a plan.

I don't know what they said to Veerie: the young boy we met twice, and my so-called Uncle. I don't know, but they told him something and he never showed up underneath the bridge where he said he'd meet me the next day.

***

I followed him for three days.

On Saturday afternoon, he wasn't just tipsy, but drunk, he could barely walk. I followed him from the pub to his house. He never locked the door. I reached the window on the tips of my toes, he didn't undress himself; he just tossed his body on the bed and fell asleep, or unconscious.

What a stench! I slammed the window in an attempt to wake him up—his body never moved. Knowing that he was numbed by alcohol I walked in and unbuttoned his shirt, then took it slowly off. I unzipped his jeans and with great difficulty took them off. I took off his underwear. There!

I took my clothes off.

I smashed glasses and a bottle which was on the table.

With a piece of broken glass, I cut myself on various parts of my body.

I took a chair and smashed it against the wall whilst my so-called Uncle was in an unconscious slumber, and with a chair leg I smashed my head several times until it started to bleed. I called the police and told them the neighbouring house experienced domestic violence, gave them his address and hung up.

Then I tried to wake him up.

My blood all over his body!

I was crying, hugging him, waking him, and staining him with the blood. He vomited twice, then he asked what was happening.

I couldn't talk, for I was crying.

By the time he got to his senses, police officers were at the door. They ran into the room and the three of them jumped on my so-called Uncle, who was so drunk that he couldn't grasp any meaning of the unfolding drama.

I was covered with someone's long white shirt.

An ambulance was heard and I was taken to the hospital.

My mother and Aunt Clair came.

My Mother said:

"I knew that would happen sooner or later. He is mental."

"He is mental? What about her?"

"The apple doesn't fall far from the tree."

I looked at them in disbelief.

"Isn't he just my so-called Uncle? Isn't he?" I screamed.

Aunt Clair said:

"She inherited his madness. I told you she did."

Randall and Abigail, a Love Story

How shall I start this story? From the beginning, one would say, but where is the beginning of this story? It isn't an ordinary story. Randall had never had a family, yet he wasn't an orphan. How is that possible? Well, at the age of three he was adopted, never loved though. At the age of seven, they handed him over, in the way one would hand over an unwanted, cheap gift.

Mrs Swinton was not *'a child friendly person'*, she preferred cats to kids. Why did she adopt a child, then, one could ask? To this question, I had never found the answer. I know that Mr Swinton couldn't care less about the adoption, he just wanted to proceed with his wife's plan or whim as he was inclined to fulfil all her wishes regardless of their validity and reasonableness. Mr Swinton wasn't a weak man, he just simply couldn't confront his wife, for she had a temperament he preferred not to question or challenge. With the same calmness with which he agreed when she propounded the adoption, he met her decision of handing him over, because he had been a father for almost four years to a child he never really wanted to father. Randall never called him father. Yes, I forgot to mention who they handed him over to. I'll explain that as well, but first I'd like to point out that Mrs Swinton had an excellent excuse for such an extravagant deed of handing the kid over: they moved temporarily (or they intended to) to India where she planned to take up studies of Sanskrit. No one questioned, no one challenged this story, and she claimed the doctors told her Randall couldn't survive the Indian climate with his condition. So, she knocked on the door of Lorna, her younger sister and her husband Clint. They owed her! A big favour, they owed her, therefore Lorna accepted the child *'temporarily'*, knowing in advance that she would never really get rid of that child, knowing her sister's sinister ways too well. If you ask me, *'What did they owe her?'* I know that story as well, and I might narrate it sometime later. But first things first!

By the age of seven, Randall lived in the house of his *Aunt* Lorna and her husband Clint. He called her *Aunt* Lorna, whilst Clint was simply Clint, for he would never allow a child to call him *Uncle*.

One year passed, they heard nothing from the Swintons. Not a word! They didn't even know if they were in India or—or if she had just made a quick, lame excuse.

They rarely talked to Randall; they didn't know what to say to the seven-year-old odd child who was mostly silent. Not a word!

He never, ever heard again about his, let's call them parents as they were the first people he remembered who had adopted him. He even carried their name: Randall Swinton.

When yet another year passed, *Aunt* Lorna and her husband handed Randall over to the local priest. I think they were some sort of friends, but I am not so sure about it. In my personal view, it wasn't an ordinary church, it was some strange group of people gathering in an old abandoned church once a week singing songs to the Lord. Who was their Lord, I had never managed to find out, but I am positive that Randall ended up in the custody of a man who called himself a priest.

Randall Swinton was nine years old when he involuntarily became a member of a group of people, a group so weird that even nine-year-old Randall was in disbelief when they prayed or talked. He planned to escape, leave this abandoned church where he lived with the so-called priest, his two girlfriends and two billy goats who were tied to the hornbeam tree. Both billy goats were violent and unpredictable, Randall would avoid them in wide circles. When the priest, who became Randall's legal guardian, used to tell him to feed the billy goats, Randall threw food from a distance. He was never punished in the way kids were punished back then, but if he disobeyed, no one would talk to him for days. That was exactly what he wanted, hence he was often wilful and disobedient seeking punishment, but the priest was a clever man! When he understood Randall's ultimate purpose, he changed his tactics too. Instead of isolating him from group discussions, he asked him to read aloud from their Bible. I say, *'their Bible'*, for you have to know that this group, or shall I call them a sect, wasn't reading the ordinary Bible, but an adaptation of the Bible which their priest re-wrote for his own purposes (or dare I say—agenda?). Even though he was exposed daily to a heavy dose of brainwashing, Randall was an intuitive boy, I'd say, if I can't say a clever one. Intuitively, he knew they were a bunch of lunatics and their teaching were wrong in the eyes of any god. Any god would be disgusted by their way of living, by the way they treated women and young kids. Randall thought even if the Devil saw them he would raise one eyebrow, thinking: *'What the hell!'*

So, that was the environment where Randall lived from the age of nine to thirteen.

A few days after he passed his thirteenth birthday (which they did not celebrate), he made a plan with Abigail. She wasn't living with them, but she was a part of the *'congregation'*; she came with her mother almost every Saturday. She would sit in a corner and read a book. She couldn't care less if the priest was upset by her behaviour; even if her mother asked her to come closer and sit with others, Abigail just smiled and did what she wanted to do. She was sixteen.

The first time they talked, Randall remembered it so well, that conversation remained engraved in his brain forever. She asked:

"Why do you live with them? They are not your parents."

"I have nowhere to go."

"Where are you parents?"

"In India."

"Why aren't you with them?"

"I had asthma, back then, so they left me with Mrs Swinton's sister."

"Who's Mrs Swinton?"

"My adopted mother."

"You call her Mrs Swinton?"

Randall said nothing; he was picking the skin from the top of his finger, Abigail grabbed his finger and said:

"Stop picking it! You have an anxiety disorder!"

"How do you know?"

"My mother has it; she picks her fingernails, her skin and she lies. When she tells too many lies, she falls on her knees and prays. She prays to different gods. She prays to Hindu gods, to Christian gods and some others ... she is confused about which god to pray to in order to be heard."

"You carry a soberer head on your shoulders, don't you?"

"Yeah! I think we swapped our roles. She comes here believing, somehow magically, her bills will be paid if she prays hard enough, that she will find an easier job or a kinder man."

That was all he learnt about Abigail, but at first sight he liked her, at first sight he trusted her, believing she had a similar soul to his, because they might have had similar experiences, whilst growing up, of being exposed to utterly irresponsible and self-centred people.

Randall couldn't wait to see Abigail next Saturday.

He decided, without knowing the reason, he would be a bit kinder to the priest, his two girlfriends and to both billy goats. He decided to feed them better and to stop beating them with a long thick stick when no one was there to see.

On the following Saturday morning, he washed his hair in cold water. He rarely washed his hair as there was no warm water, one of the commodities he had at Mrs Swinton and later at her sister's. He hated washing himself in cold water, plus he never saw a valid reason to do it. As if the billy goats cared whether he had washed himself or not.

But on that Saturday, he woke up in a better mood; he fed the billy goats, he made breakfast for the priest and his two girlfriends; he never ate with them, so he took a bowl of porridge out and finished it clean.

When the flock gathered, he anxiously looked around. He was proud of Abigail's discernment and her easy diagnosis of his mysterious condition: anxiety disorder.

He thought her a seer!

Abigail seated herself right there where he met her last time with a book on her lap. It wasn't the Bible re-written by the priest. It was a book with a colourful cover.

He walked there hiding a daffodil behind his back. She took it, smelt it and said:

"It doesn't have any fragrance, but what counts is the thought. You are such a thoughtful boy. How was your week?"

"As usual: horrible."

"Really? Is it that bad?"

"What do you think? Living with the violent billy goats and the priest, who pretends not to be violent, and his two brainless, obedient girlfriends. So weird! They are weirder than my so-called family."

"What are you going to do?"

"Tell me! I have no idea."

"Run away."

"How?"

"When they have their orgy, you just leave."

"Where can I go? The Swintons are the only people I called family. I don't even know if they are still in India or, maybe, they came back; here, several blocks away. Mrs Swinton's sister doesn't want me either ... I have no idea where I can go."

"Do you have a cell phone?"

"No."

"OK. Next Saturday, I'll bring you one."

"What am I going to do with it? I don't know how to use it."

She took out her cell phone and pointed:

"You see this? You press here when the phone rings, all right?"

He shrugged his shoulders.

"What then?"

"We can organise your getaway."

"My what?"

"Do you wanna run away from those idiots and the billy goats, or you wanna stay stuck with them until you are of age?"

"But ... where am I going to go?" Randall asked, scratching his head.

Before Abigail answered this question, Sunflower, one of the priest's girlfriends, walked to them and said:

"What are you two planning?"

"Nothing!" said Abigail.

Sunflower grabbed Randall by his ear and walked him down to the altar, holding him the whole time. All eyes were on them; the priest was praying incessantly whilst they walked, lifting his outstretched arms to the heaven, repeating imperceptible words. Later, they said the boy was possessed. That the ghost of one of the billy goats entered Russel's body.

The gathered crowd started bleating. The bleating became so loud as if, there in the church, a huge herd of billy goats were performing an undesirable, unbearable concert.

The priest was preaching about various miracles that had happened to him, to some members of the congregation, but somewhere else, in some other parts of the world; no one ever witnessed any miracle in this church, but their faith was strong and undivided. They all believed the priest was a holy man, all his words were graced by truth and wisdom. They knew, deep down in their souls, that one day, a miracle would happen in their church, in their ordinary lives, and they would be lifted, elevated to the higher planes of existence.

As Sunflower was dragging Randall by his ear, the crowd continued to bleat, the church door opened and the light entered from the West. Abigail stood up and shouted:

"Let go of him!"

She ran from her back seat and charged, like a little ram, at Sunflower and knocked her down; through the open door, the sun came in, and the two billy goats ran into the church and the bleating crowd went mute and their mouths stayed wide open. The billy goats charged at the priest and his other girlfriend Raindrop, digging their horns into soft flesh.

Abigail, in a firm, strong voice commanded:

"Stop!" and the billy goats stopped at once.

The whole group of people were still in a state of total shock, tongue-tied, with tears in their eyes. Someone shouted:

"A miracle, a miracle has happened!" then cheering took place.

Someone shouted:

"It is not a miracle! It is an evil omen: the billy goat represents the Devil. This is blasphemy, look at them with their bloody horns. They almost killed our priest."

As a commotion took place, the billy goats walked out of the church, Abigail took Randall's hand and said:

"Run!"

They ran out of the church and instead of the sun, which had graced the whole scene, now a kind, warm rain was coming down from the sky like a mellow melody bathing their bodies with drops of hope.

They ran and ran and ran … all the way to the river bank where they finally sat down and watched the sunset, hand in hand.

No one ever found the billy goats, some said they were the sign of the Devil visiting the church, some said God's justice had been done.

No one ever found Abigail and Randall, not even I, who knew them both, had any clue what happened to the two of them.

I'd like to say they got married later on … but it would be irresponsible to say so; I will just stop here and leave it up to you to give a logical or pleasing conclusion to this true love story.

Mitch and Loretta Steel's Roma

"There is a great favour I'd like to ask you, brother."

His eyes stayed focused on the sunray that shone on his brother's seemingly polished forehead, which looked like a bright-yellow-painted billiard ball.

"Is it about my student?"

"I wouldn't call her ..."

"I asked, is it about my student?"

"Why are you calling her your student?"

"Because she is my student."

"She is a young lady..."

"Stay away from her. Never start your sentence by asking a favour from me ever again."

"We are brothers."

"It was a random chance. It was a random mistake."

"Was it a mistake?"

"Is that even a question; yes, it was."

"Why would you assume I was about to ask you a favour which was in regards to her?"

"I know you too well."

"I am an ex-offender."

"You are an offender. There is no such thing as an ex-offender. Once you did it, it stays with you. It is like a title."

"Like your title, Doctor of Philosophy."

"What a comparison! You can go now!"

"Are you going to tell Mother that I visited?"

"No."

"You better not. Are you going to tell Loretta I visited?"

"No."

"Are you going to mention it to anyone?"

"Not really."

"I wanted her to testify."

"I know what you wanted, I know why you came. You didn't have to tell me, and because you didn't utter a word about it, or shall I say I didn't let you speak, it looks as if we never spoke about it. You can leave. Right now!"

Mitch Steel was about to leave the room without a handshake when the front door opened, and in about ten seconds a tall woman, with a small blonde bun on top of her head, came in saying:

"You are still at home, how come?"

Her eyes met Mitch's and she stood frozen.

"Loretta, I was just about to leave."

"Is that you, Mitch?"

"I know; I look nothing like the old Mitchy. I have aged rather quickly", he said winking at her and smiling a smile of mockery. Shadows were playing in his eyes, changing quickly between shades of blue.

She stared into his deeply-mocking eyes for a long time, which were also filled with obvious lust. She stared long enough at him, she opened her mouth as if she wanted to say something, then she changed her mind and changed her direction—instead of going to the lounge room, she went out on the verandah.

"Go, now. Go!"

"It looks like Loretta is upset. Are you going to leave her upset and all alone on the verandah? It is cold outside. Go and get her in."

Stanley Steel's voice became harsh, almost hostile:

"You have worn us all out with torment because of your hatred and bad temper."

"It is out father's temper, don't you remember? He had that temper. Only you were perfect."

"You can leave now."

"I bet you will forgive me for tormenting you. You will forgive me for staining your name, for we share it, do we not?"

"It is not a matter of forgiveness. My forgiveness means nothing to you, even if I decide to liberate myself and forgive you your deeds."

"I hope you are going to change your mind ... now that we understand each other a little bit better, since Loretta came in."

Loretta stayed on the verandah, her elbow against the railing, her right hand holding her head, the other hand holding a cigarette. Mitch Steel tilted his head, looked at the scene and said:

"You'd better go out and calm Loretta down, she appears to be very distressed."

"You know you are the cause of her distress. Leave now. Right now!"

"But you go out on the verandah and say something soothing to her. Say that I will be leaving soon. Tell her, I wish I could speak to ..."

"You are not going to speak to ..."

"Your student?"

"Yes, my student."

"All right! You go and calm Loretta down, and I'd better be off, but ..."

"No, just go!"

Mitch Steel was about to leave the room without a handshake when again the front door opened, and Mrs Steel walked in. On entering the room, anticipating only Loretta to be somewhere in the house, she called her name out:

"Loretta, why was the door unlocked ...?" but when she saw the two men, she stood still, and the handbag she was holding in her hands dropped on the polished floor. The buckle made a sound which sounded as if it were announcing the imminent trouble. She squinted and said in disbelief:

"Mitch? Is it really you?"

"It is I! Mitch Steel. May I get a hug from you?"

The woman came closer and hugged him. He smiled, and just for a short moment the room started to spin around him as if in delirium, he lost his balance and almost fell on the floor embraced in the arms of a short, slender woman, his mother.

She regained her senses, let go of him, she straightened her blouse, looked in Stanley's direction and stated the obvious:

"You are still here."

"Yes, Mother, Stanley is still here. When I came in, he was listening to music. He secretly listens to Amy Winehouse; secretly, as he likes to leave the impression that he cares only for sophisticated, classical art ... classical beauty."

Saying that, he looked at the verandah where distressed Loretta smoked her third cigarette.

"Loretta is smoking again. You'd better go out and calm her down; cigarettes will only harm her... aggravate her temper."

In a very low, and harsh voice, Stanley said to his brother:

"Go before you upset us all. You've made Mother upset as well."

"Oh, yeah? She was so upset that she had to hug me."

Mrs Steel opened the verandah door and sat next to Loretta, who lit yet another cigarette.

"You are chain-smoking again."

"Why did he come?"

"I don't know any more than you do. They were talking about ..."

"About my daughter?"

"I wanted to say, about something important."

"And now, for the disgrace that had occurred we must all bear and share the guilt."

"Don't you talk about the disgrace, about shame and guilt!"

"Are you implying ...? Oh, how dare you ..."

"I am implying nothing. I am just saying, we must all bear the guilt."

"You don't have to! You knew nothing! Yet you always tended to protect Mitch. He was your favourite son, always."

"Nonsense. I never had a preferred child."

"You liked him better."

"How would you know? You were not with us back then."

"Stanley told me."

"Stanley was a jealous kid."

"But why?"

"Such was his nature. For no apparent reason."

"He was smarter, better educated, why would he be jealous?"

"Mitch was a charmer, the eloquent one. He was better looking too, even now, bold as a pistol, he is a stunner. Wasn't that the reason you fell for him?"

"Don't talk about that!"

"Oh, no? I think that was in the same parcel of guilt."

"I don't feel guilty."

"Then who is guilty? And to what extent?"

"You pity only Mitch."

"No. It is not about pity. It is about our collective guilt."

"You can walk away, there is no guilt on your side."

"I am their mother. I should have known what was going on."

"How?"

"I knew my boys, I read their souls ... and then ..."

"Then what? I happened, then? That's my guilt. Only mine."

"Then let her testify."

The two women sat on the verandah in silence letting the cold mist touch their eyelids. The cold mist touched Loretta's hands and her heart whilst the older woman kept her hands in her lap, giving no sign of coldness in her hands or in her heart. Her face was calm; she resembled the face of an unnamed saint from a fresco she saw in her youth on some of her travels.

Martin Steel, her late husband, took her to Europe every year; he wanted to visit other places, but Mrs Steel believed that only Europe was worth visiting. Even hundreds of times, even thousands of times, it always had to be Europe. She used to buy beautiful and expensive ornaments and the finest clothes, as she believed that those ornaments and clothes made her stand apart from her friends. It added value to her social standing.

They took the boys on their travels when they were a bit older. The first time they took them, Stanley was seven and Mitch was five years old. The boys had different needs and tastes; standing on the verandah she remembered, to which extent Stanley was impressed by German bridges, buildings, public parks and open squares whilst Mitch loved Italian galleries, antique shops and rare bookstores which kept old books written in Latin and Ancient Greek.

Nevertheless, they used to hold hands all the time. They would let go of their hands only when they were eating or unwrapping an ice cream. That memory brought tears to her already watery eyes. Loretta looked at her, moved her cigarette further and said, *"Sorry!"*

"You never really were sorry."

"Are we going back in time? Back to the past?"

Mrs Steel wiped off a tear and Loretta moved a little bit further in order to prevent the cigarette smoke irritating Mrs Steel's eyes.

"You were never sorry, am I right?"

"Sorry for what?"

"Causing a rift between my boys!"

"... a rift ..." mumbled the younger woman, *"... a rift ..."*.

"And how would you call it? A competition: who loves me better."

"Is this what you think I did?"

"You ripped his heart out."

"He never had one."

"Shameless woman!"

"It is cold out here, why don't you get in and warm up your head, icy words are forming in there ... as always."

Without any further discussion, Mrs Steel stepped into the living room where the two brothers still argued about things that happened eleven years ago. Seemingly eleven years ago, for their real troubles had started twenty-four years ago, when they met Loretta back in Rome, that rainy summer in 1991.

***

They were about to visit Patrick Garrett, to have an early dinner with his family, when, right there, on the driveway, a young woman fainted in front of them all. The first one to react was Mitch, the youngest of the group. He knelt down and unbuttoned the woman's shirt, and only then did he notice that the woman was heavily pregnant. The late Martin Steel ran into the house of the Ambassador, Patrick Garret, his close friend, and in an alarming voice urgently demanded an ambulance to be called. It turned out that the woman in question was Mr Garrett's daughter. It turned out that Mr Garrett wasn't upset at all, but rather cold as a gun, he shrugged his shoulders saying, *"I was expecting something similar to happen. She never ceases to impress us."*

Mr Steel, being a dentist, was qualified enough to comment:

"Let's give her due attention and we shall judge later what's what."

Needless to say, the evening was ruined and the dinner turned cold and unappealing. They were sitting and sipping whiskey; Mitch was sitting next to a girl who possessed the most beautiful pair of glassy-blue eyes and a little nose decorated with a number of freckles. She looked stunning even in such a circumstance, but what amazed him the most, was the cold fact that the young lady wasn't concerned about a thing. She was lying on a low sofa, pale but relaxed as if she had been the closest friend of Maharishi Mahesh Yogi for a lengthy period of time. Absolute nirvana! Mitch's mouth was as dried as the dry fig on the fancy plate in front of him; back then he didn't drink whiskey in his father's presence, hence he kept on swallowing his saliva and staring at the pregnant girl who appeared to be weirdly content and amused by the whole situation.

When Mr Garrett said she fell pregnant to a *'bloody nobody'*, as he called the man who impregnated his daughter, Mitch, who fell in love immediately upon seeing Loretta and felt obliged to defend the strange but beautiful girl, got up and said:

"I am not a bloody nobody."

"What?" came out like thunder shouted from five mouths simultaneously.

"Yes, I am not nobody! Loretta, am I nobody?"

"You are not." She said showing a wry little smile, looking in the eyes of her father, then alternatively in Mitch's. Mitch was a stunner! He looked older than his brother, even though he was two and a half years younger: his body was strong and well built; his hair thick and dark, dimples in his cheeks and big healthy teeth shone when a smile revealed them.

And this is a story of—How the Steel family brought home a pregnant girl, Loretta Garrett, Ambassador Garrett's daughter.

She was as spoilt as a Persian cat who lived with a lonely wealthy widow, but Mitch was keen to treat her exactly the way a lonely widow would treat her Persian cat. Instead of meals she ate only Ferrero Rocher chocolate balls all day long, she drank the most expensive wine, she watched trashy shows and films all day long and she sang from the top of her lungs when in the bath. She loved spending time in the bath where she demonstrated the average talent of her musical achievements. Back then, when she was almost obedient, or to phrase it better—tolerantly-spoilt, she attended the best musical schools and private teachers, for her father, Mr Garrett, believed his daughter was going to be nothing less than the new Maria Callas.

She never even fell in love with her Italian teacher, who was, as they claimed, seventeen years' her senior, who had a wife and adult sons. He wasn't even rich, he wasn't even famous … but, when Loretta met him at one of Rome's operatic events, she, like a spoilt child, flirted and played with him for the entire evening, demanding to coach her instantly. They sang that evening together; sitting on the big rocks, he held her hands, trying to convince her of that extraordinary talent she never really possessed.

When she told her father about her plans to get herself a new singing coach, he was keen to learn about him as much as possible, but his research led nowhere. He said:

"He is a nobody. No one has heard of him."

But no one could talk to Loretta like that anymore. Instead of reasoning and trying to find common ground, Loretta got pregnant to her Italian instructor. There you have it!

Even before the child was born, Loretta fell madly in love with Mitch; and for Mitch, he couldn't even breathe if Loretta wasn't in his immediate vicinity. He fulfilled each and every wish of hers; each and every extravagant choice she had made, he followed blindly.

Seemingly everyone was happy, everyone profited in some way, and Loretta made up with her father, Patrick Garrett, who was still serving his term as Ambassador in the city of eternal love.

She gave birth to a little girl that looked nothing like her or anyone from the Garrett or Spencer family, her mother's family. She couldn't look like Mitch either, even though Mitch called her *'my girl'*.

Mitch became a young father, whilst his brother Stanley enrolled into University.

Mitch started struggling to keep Loretta's moods in check; he struggled to deliver when her demands, increasingly, became unreasonable. If, and when, he couldn't deliver, she would go ballistic! She had the temper of a hungry she-wolf who roamed deserted and hostile planes, in some places far away from any civilisation. That was Loretta, when in distress or when she wasn't the centre of everyone's attention.

She wasn't a good mother either, for she payed attention to her own needs rather than attending to the child's needs. Mitch was there to play both roles. Mitch was there to play many roles, perhaps too many, but for the time being he wasn't aware of being *'the fool who had to play a million roles'*, as his mother would point out to some of her closest friends.

Seeing Mitch, vastly changed by his latest experience, his mother kept her tears on the edge of her eyelashes, the memories flooded her inner screen and she lashed out on the verandah, where Loretta was smoking her countless cigarettes, one after another as if she was shooting a commercial for a tobacco company.

"Mitch did everything for you and the girl."

"Your granddaughter?"

"Your daughter."

"You used to call her granddaughter."

"He did everything he could possibly do for her since she was born, until the ..."

"Hang on! He claimed she was his daughter."

"He loved her as if she was his own."

"Wasn't she?"

"No, she wasn't!"

"Now, you said it."

"You know, Loretta, what you did to this family!"

"Wow! What I did to this family! You have some nerve to say that! You, the one who threatened to sue me if I took Roma with me. Don't you remember? You were ready to take me to court if I only ..."

"Enough!"

"Yeah, enough!"

When Mrs Steel entered the living room once again, the two men were sitting around a coffee table, where two whiskey glasses stood together, one a quarter-filled with a dark brown spirit, the other empty, she noticed their voices were lower than before. They looked a bit calmer. Their facial expressions were smoother. Whiskey had relaxed their facial muscles, therefore they resembled more the boys she had known before the tragedy took place.

After a very short period of time, Loretta walked in, came close to Stanley, took the glass out of his hand and said:

"Don't you remember what your doctor said? Your blood pressure is ..."

"Loretta ... Loretta, give me back my glass."

"No! If you are going back home with me, that's enough!"

Mrs Steel stood up; she brought another glass and filled it with whiskey. She took a good gulp and extended the glass to her older son. Stanley took the glass and left it dry in one gulp.

Loretta cleared her throat.

Mitch looked at Loretta keeping his gaze on her.

Loretta cried:

"What! What are you looking at, now? You don't deserve anyone in this family to talk to you, let alone ..."

Mrs Steel cut into her sentence:

"And what do you deserve, Loretta?"

"Justice!"

"You'll get your justice, when my family gets it first."

"Where do you want to go back? To ancient Rome?"

"Ancient it isn't! Don't you think I regret meeting you in Rome?"

"Mother! Please, we don't need more confusion."

"There is no confusion here, my son. She came back with us from Rome pregnant. Thanks to Mitch, thanks to my kind heart ..."

"Kind heart ..." mumbled Loretta *"... your kind heart! I heard it every morning; every morning the same story of 'How Mitch was tricked', I can't tell if I was vomiting because of the pregnancy or because of that story she served me every morning whilst sipping her morning tea and leafing through her glossy magazine."*

"Ungrateful, spoilt brat!"

"Mother! Don't let yourself get into this kind of conversation."

"I have been silent for too long. I have never said, what I really thought of her pregnancy, of Mitch's mad decision to marry this trollop ..."

"Trollop! Now you call me a trollop!"

"Yes!" screeched Mrs Steel, *"A trollop! He married you; he looked after your child; he stopped his studies because of you; he did everything you ever wanted whilst you treated him like a piece of garbage. It all played out in front of me every day! I have witnessed all your wickedness."*

"My wickedness! My wickedness? And what about your wickedness?"

"You know what was my wickedness? I was wicked because I let you into my house. Yes, back then, when you were carrying someone else's child. The child that brought many troubles to our family. The child who was a liar and a thief, just like you were back then when we met you."

"Mother, please!"

"No, no, Mitch! I am now going to tell it, exactly as it was, and as it is right now. She came with us only because you were young and fell

under her spell in no time. She did horrible things behind your back. You don't even know what she was ready to come up with. Her daughter, the girl I called my granddaughter, the girl you used to call daughter, the girl she named Roma after a city where she conceived her, was a liar and a thief who stole from us. She stole everything: from money to antiques and my jewellery. What did she do with it? Did she give all that to Loretta? Did she sell all my pearls and rings?"

"Mother! This is not the moment ..."

"Oh, it is the moment. The right moment, right now! Loretta stole from the family, but the biggest crime she committed was to rip apart your love and friendship. She turned you two against each other, finding in it the most satisfying pleasure, yes, in seeing you hate each other, exercising her wicked, wicked superiority. Mitch, I knew, much before you did, about her 'business-dinners' with Stanley. Stanley was weak! The clever one but weak, like a newborn-kitten-weak. He was a kitten and she was a lioness. He could not resist her ways; the same way Mitch couldn't resist her gaze back in Rome when she was already pregnant with a child she was going to name after the city where she conceived it. She sold father's house and shared the money with her friend, a solicitor. You did not know that? You didn't, for I didn't want to bother you! I feared you might cut me out of your life just like you did to your father when he mentioned she might be manipulating you. You just stopped coming. You stopped answering your phone and in the end, you changed your number. Stanley, you believed each and every word she said to you. You even believed Mitch was beating them, her and her daughter. That story would be unbelievable to anyone who knew Mitch even superficially, but you bought into it. You gave her 'shelter'; you said to your brother that you'd call the police if he came near her. She made such a performance; she had a witness; her father came after and said Mitch was out of control, he said Mitch was prone to the bottle, he said Mitch's jealousy

was notorious. He had dinner with us; he was upset with Mitch regardless of knowing Loretta's ways. He had changed because of the child. He feared Loretta might forbid seeing her. Only then, only when she had left, Mitch turned to the bottle. You know, Mitch never drank before, both of you knew that. Mitch cried, and wandered off, and I had so many sleepless nights, I had sleepless nights whilst the two of you justified everything calling him an alcoholic and a woman-beater."

Loretta lit her cigarette and Mrs Steele raised her voice even higher:

"Don't you dare smoke in here! Out, get out on the balcony!"

"Mother, she used to come back home with bruises all over her arms."

"And you believed Mitch had beaten her! How naïve! They turned you into a zombie. I couldn't recognise you any longer, I couldn't get the message across to you; it was like I was trying to reach to you through a thick, blurred glass wall. They cast a spell on you and you believed the two of them, but not your brother."

"I witnessed the bruising on Roman's body so many times. Even Loretta had bruises on her cheek twice; he hit her, slapped her across her face when he was intoxicated. We know that, I didn't make up this story. We had witnesses."

"What witnesses? Loretta and Roma? Were they the witnesses? It was all Loretta's play and performance ... Roma followed her mother's script, the seed of madness was planted way back, my son."

"I'd better be going now, Mum. Anyway, we can't change a thing now. I know Lorry wouldn't let her testify, I know Stanley doesn't believe me, no one did, the jury didn't. Only you did, Mother, but what can I do right now? Just have another drink and listen to some more family garbage."

Mitch left his almost half-full glass on the table: he straightened his half-buttoned shirt and walked to the door without a word.

His mother called:

"Mitch!"

But Mitch walked out and closed the door.

Stanley took the glass and went out on the verandah; he hugged Loretta saying:

"Are you upset, Lorry?"

She just kept on smoking, breathing heavily, angrily.

Mrs Steel sat on the settee and filled up her glass.

Stanley and Loretta were looking at Mitch's back in the distance, walking down the road, becoming smaller and smaller.

When he disappeared behind the tall building at the end of a long street, Loretta threw out the cigarette butt, reached out for Stanley's hand and said:

"Let's go! It's almost 3 o'clock. We have to pick up Roma."

Before I Close

Dethroned, a Haunting Story

It was too late to find Bea and talk to her as one would talk to a woman of her age. She was gone; the best part of her had gone forever. She refused to speak, refused to argue or to write. I need to correct myself here: she refused to publish her work ever again; I suspect she kept on writing her stories aimed only for fallen angels as she couldn't care less about people any longer. She pursued that nonsense of speaking daily to her angles in a language unknown to anyone; in a language without syllables, without melody or even meaning (to an accidental intruder).

I met Bea when she was in the best shape of her life: she was a young woman who resembled an angel herself; she had a mature head on her shoulders and a gift of crafting and arranging words as if they were roses in the garden of Eden. Her words were fragrant, they resembled fresh, pleasant rain in a distant land, the mighty thunder in unnamed mountains and they had the colour of honey-haired children one meets in the paintings of the nostalgic old masters she hung above her headboard. I won't claim that she was ever happy, but neither was she sad when we met. She strived for some sort of perfection known only to her and the angels with whom she was in occasional communication with, back then, as she claimed.

(I, poor soul, almost fell in love with her words!)

I, poor soul, almost fell in love with her words, but on time I understood that love in her words was reserved only for her Muse: the dark-haired Nymph whom she inherited from the trusting sky and whom she was entrusted to keep for a short while.

She couldn't grasp the concept of borrowed love as she believed it to be eternal, a definite state; that was my interpretation, for which I was almost punished when I dared to comment on it.

When she wrote about her Nymph, she used words that confined, ones which made invisible boundaries, barbed wire territories, limited skies to where her sight could reach and monitor the movements of her Nymph. Her words were painted in soft colours as was the mellow, benevolent sky; the wire was made of honey, aloe gel and drops of roses so as to serve like perfect camouflage, the illusion of limitless freedom.

The years slipped away like pearls on a broken string. Bea curated her garden of words carefully selecting gems, stories and events. She had built the most unusual throne adorned by jewels and precious stones, pressed flowers, inscribed with sweet sounding verses and sprinkled with silent tears, then on it, finally, she placed her dark-haired Nymph. What a dream, that she had built! Even birds cried of sheer happiness or pure astonishment flying over the Nymph's head where a wreath of never-withered field flowers emphasised her ebony-dark hair. What a dream Bea had built!

Was Bea aware that the throne was built on quicksand, that her yellow-brick road led nowhere? The years slipped away like pearls on a broken string; the pearls scattered all over Bea's Enclosed Kingdom, some of them rolled and hid in the dark corners where Bea kept her deepest fears: suppressed, never verbalised, tamed and bribed.

In the shadows Bea's fears grew and multiplied, giving birth to Gamayun, a beautiful woman-bird Bea named with a three-letter name: Pia, the woman-bird who sang a song of nostalgia, a song of sadness and betrayal.

When Gamayun was born, when she was christened with the name of Pia, Bea's stories took a strange, dark turn, and her soft heart started to harden whilst the woman-bird sang her songs of sadness and revenge. She dictated the long-forgotten stories of lost youth, lost kingdoms and decayed beauty; she dictated the songs of withered flowers, lost strength and paths overgrown by grass and weeds. She whispered into Bea's ear her dreams and memories about a land where werewolves spoke like humans, drinking the blood of small animals and their children alike. Chilling stories! The land of no-one's ancestors, where the past played the same story on the celluloid tape of absurdity, a savaged land, where birds cried black tears and the Fallen Ones played trumpets and danced on unknown graves. Bea lived for exactly 1,825 days in Pia's world, dragged through the mud of wars, human cries and dead bodies, women's spells and men's brutality whilst crying the tears of all the citizens of this strange and hostile kingdom where she wasn't welcomed by anyonc, except the narrator, Gamayun, in the shape of a woman, Bea named—Pia. Pia kept on telling the stories, Bea kept on writing them, Pia drank Bea's strength and vitality just like one of the main protagonist from her stories had drunk her own. A vicious circle it was, a wicked wheel, a merciless ever-repeating story where no one really lost, no one ever won, no one was aware of the everlasting nightmare. Bea couldn't find the crack in the story and escape through it; she couldn't run away to her own reality, for the sweet-voiced Gamayun mesmerised her with her song, imprisoned her with a melody leaving no means to work out the maze and let her out of the Kingdom of Gamayun, which lay on the shores of the dark but shimmering sea.

I met Bea a long time ago; she was almost a friend, back then she won me with the kindness of her heart and her craft of telling stories exactly the way I liked to hear them. She talked about her beautiful

Nymph, the one I met long ago, and I never questioned, not even once, why she had so much love and admiration for a dark-haired Nymph. Her smile was the smile that kept Bea's world together, it was like the brightest ray of sunshine that never faded. Bea built an altar for her Nymph and celebrated every day as if it was the most important or the most beautiful day ever. The celebrations continued until she found Gamayun in that dark corner, when she sucked her into her world of dark matter, dark stories and songs, asking her to write them down one by one, asking her to forget her dark-haired Nymph and to dethrone her.

Bea obeyed! She kept on writing obsessively day in and day out; she never slept in her bed again, she never ate a meal again and never combed her hair. This obsession lasted exactly 1,825 days, the Nymph left, she flew to unknown freedom, when Bea came to her throne there was nothing left: all the jewels were taken, the inscribed words faded, washed by stormy rains and the Nymph's tears. Nothing was left! Bea put her head on the throne and prayed to unknown angels, but no one answered.

Gamayun flew off, back to the land she had spoken of in Bea's stories, she flew back home to her dark Kingdom leaving Bea's tired body on the empty throne.

When I found Bea on the throne there was nothing in her eyes any more: her soul flew off in search of the Nymph she had dethroned for the sake of Gamayun's stories. She couldn't even cry, she couldn't call anyone for she had forgotten how to call those that were lost, including her own soul that was betrayed. I talked to her body, I talked to her mind, but she wasn't that body nor that mind … she had gone forever in search of her eternal soul, in search of her Nymph … or maybe in search of

Gamayun to make her pay with her life for the lost time: the 1,825 days that she was imprisoned in her stories.

No one knows what happened after; no one saw the Nymph or Bea, no one talked about Gamayun anymore. After all, it is well known to be only a mythical creature who returned to their original story.

On Sale Now!

For more information
visit: www.SpeakingVolumes.us

On Sale Now!

For more information
visit: www.SpeakingVolumes.us

www.ingramcontent.com/pod-product-compliance
Lightning Source LLC
LaVergne TN
LVHW091031080826
845145LV00002B/448